PEDRO THE KID

Carla —

I always knew you would make the right turns in life. It was easy to see!

Always —
Paul Bunyans
3-23-95

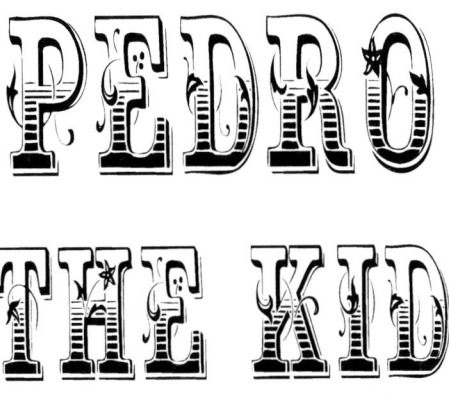

PEDRO THE KID

PAUL PROVENZANO

Northwest Publishing Inc.
Salt Lake City, Utah

Pedro The Kid

All rights reserved.
Copyright © 1991 Paul Joe Provenzano

Reproductions in any manner, in whole or in part,
in English or in other languages, or otherwise
without written permission of the publisher is prohibited.

This is a work of fiction.
All characters and events portrayed in this book are fictional,
and any resemblance to real people or incidents is purely coincidental.

For information address: Northwest Publishing, Inc.
6906 South 300 West, Salt Lake City, Utah 84047

JAC 2.24.94

PRINTING HISTORY
First Printing 1994

ISBN: 1-56901-269-5

NPI books are published by Northwest Publishing, Incorporated,
6906 South 300 West, Salt Lake City, Utah 84047.
The name "NPI" and the "NPI" logo are trademarks belonging to
Northwest Publishing, Incorporated.

PRINTED IN THE UNITED STATES OF AMERICA.
10 9 8 7 6 5 4 3 2 1

To my loving Ester Mae,
whose dedication, sincerity, understanding
and loyalty has made me realize
how bountiful life can be.
Dear God, I owe you.

ACKNOWLEDGEMENTS

In appreciation for their help, support and ideas:

The Rev. James E. Daley, C.S.B. (Deceased)
Holy Family Church, Missouri City, Texas.

Harley Evans, Portland, Texas.

Candy Moulton, Encampment, Wyoming.

CHAPTER 1

In the year 1861, Benito Juárez, president of Mexico, and his cabinet voted to cancel the large debts owed to France and Spain, and the small debt owed to the British. During these same times, bands of outlaws roamed through Mexico and many of their citizens were robbed and murdered. Meanwhile, the Civil War erupted in the United States. On the edge of a small village, just a few miles south of Matamoros, Mexico, an eight-year-old youth had more important things on his young mind.

The little cork bobbled. The young fisherman watched it closely. Again it bobbled, sending out small circles around it. In Spanish, the young man whispered to himself, "Come on, hit it, I dare you."

The sun was setting behind the trees across the small

stream. Shadows from them had gradually come across the water to the bank where the young man fished. A slight breeze from his backside helped to keep it livable but the sultry heat was still prevalent. A very recent downpour had quieted down the dust that usually was a partner of the hot temperatures.

Pedro was feeling disappointment as he had promised his mother a nice fish for their supper. The fish would have to hurry if he was to keep his word. He lifted the small pole out of the water to check the bait, but it was still intact. As he dropped it back, the cork was suddenly jerked under with a lot of force. The youth pulled back on his pole and for a moment thought it was just caught on some debris on the bottom. When it started moving away with vigor, it dawned on him that he had a nice fish on the line. It began to pull with such force, the youth decided to follow it down the bank so it would not break his line. He kept just enough pressure on the fish so that it could not get slack in his line and escape.

Coming to some bushes along the bank, the youngster walked out into the water, around them so as to not get his line tangled. After a few minutes, it became obvious that his possible catch was tiring. Pedro could feel beads of perspiration on his brow as the excitement began to rise as to the possibility of how large his catch would really be. He stopped along the bank and the tired fish offered only a little resistance. Backing away from the water, he dragged the squirming spotted prize onto the dry bank. Dropping his pole, rushing to grab it, Pedro Zamora was never happier in his life.

It was a large perch, and by far, the biggest of his young fishing career. His heart was racing as he looked it over. As he began to study the size, his first thought was it probably weighed five pounds. However, a second glance forced him to drop that estimate to maybe almost three.

Doubling a piece of string, he ran it through the gills on one side and out the fish's mouth. With the pole in one hand and the fish on a string in the other, Pedro proudly started toward the little shack that he and his mother called home. Humming as he walked, the slender broad shouldered youth moved at a fast clip as darkness was about to become complete.

After about 300 yards, he pushed his way through some high weeds and as his home came into view, the youth became immediately alarmed. A group of horses were outside his home, and his young horse, Speedy, was nervously running around his small corral. A few more steps and his thoughts turned to horror as he heard a scream that he believed was his mother.

Racing to the small window, he could hear several men laughing. Peeping inside, he could see his mother lying on the bed, with a large man moving on top of her. Two of the men were holding her arms outstretched, while the other two were just watching and giggling. Pedro became frantic, and for the first time in his young life, felt fear in his small heart. His first thought was to run in and try to stop it, but he quickly realized he would have no chance. They kept calling the big man "Toro" and that name would be embedded in his mind forever.

Then he made a dash for the nearest neighbor's house about 300 feet away. As soon as he could see the house was dark, Pedro crossed the small road and ran down another 100 feet until he could see the only other neighbor's house was also in total darkness.

Breathing hard and with sweat pouring out of him from every part of his body, the lad ran back, crying more with every step. Hoping they would be gone did not come true, as the horses were still there. Looking into the window again, his mother was alone on the bed with her arms outstretched. She was covered with blood, while the men appeared to be searching the house. Pedro wondered what they were looking for as they had nothing of value.

Then he saw his little dog, Bosco, lying still just outside the doorway, covered with blood. It was the first time that the dog had not followed him fishing. All at once a thought hit the youth that would change his entire life. He would try to remember their names, and study their faces. Some day he would make them pay the price for what they had done to his wonderful mother. He could never forget the fat one that he saw on his mother. He apparently was the only Mexican, though two of them had on small masks. Toro had large teeth, thick eyebrows, a heavy mustache, and a flat nose making him an extremely ugly individual. Of the two without masks, one had the top of his left ear cut off, and they called him Luke. The other was ordinary looking, and they called him Gabby. He would be hard to remember. Of the two with the masks, one had white hair and was called Silver. The other one would be impossible to ever recognize as he never heard his name. So he had two that he could recognize by looks and four first names. Not a lot, but it was something.

They all looked to be fairly young so maybe some day he could find them. At this moment, he felt like he would never give up the search.

Suddenly, they started to come out. Pedro slipped under the wash basin below the window. They took his horse, Speedy, mounted up on theirs and rode away. Then it came to Pedro how stupid he had been. He could have chased their horses away. While it may not have helped his mother, it would have made it difficult for them.

Running inside, to check his mother, the smell almost took away his breath. Pedro forced himself to check his mother despite the fact that he wanted to vomit. The smell of blood, sweat, and tobacco was just unbelievable. His mother had taught him many handy and sometimes necessary procedures including how to check a person's pulse. He became frantic as he realized the worst. Rage inside his heart came out. Death to those scum! Then he ran outside and vomited.

Checking the lifeless dog was next, and he picked him up and laid him under a tree away from the front door. He would bury him later. Pedro completely forgot his prize fish as he went back inside. He opened a drawer, and pulled out a sheet and covered his mother. The youth could not look at her like that.

Dropping to his knees, he prayed to God with all his broken heart. Tears rolled down his cheeks as he realized that not only was his mother gone, but that he had no one else in the whole world. His mother and the Priest, Father Frankie, had taught him well about the life of Jesus Christ. He believed in God, and at this moment, needed him more than ever. Then a chill went down his spine as he thought of her killers and his plan for revenge. One minute he was praying to God and the next he was planning murder. He got off his knees and sat in a chair. This is going to require a lot of thought. Could God understand his problem? He would pray for that.

Sitting in the squeaky chair, the lad looked around. Now he owned what was in the house but really it was nothing. An old iron post bed, three old wood chairs, a weak round wood table, pots, pans, and some old pieces of furniture.

Tonight had brought out a trait in Pedro that he did not like. Fear. He was ashamed of it.

Lupe, Pedro's mother, had confided in him only a year before that his father was an Anglo-British, she believed. She had met him only that night and never even knew his name. Yes, she had told him that she was embarrassed to tell about it, but it was the truth. Her final words on the matter were, I guess none of us are born who are free of committing sin. Father Frankie said God had forgiven her and deep down she hoped it was a fact.

Pedro knew he would eventually go into Texas to look for those men. Maybe the fact that he was lighter in complexion than his school mates would be a help. From what he had heard, Mexican people had a tough go of it there.

It was time to go back to the neighbors so he ran all the way with the tears flowing as fast as he ran.

CHAPTER 2

During the following year, there was quite a change in the life of little Pedro. Although he lived with the neighbors for a few weeks, he soon moved into the Catholic orphanage, that was supported by the small church in the village.

Father Francisco de la Perez was aware of the financial problems of Pedro's neighbors, and soon paid them a visit. Using all the finesse of his many years of experience, the old priest informed the youth that he needed him at the orphanage. Aware that the lad's mother, Lupe, had taught him to work a garden, he appealed to him that they really needed him. Then he went for the clincher, by telling the youth that directly behind the orphanage was a stream full of fish and no one knew anything about catching them so they could have more food. This bit of information lit up Pedro's eyes very brightly.

It was the most magic of words, and it was obvious that the lad was hooked.

The only help the aging priest had at the orphanage and church was Sister Theresa, a young nun, who had been with him since she had taken her vows five years before. With his health on the decline, she became his backbone and the center of all activities. The sister loved the old priest for all the wonderful deeds she had seen him accomplish in her years with him. All seven of the orphaned children were treated as if they were her own, and when Pedro became the eighth, she had no idea that he would eventually become both Father Frankie and her favorite.

Pedro was surprised that the old orphanage, so run down from a lack of paint and repairs on the outside, could be so clean and well kept on the inside. Each of the children had their own small room, that consisted of a single bed with wooden posts, a small dresser for their clothing, and a little table and one chair. There was a small library, with a nice selection of books, though many were very old. The kitchen and dining room were all one but very roomy. The sister's room was next to his, while Father Frankie lived in the back of the separate church building. As a growing young boy, Pedro's favorite room was the kitchen, where the aroma of the coming meals always pleased his nostrils as he anticipated how good the meal would be.

Ricardo, a twelve year old, was the only one that was older than Pedro. However, the pudgy lad showed no interest in anything that resembled work so as Pedro actually took over the garden, all the other children began to look up to him, not only as their leader, but also as their boss. Ricardo ignored the sister's requests so that only the father could get him to do anything beneficial. The priest and sister spoke of Pedro often and hoped that some of his desire and disposition would rub off on their problem lad, Ricardo. The only time he ever smiled was when he spoke to María, a beautiful eight year old, who never paid him any attention. Now, the long black haired girl was paying attention to Pedro, and this bothered them for they were afraid of trouble between the two.

Pedro was teaching all the children to fish, and even María, who had never tried before, was now making the effort. However, most of the children felt she was fishing because of who was doing the teaching. Ricardo usually watched from a distance, and despite the fact that Pedro showed María no more attention than the others, jealousy was engulfing him. Finally, one day when Father Frankie had left the premises, and Sister Theresa was cooking supper, the matter came to a head.

Having caught several nice fish, the children were all watching and making over him with admiration. Suddenly, Ricardo came up behind the fisherman, and slapped him behind the neck so hard that Pedro fell to his knees, with the pole tumbling down the bank. As he got to his feet and turned around, with no warning, Ricardo hit him squarely in the mouth and the youth was down again. This time, he could feel the warm blood seeping from his busted lip. "What is the matter with you?"

Ricardo flashed one of his rare smiles. "Get up, yellow belly"

With a fury, he came off the ground and tore into the bigger but out of shape lad. It took Ricardo by surprise as Pedro hit him two blows in his pudgy stomach, and he doubled over in pain, mumbling, "Ooooh."

Pedro hit him a right cross on his jaw, and the much larger boy fell to his knees. The other children were completely awed by what they had seen. Ricardo raging with anger, got to his feet and yelled, "I'll kill you for that!"

Grabbing Pedro by the neck, they both tumbled onto the ground, rolling over and over in the dirt as they fought.

Suddenly, a scream rang out. "Stop that now!" It was Sister Theresa, and they knew the voice. Both jumped up as she arrived on the scene. The fight was over but now Pedro's stock had risen even more in the eyes of the other children. His valiant fight against the bigger and older Ricardo had won over their hearts. Joey, a seven-year-old, who was fast becoming Pedro's pal, was so proud that he was speechless. Millie, a six-year-old, ran over and hugged his neck. María wanted to but decided against it.

"Both of you will see Father Frankie as soon as he returns. Now, follow me into the kitchen and let me nurse your wounds."

Both boys, with their heads hanging, followed the sister into the orphanage building, hating to think about the upcoming talk with the father.

When Father Frankie returned and learned of the incident, he went out to speak to each of the other children first. Although he knew they would be partial to Pedro, he decided to see how their stories matched. Their stories were so similar, the old priest smiled as he realized he already knew the truth before he questioned the two scrappers.

To their surprise, the father called them both in together, and seated them face to face. "Now boys, I want the true story of what happened that caused the fight."

It was Ricardo who spoke up first, "It was my fault. I guess I just got tired of him getting attention and praise. He's too damned perfect." The priest butted in, "Watch your language. You know better than to use that word."

"Sorry, Father."

Then Pedro spoke up, "I must be at fault too. The children do favor me more than they should."

Ricardo broke into a laugh. "Mister Pedro Perfect."

"Ricardo, you have caused enough trouble for one day."

With a serious look, Ricardo calmly and quietly answered, "It was all my fault and both of you know it. I apologize and I also owe one to Sister. After today, I believe maybe I might grow up some."

The apology was quickly accepted by the other two.

Then Ricardo surprised them again, "Pedro, if you will teach me to fish, I will be your best helper in the garden."

As the two walked out of his office, laughing and talking, Father Frankie leaned back in his chair with his head looking up. "Dear Lord, thanks again." A big smile crossed his face as he got up and headed to speak with the sister about the outcome.

The change in Ricardo over the next few months was truly amazing. He worked side by side with Pedro in the garden, and with the heat of the summer sun bearing down on them, the pounds just rolled off the pudgy Ricardo. It wasn't long after this that Pedro had to smile as he glanced at him at work. No longer just a fat boy, he was now all boy. Pedro grinned as he thought about their earlier fight. He was glad they were friends, for to tangle with him now would be really tough. In the meantime, Ricardo realizing he could never attain the popularity that Pedro had with the children, was nevertheless happy with the respect that the children all showed him now. Even María was friendly, but it was obvious that she had a girlish crush on his friend, Pedro. George, a six-year-old youngster with curly hair, had become a buddy of his. Even Laura, a five-year-old Anglo girl, became his friend. Ricardo was happier now than ever in his entire life.

As the months passed, the church and orphanage became poorer by the day. Many of the citizens of influence, the main supporters of the church, were robbed and many slain. People lived in fear, as the bandits caused more trouble than the war with the French.

The garden kept the orphanage in vegetables, but the fishing had slowed, so Pedro and Ricardo fished late into the night in an effort to supply the orphanage with enough food.

CHAPTER 3

1867 was the year the French army gave up and departed Mexico. Not only had Maximillian surrendered, but he also had been executed. Once again, Benito Juárez had become the president of Mexico.

Helped tremendously by the two hard working youths, Father Francisco de la Perez and Sister Theresa still managed to keep the little church and orphanage open. The old priest had fought hard for his life, but now was barely able to stay out of the bed for any longer than two hours at the time. The slender attractive sister had lost weight in her solid and tireless effort in keeping her beloved children healthy. The orphanage had taken on no new children.

A strong rumor that the church and orphanage would be closed soon, with the children being transferred to a larger place in Monterey was confirmed today when Sister Theresa received the formal notice of the closing and transfer. She was very thankful that she would be going with the children. It was assumed that Father Frankie would also go provided his health would permit the journey.

"Pride has kept us here, but in reality, it will probably be better for the children," added the devoted nun in an attempt to make the ailing Father feel better about the matter.

He smiled slightly, "I am especially worried about Ricardo and Pedro. Both have been hinting that they will run away before the transfer."

The sister looked at him sadly, and with tears in her eyes. "Yes, I know they will, Pedro has that revenge thing embedded in his mind. When he does run, it will be to Texas. That worries me as they are tough on all Mexican people there; although he is much fairer than most. It is a shame for he is such a wonderful youngster." This really brought a smile to the face of the father.

"Yes, and as you know, he has been a wonderful influence in the development and change in Ricardo's way of life."

After a hesitation, the old priest continued, "What's with him?"

Sister Theresa blushed slightly and looked away for a moment. "I thought maybe you might already know. He is involved with Rita Guadalupe, who has two young children. Her husband was killed over a year ago."

Father Frankie stared at her, which did not exactly help the situation she found herself in. "How old is she?"

"Twenty-three, or so," Ricardo said.

Now a strong look of surprise came over the priest's face. "You mean he told you of this?"

The sister blushed more deeply now, but gradually forced a thin smile on her lips. "It is very hard to keep things secret in a small village such as this. I heard about it from one of the women at the market recently. At first, Ricardo tried to deny it, but he is not good at telling stories. In fact, he could not even look me in the face. Then he settled down and told me the truth.

This young woman's family have a nice farm near Monterrey, and he plans to go there with her as they need help. He even spoke of marriage."

The priest was silent for a few moments, obviously thinking about what she had just told him. "Did he mention that maybe he would check on the children once they get there?"

A big smile crossed the sister's pretty but thin face. "Yes, he volunteered that before I could ask him." This pleased the old priest. Then the sister continued, "The only thing that concerned him was the fact that being a runaway, he might be in trouble."

"He's eighteen. They can't hold him, and neither can we for that matter. Explain it to him, for if by chance they decide to send you elsewhere, it would ease our minds to know that he would look in on them. Meanwhile, I will pray that they keep you with them."

"I appreciate that, since it is already in my prayers each night."

Getting up out of his chair, the father paced the room. "Now let's talk about your boy and my boy." Seeing her face light up, he continued, "He is the one keeping me up at night."

"Would you like to rest first, and talk later?"

"No, let's talk now."

She thought for a moment and began, "Well, the fact that he speaks such good English will be a tremendous help to him. He has no Mexican accent when he speaks English, yet he speaks Spanish as well as anyone. This is because of your valuable teaching."

He gave her a look of genuine affection. "And yours, my dear. Everything good that has come from this church and orphanage bears your influence on it."

The sister lowered her eyes and then looked up, "You are too kind. I only hope I will not be lost at Monterrey if you do not accompany us."

Father Frankie's eyes gleamed with pride at her. "My dear, you could make it anywhere without me. I am proud to have worked with you these past years."

By now, the sister was almost bursting with pride. "Sister, I am truly worried about this revenge idea he has. I have spent many hours on this subject. It is as you said, embedded in his brain." A look of concern was on the worried faces of both.

"It is a shame a wonderful young man like Pedro had something like this happen to him as a youth. He is the type of young man that Mexico needs very badly these days. We have put six years into him, and last night I wondered if maybe we have failed him." A tear rolled down her cheek as she finished the statement.

"Wonderful Sister, listen to me. No, we have not failed him. I believe that he loves Jesus as much as any young man wherever he might live. Revenge may be in his brain but the love of God is in his heart. These two contrasting thoughts will cross many times in a battle of his conscience. If he finds any of them, which is extremely doubtful, I believe the feeling he has for God is going to affect his actions. How much I don't know, but surely some. All we can offer him now are our prayers."

Sister Theresa wiped her teary eyes, moved over to the priest, and hugged his neck. It was an emotional show of affection that was very rare. She had seen the many wonderful deeds this man had performed for the poor in this area. Never would she encounter his equal on this earth. "I must rest now, but when I get up, please send in Ricardo first and then Pedro. I want to give these two young men all the advice that I believe will be of value to them. With a fresh mind, I will be more successful."

"Yes, Father," smiled the nun as she left the room.

Meanwhile, Ricardo and Pedro had gone up the stream farther than they normally would, in an effort to be able to have a talk in complete privacy. They brought their fishing poles along as it was a habit never to past up an opportunity to fish. The brush along the stream was thicker here so they had to weave in and out in an effort to stay close to the edge. Both knew about snakes and the young men kept their eyes peeled for them as they made their way through the brush.

As they finally reached a small clearing on the bank, both youths tossed their lines into the water. "Do you really feel that strongly about Rita? It's a big move for someone your age to commit to a woman with two kids."

"I can't think of anything else," smiled Ricardo.

Pedro looked at him without answering, and the big youth did something new for him. He blushed and never really knew it. It was probably his first time.

Then Pedro grinned. "There is a whole lot more to it than what you are thinking about." Pedro fully knew he was not experienced enough to give this type advice, yet he wanted to help his friend, and try to make him understand how serious the matter was.

"Maybe I know more about it than you think. Her folks own this large farm. Having trouble getting decent help, they have invited Rita to move with them and help."

"But they have not invited you."

Now it was Ricardo with an even bigger grin. "Since we talked last time, Rita got another letter. This one invited me to come along. You see, they only have one large empty room in the farm house. They were against me coming with her, until she told them that we would marry soon after we get there."

Pedro mulled this over before attempting to answer. Meanwhile, Ricardo caught a very small fish, and carefully took it off the hook and tossed it back.

"Grow up, little fella, and then come back."

"So they know about you and Rita. How about her brothers and sisters?"

"She is an only child. Someday the farm will be completely hers. It is a great chance for her, and also for me."

Pedro now flashed the big smile. "This sounds really great. One thing though, buddy of mine, I hope the kids don't ask why the springs squeak at night before the wedding."

Then both had a big laugh together. Then they both caught a nice fish each.

"Pedro, let's talk about you. First, bring me up to date about María." Pedro looked at him without expression. It was more blank than anything else. "Little buddy, you are known as the most honest and truthful of anyone at the orphanage with the exception of the father and the sister. The other night I thought you were alone in the library room, so I came to visit. You were not alone, friend. I only glanced and shut the door, but it looked like María and you were on the couch together."

Pedro stared at Ricardo, and turned a little pink.

"Well, you two were not reading, or saying your prayers," laughed the big youth.

The embarrassed kid gulped, and suddenly a good sized fish hit his line and he pulled him in. "She had come in right behind me. We had been stealing kisses for a year or so. Being alone, we sort of went crazy for a few minutes. Hugging, kissing, feeling each other everywhere something fierce."

At this second, Ricardo interrupted , "Keep the rest to yourself, it's better that way."

But Pedro quickly responded, "No, you need to know the whole truth. Nothing happened, I swear. Somehow I pulled myself together and crawled off that couch, putting on clothes as I did. María did the same a second or two later, and thanked me from the bottom of her heart the next morning."

Ricardo could see the sincere look in his friend's facial expression. At this moment he was proud to be associated with a person of Pedro's caliber. "I believe you, buddy, but you are about the only one who could make me believe such a story."

Pedro, with a very serious and determined look on his young face, muttered, "Thank you, Ricardo, I appreciate that."

Then a fish nailed Ricardo's line, and the burly young man had a tough time in getting it on the bank. It was the biggest one in a long time, and it left him feeling proud of himself. "Let's just see if the champ can top this one," as he held the large fish up, waving it in Pedro's face.

"We're not finished yet. I never give up."

"I know. That's why you're the best usually." Then with a smile added, "Not today though."

The kid smiled, and for a few minutes there was no

conversation as the competition continued. "Tell me more about your plans when you leave for Texas."

"I plan to cross the Rio Grande well on the west side of Brownsville. Depending on my hunch then, I will either go up toward San Antonio, but it is possible I might go right toward Corpus Christi."

Ricardo had another good bite but missed hooking it. "Go on, I want to hear more."

"Well, I plan to bring my backpack, with a change of clothes, a blanket, a nice sized piece of canvas, and all my fishing needs. I might have to live on fish for a while. A lot depends on me being able to find part-time jobs in small towns on the way."

The big lad looked sadly at his friend. "Really, honestly, do you have any real hope of finding those scum?"

"I don't know, but I have to try for a while."

A look of genuine feeling passed between them. "You are invited to Rita's anytime, you could earn a living. They really need good help."

"Thanks, but I have to try first. My conscience would not allow anything else."

Then came the question the larger boy was anxious to ask. "What happens if you do find one or more of them?" With a look Ricardo had never seen before, Pedro replied, "Something, I promise you. What, I am not sure."

"I owe you. That day you whipped my butt changed my life."

Pedro put his pole down and hugged his friend. "I never whipped you. If the sister hadn't stopped us, you know I didn't really have a chance."

With a smile, Ricardo came back at him. "It was the eyes of those kids that told me you had won. Their feeling for you, and our talk with Father Frankie were what I needed. I will be eternally grateful to you."

Just as they hugged again, Pedro's fishing pole went jerking down the bank. Quickly, he chased it, and feeling the size of the possible catch, played it with all the finesse he had acquired in all his fishing experiences.

When he finally drug it out on the bank, both boys realized it was the biggest fish ever caught from that stream since they had fished it. "I am not sure if you are really the champ, but you are also damned lucky." They both had a genuine laugh together.

Finally, when they walked back together, Pedro whispered to his friend, "I wonder who's the luckiest. Every night when I curl up in that blanket, and hope a rattlesnake doesn't decide to slide in there with me. I'll think about what you are curled up with."

"I told you already. I can't think of anything else."

CHAPTER 4

After hitching a ride on an old hay wagon, Pedro lay on his back totally relaxed. An elderly Mexican was guiding the two slow mules, who looked to be as old as the driver. The man wore a very wide-rimmed straw hat that appeared to be coming apart. Slowly the wagon moved down the small dirt road, and it was the dust that bothered Pedro and kept him from really enjoying his first ride in three days since he crossed the Rio Grande. He was northwest of Brownsville, and soon must decide between Corpus Christi and San Antonio.

Pedro was ready to stop at the first small town and attempt to find a part time job so he could eat something besides fish. He had done poorly on the fishing, so hunger was upon him.

Stretched out in the back of the wagon, his mind went back to the orphanage, and the good-byes that almost broke his heart. The night before his early departure, the youth had gone around to all the beds to hug and kiss each one of his friends. He had to promise that soon he would visit them in Monterrey. While Joey had cried the most, it was María who was the hardest to leave. Two days before he planned to leave, she had decided to run with him, so he had a world of talking to do to keep her contented to remain behind. It didn't take long before his mind drifted to the talk that Father Frankie had given him. It only made things worst. He did not want to think about what he would do if he found them. The old priest had worked on his conscience, and Pedro felt he had enough problems with that already. He knew no one had even tried to find his mother's killers. Well, he certainly would. The toughest good-bye was to Sister Theresa. She hugged and kissed him until he was totally embarrassed. God had worked a miracle in making this woman. She was a cinch to enter the gates of heaven. Sadly, he thought, this revenge thing could send him straight to hell.

Later, as the wagon turned onto a small trail leading to a little shack, Pedro jumped off, waving and thanking the old gentleman. The use of Spanish, as well as English, had proven very valuable to the youth.

Again, he found himself walking along a very dusty road. For some unknown reason, the youngster felt a little happier and less lonely, and found himself whistling a tune as he moved down the long road ahead.

About an hour before dark, the lad came to a small wooden bridge that crossed a narrow stream. Looking both ways, he spotted a group of trees several hundred feet down that appeared to be on both sides of the water. The youth was totally bushed and hoped to catch a fish, cook it, eat it, and get in his blanket and canvas to attempt a good night's sleep. Crossing the bridge, he went off it to the left toward the group of trees. The cover was heavy, with cactus and thick clusters of grass that seemed to invite rattlesnakes. Slowly easing past the many obstacles, he realized how afraid of snakes most people were. Well, he was no exception, and with a smile, decided it only meant he had good sense. Finally, reaching the cluster of trees, he only had about thirty minutes before darkness would set in.

Quickly, he took a small branch and tied on his fishing line with the hook already on it. Reaching into a small leather packet, Pedro took out a small piece of smelly meat and placed it securely on the hook. Dropping it into the water, he spoke out loudly in English, "Come on, you Texas fish, meet the champion fisherman of all Mexico."

At darkness, he began to doubt that statement. Just as he decided he would have to go to sleep hungry, a fish took his line, and Pedro easily pulled in the small fellow. It certainly was not enough, but sometimes a little is better than none, thought the hungry youth.

Later, wrapped in his blanket and canvas combination, the lad licked his chops as he thought about how good the little fish had tasted. Despite fighting off the thoughts, his mind drifted again to the snakes. He had seen four in three days in Texas. Thank God they were all in the daytime. Then he thought of his buddy Ricardo, probably all curled up with Rita. That lucky devil, for Pedro remembered how pretty and mature she looked the day he had met her.

The following year was a difficult one for young Pedro. It was also a learning experience as there had been many sad ones. The worst part of it all was that he had not found a single clue in his search for the killers. Born and raised near Matamoros, the youth had never been out of that area. He watched through surprised eyes at the hatred the Anglo Texans had for all other races. They punished and lynched good Mexican people because bad Mexicans had plundered and raided them. He saw firsthand the plight of the black man. Although no longer a slave, in most cases they were worst off. He had found a few odd jobs in Corpus Christi and in towns on the way to San Antonio. This way he had been able to stay away from fish. By the time he reached San Antonio, where many wagon trains left for the West, Pedro had been gone for well over a year. He was now close to sixteen years old.

There were many stories of the fierce Comanche Indians. He had seen a few Indians at great distances, and was not sure if they were Comanches or not. In fact, he was not anxious to find out. Their reputation preceded them. He hoped to stay completely out of their way.

Pedro had hustled jobs in stores, banks, saloons, and any other place that needed scrubbing or anything else done. He slept outdoors usually, but worked very hard in keeping up his appearance. Clean clothes and combed hair were vital. His light complexion and the use of both languages were all big help aids to him. He had only been called a "greaser or pelado" several times, and had managed to stay out of trouble so far. Whenever possible, he visited a church to pray. It did not matter what denomination, as he prayed to Jesus regardless.

After six weeks in San Antonio, where there was a tremendous turnover of visiting people, Pedro still had not a single lead on his revenge mission. Whenever he made a new acquaintance, at the first possible chance, the youth asked about them, but never took anyone into his confidence.

He wrote to Sister Theresa, Ricardo, and all the children. Enclosed in the sister's letter was one for Father Frankie, not knowing where he was or if he was still alive.

Working on several part-time jobs, Pedro made friends with two former slaves, Jebb and Sambo. They were sincere hard working men, who admired the way the kid worked along side of them.

Late for work in a saloon one morning, Jebb, trying to run through the crowd, bumped into a large white man and knocked him down.

"I'se sorry, sir," apologized the scared Jebb.

The man stood up. "You black bastard, I'll kill you for that."

Pedro and Sambo moved toward the man. "I'se just made a wrong step, sir."

"You got that right—get a gun and step out in the street." Jebb was shaking with fright.

Pedro stepped forward. "Sir, he meant no harm to you. He is just a harmless old man."

Before he could finish, two rough looking men grabbed him and both hit him at once, knocking him down and out. Sambo watched in fear.

Meanwhile someone strapped a gun on Jebb, and motioned him toward the street.

"Sir, I'se no gun shooter. Never had one to shoot."

All the men around him laughed. "It's time to learn fast," said one of them as they pushed him toward the street.

Before Jebb realized what was going on, the gunman drew and shot him to death. No one bothered with the body.

As soon as Pedro revived, Sambo and he rented a wagon, placed the old man in it, and took him out of the city and buried him. Pedro had a pain in his heart. He was tired of being pushed around. He never learned the gunman's name, only that he was known as a "nigger killer." Shortly after this incident, both Pedro and Sambo left San Antonio. Sambo hired on as a cook's helper with a wagon train headed west. Pedro, losing his desire for what he was trying to do, heard of some outlaw places north of the city, and headed that way. This would be his last stops before he would go back to Mexico and his friends, hoping to decide what to do next after that.

Leaving San Antonio, Pedro soon came into the hill country, easily the prettiest land of hills and grass that he had observed in Texas. On the third day, he saw a group of Indians in the distance. Forced to hide for some time, he eventually decided to spend the night there since a stream nearby offered a possible meal for that night.

He slept well, but upon awakening, there was the shadow of a man blocking the sun from his eyes. Barely awake, it was still easy to recognize who was standing over him. An Indian and probably a Comanche. Many of them were said to be in this area. For just a second, Pedro decided to make a run for it, but just as quickly changed his mind. There were four others also around him.

The lad sat up and spoke in Spanish, "How are you?" There was no reply. Repeating it in English, he still received the same quietness.

The one nearest him had to be the leader or chief. He was broad shouldered, yet lean and very bronzed from the sun. He wore no shirt, and on his head was a set of horns, probably buffalo, that were attached to a small cap that was surrounded with feathers around it's base. Instead of trousers, he had a cloth in the front and one in the back, that almost reached his knees. While the others were dressed similarly, they had no horns, although one did have a single feather held by a band of hide around his head.

Since they made no move to hurt him, Pedro rolled up his blanket and canvas, placing it in his backpack. As he slipped it over his back, the Indian with the horns pointed to a beautiful brown and white horse that Pedro always knew as a paint. The Indian spoke but it meant nothing to him. However, he understood what he wanted.

As he walked toward the horse, the Indian quickly and expertly jumped on him, pointing behind him. As soon as this was done, the five Indians took off with a yell that sent chills down Pedro's spine. He was their captive, and knowing of their reputation, the youth had no idea what his future was, if he had any. It would probably be safer if that rattlesnake had crawled into his blanket on one of those nights. Just the word *Comanche* put fear into the hearts of almost everyone, and Pedro knew at this moment that he was no exception.

CHAPTER 5

Although he was trying to study the direction in which he was being taken, Pedro was confused very quickly. Heading northwest, crossing streams and riding down the center of some, finally they entered a few small hills with the cover extremely heavy along with an occasional tree. As several hours passed, Pedro was convinced that despite all the twists and turns, they are still basically northwest of where he was taken captive.

One of the warriors lagged behind, and with the horses turning on different angles through the dense brush, the youth could see him occasionally, dragging a large tree limb obviously covering their tracks wherever possible.

It was clear now, he was riding with the leader of these warriors. Although he could not understand the language, this

Indian was obviously giving the orders. As it became warmer with the sun fully exposed, Pedro hoped they would soon arrive at wherever they were going. He did not exactly appreciate the odor from the back of the sweating Indian. The horns on his head must be from the buffalo and the claws on his necklace looked like they might be from a bear. Where in the world did he kill bears? Pedro had never even heard of one in this part of the country. Maybe these were Indians from a more northerly region. While the other warriors seemed to be younger, this one was deeper muscled and stronger looking. All of them wore silver looking trinkets hanging from their ears, with some of these so heavy it contorted them. Their long black hair looked greasy, and was tied with a small piece of leather to hold it together in the back. Pedro was amazed at the ear pieces, as there was no way they could be comfortable.

After three hours of hard riding, they stopped at a wide stream and everyone dismounted. As the horses drank, Pedro pointed to the water, and the strong Indian smiled and nodded. The sight of the smile did more for Pedro than the water. After a short rest, they all mounted up again, and the trip was resumed. The sun was bearing down even more as it now was directly overhead.

Then they entered the stream and began to ride straight down it. As time progressed, the water became deeper and the brush heavier. They came out of the stream, where the cover was high and very thick. It was a far more rugged looking place, as the terrain was more than rough.

After another two hours, the land began to smooth out some. Gradually, the heavy cover was disappearing, and soon they were in the open. In the distance, the youth could see the teepees along the bank. They were all on one side and appeared to be spread out for a long way. Hills were not far behind them and the cover was thick in this area.

As they neared the village, the people had come out to meet them. The smaller children were all excited and ran up and down. Most of the women appeared to have short hair and all seemed to be wearing loose fitting blouses. Everyone seemed to be happy to see them and Pedro was feeling many of their eyes on him. After passing about a dozen teepees, the warriors stopped their horses. Everyone dismounted and most of them walked off with apparently their happy families, leading their ponies along.

So far, these people did not look so vicious to him. Several women embraced the leader with the horns, and from what Pedro could tell now, this muscular warrior must be the chief of the entire village or tribe. Then he saw her, the last one to hug the leader. Pedro had to take a deep breath. She was the most gorgeous young woman that he had ever seen. Being younger than the others, the lad immediately began to wonder if she was the chief's wife, daughter or who. Not familiar with Indian customs, he had heard that the warriors usually had more than one wife but he had no idea about the ages of the women.

All of the women looked at him as he was led into the closest teepee, but none with the intensity that came from her. The long-haired beauty's piercing gray eyes stared, seemingly consummating him. She had no smile, but her beautiful face did not need it, thought Pedro. In the teepee, the chief pointed to a pallet toward the back of it and Pedro understood it was to be his bed. Then the women brought in food, and as soon as the leader started eating, he said something to the women.

Soon, one of the short fat women brought him some dried meat and a couple of stale looking biscuits. They were treating him as a guest as the chief's food looked the same. A circular pit, either used for cooking or warmth, was centered, with a large type pallet next to it. The other flat bed places were smaller so he quickly assumed this was the chief's and his wife's bed. All of the others, including his totaled about six and they were spaced around the middle to backside of the teepee.

He was disturbed, as while he ate, the gray-eyed beauty never took her eyes off him. Pedro did not know what to think of it, but one thing he was sure of, it was a sign of either hate or fondness. The latter thought intrigued the youngster. It became difficult for him to look around with those staring gray eyes on him continuously. The young lad did notice, that despite the rug type doorway propped open, it was not only warm but the odor was not pleasant. There was another attractive woman, who looked to be near the leader's age, and several others who were mostly short and fat. Another attractive one came in at that moment, and from behind the chief's back, smiled broadly. As the warrior motioned for him to join them in the circle they had formed, he quickly moved and crossed his legs, sitting as they were. Now, everyone smiled except the one with the piercing steel gray eyes. Her expression was unchanged but the stare remained.

The warrior spoke to one of the short fat ones, and she left the teepee, returning in a matter of minutes, a young boy of maybe twelve came in with her. It was hard to tell, but to Pedro, this lad looked more Mexican than Indian. He came to Pedro smiling, and when he spoke in Spanish, it sounded like music to his ears.

"You speak Spanish or maybe English?" What a relief to be able to speak with someone! He smiled back at the young boy, a slender youth with attire similar to the Indians, bare chested, with the cloths in front and the back, long hair tied in the back. "Both—you prefer Spanish?"

"Yes, I no speak English, I am José."

"Good, I'm Pedro. Let's talk about all this."

The youth sat down beside Pedro as the others watched. "You are lucky like me. This great warrior is Wounded Bear. A Comanches chief, ruler of this entire village. We are his property, his captives."

"Maybe so, but I was brought here against my will."

Now the youth's expression changed and the friendly smile was gone. "Take my advice, act happy. Things can be bad. I have seen it."

Pedro did not answer, and the youth continued. "I work hard for reason. Someday, I might get to be warrior. A small tribe needs warriors. Your chances good."

The chief then spoke with José, who turned to Pedro again. "He wants to know where you from. Do not lie, he no fool."

Then after a slight pause, he continued. "Treat him with respect."

Pedro looked over at the chief. "I am from Mexico. I ran away from an orphanage well over a year ago, and have been just town hopping, doing odd jobs since then."

José relayed the message to the chief, and then a little conversation took place between the two. Pedro realized how well this kid spoke the Comanche language, and his need to learn a third language.

"Chief Wounded Bear will make you no promises now. You work hard for him, show his people proper respect, and later he will speak again since no harm will come to you." Pedro smiled and nodded his head to the chief. Then Wounded Bear spoke again, this time with a vicious look on his face.

"He wants you to know that if you try to escape and they catch you, there will be no second chance. Like everyone else, you will be put to death."

Pedro nodded to Wounded Bear. Those gray eyes were still putting holes through him. Does she ever even blink them? What a gorgeous creature she is but those eyes, wow. The young Mexican youth was waiting for Pedro's reply.

"Tell him I give him my promise that I will not try to escape. Working hard is the only thing I know, so that will not be a problem."

As the boy relayed the message, the pleasant look on Wounded Bear's face returned. Then he spoke with the young boy again.

Turning to Pedro, the lad repeated what had been said. "He says good. We will see."

CHAPTER 6

Later that day, the boy took Pedro into the woods and supplied him with his new clothes. Cloths almost down to his knees in the front and one for the back. This was it except for a pair of moccasins, which were well-made. There was no shirt as long as the weather was this warm. Pedro rolled up his clothing and planned to stuff it into his backpack, which he had placed by his pallet.

Pedro was pleased there was someone like José to speak with, while trying to learn the Comanche language. His success with English and Spanish made him confident he could also master this language.

"Boy, you are strong. Where did you get all those muscles?"

Pedro laughed and it felt good to do that again. "I guess it comes from just good old hard work. Scrubbing floors, walking for miles, and other things. You are also strong looking."

José was proud to hear Pedro say that. "Maybe, but I am only twelve. How old are you?"

"Fifteen, but close to sixteen"

José looked surprised. Then he looked the older boy over. "I would have thought you were older. I bet Running Fox thinks so."

Now Pedro looked surprised. "Who's Running Fox?"

José came up with a foolish looking grin on his face. "Do not tell me that you are strong but stupid." A pause followed and when Pedro did not say anything, he added, "The long-haired beauty, who has not taken her eyes off you. She's Wounded Bear's daughter."

Somehow Pedro was glad to hear that. "Surely she is spoken for. A warrior or boyfriend?"

José was smiling broadly now. In the orphanage, Pedro had experience with children younger than he, and this was a likable kid. He knew they would become good friends. "Many warriors, five I think, have offered Wounded Bear many horses, pelts, much food and more. He is the only chief willing to let his daughter pick her mate. She has refused marriage every time so far."

Pedro listened with attentive interest. "Is she seventeen or eighteen?"

"Sixteen."

His sudden, "Oh," brought a grin to José as they continued to gather the wood. "Does she always glare at strangers?"

With a chuckle, "You're not dumb. You just want to hear me say…no, she doesn't." Now Pedro flashed a smirk.

"She really hates or has it bad for you. I'm bettin' it's not hate, but don't get the swell head yet." Pedro was speechless for the moment.

José continued, "Pedro, take my advice and be careful. She, a chief's daughter and you, a captive—that's risky, very risky. Maybe you can become a warrior. That would be different. Maybe she might approach you. It's all dangerous. Be careful, it could cost you your life."

Pedro was totally confused, and preferred she not look at him like that. With her beauty, he knew it would be difficult not to look at her. The whole thing needed much thought. He decided to change the subject. "Tell me more about these Indians."

Meanwhile they had gathered a large pile of wood that needed to be carried back to the camp. "Well, this is a small Comanche tribe. There are only about twenty-five warriors, and except for two or three, all are married. Most of them have two or even three wives. The only other captives are two small girls, one about five and the other only about three."

"Go on."

"In simple Spanish, this means that you and I are important to the chief. Even most of the Indian boys are younger than I. He needs warriors badly. You are also important to another." He was smiling before he even got the words out.

"José, let up. I'm worried about that. Tell me about Wounded Bear's family."

"Wounded Bear has two wives and two teepees. The first wife is the more important, bossing the others. Brush Fire, the mother of Running Fox, is his first wife. I'll bet you noticed her, she's no dog."

"Yes, I did," chimed in Pedro.

"Short Duck is his second wife. She is an Apache captive, fat and short, very fat and very short. There are no secrets here. Wounded Bear has two others who share his bed. Red Bird, another Apache captive, also short but not as fat, and Little Elk, a true Comanche. Slender, real nice tits, and the other who smiled at you."

Pedro looked at José with amazement. "Do you miss anything?"

"Well, not usually." Then they both smiled. "Little Elk is the kindest woman in the whole camp. Many believe she will soon be number three wife. Let us hurry with the wood, as we have to help the women work on hides soon."

Pedro and José joined Brush Fire, Short Duck, Red Bird, Little Elk, and even the beautiful Running Fox as they jointly worked on the hides. The group sat in between Wounded Bear's two teepees, and most of the work was sewing along the edges of older hides needing repair, while the two boys were given a greasy substance to rub into some of the fresh hides.

Despite the fact that she was obviously the boss, Brush Fire was working as hard as any of the others. The women laughed and spoke Comanche, and this kept Pedro in the dark, but he knew some of the laughter was about him as their eyes gave it away. With José involved in the laughter, he would find out about what was said or his friend's neck would get twisted. Running Fox, while working, could not stare as much, but she still got in some piercing looks. She did very little talking and no smiling with the others. He wondered if maybe she did not like their remarks.

Finally she walked behind the teepee, and came into view riding a paint horse, that was even more beautiful than the one her father rode. What a beautiful pair, thought Pedro. Now, with her gone, he could relax and get more work done. Obviously she was affecting him and he resented it. He had no delusions about ever becoming a warrior. He had business to take care of and it was not with these Indians. Escape was in the back of his mind. It would have to be well-planned for there would be no second chance. Wounded Bear had made that clear.

The greasy substance was probably to soften the skins as they appeared to need something. After Running Fox left, the laughing and talking increased. He was determined to learn their language as soon as possible. The youth was pleased as to how he was being treated so far. It was becoming hard to believe the tales that had been told about these people. He decided it was the action of the warriors that bought this talk on. They stole, killed and scalped people, and goodness knows what else. Another reason that he could never be a warrior. How could he ever kill innocent people when he could not get his mind settled on how to get revenge on his mother's killers without actually committing murder. However, he was becoming fearful there would be no other way. Only time will tell that tale, and meanwhile he would continue to pray to the good Lord.

Pedro had decided, by the time they finished work that day, that some talk was complimentary toward him. Brush Fire had corrected him a couple of times but it was only to show him the right way. He could understand that, and by increasing his speed, it left him in hope that the chief would get a good report on him.

That first night brought on several more surprises in his life with the Comanches. Because it was warm, the lowest part of the skins nearest the ground were raised to let air in. Pedro was on the pallet that had been first pointed out. Wounded Bear's pallet, a double sized one, was in front of the fire pit, being the closest to the front opening. Little Elk was behind the fire pit, near the back, while opposite Pedro across the teepee was, believe it or not, the very long-haired beauty, Running Fox. Wounded Bear's teepees were smaller than most of the others for they only possessed the one.

José slept in the teepee with the other women. He had been right, thought Pedro, as he saw Red Bird slip under the light cover with the chief.

After three nights, it became clear to Pedro that the chief alternated his women, sleeping with a different one each night. Tonight had to be Little Elk's time. He doubted that he made love each night but they did share his bed. One thing was for sure, he had made love to Short Duck the second night because her moaning and gasping was so loud that people in other teepees could probably hear her. Maybe that is what he liked about her. Pedro could not see anything else. He was right about Little Elk.

Shortly after Pedro had moved into his bed, she came in, stopped at Wounded Bear's bed, and began to undress. The surprise was she kept taking it off until she was totally nude, then smiling at Pedro, slowly slipped under the light cover. She got into the pallet before Wounded Bear came into the teepee.

Later, Running Fox came slipping into the teepee. She slowly began to undress, and Pedro was squirming in his bed, unbelieving what he could barely see in the dark teepee. She knew her father and Little Elk could not see her from their position.

When finally naked, while still standing, she placed her hands over her firm, slightly oversized breasts and gently rubbed them around while poor young Pedro could feel extra dryness in his lips, and his arousal, reaching its maximum, had begun to ache. It almost appeared that he could see a slight smile, but in the poor light he was not sure. With one last movement of her hands, she slid them slowly down to her pubic hair, covering it. In slow motion, she descended down.

With his eyes open so wide, the youth felt for the moment they would never close again. Then trying to relax, he decided she was some tease. Never had she spoken or smiled at him, yet she puts on a show for him. She was even more beautiful than he could have even imagined. That beauty better stay over there, as he did not want his scalp hanging in front of Wounded Bear's teepee. A puzzled young man tried to forget it but it was in the early hours of the morning before sleep overtook him.

CHAPTER 7

Three weeks later found Pedro beginning to get used to some of the Indian way of life. The work was not as hard as he had imagined it would be, and overall, it was not a bad life. The problem was still there for him. Revenge, and he felt it would plague him all his life unless he could do something about it. His mind also drifted to his friends at the orphanage, especially the wonderful nun and the gentle old priest. He decided that Ricardo was probably married by now.

There had been no more nude displays at night. The opportunity had not been there for either. Tonight would be Little Elk's time to be with the chief, but with what was happening, it looked like Wounded Bear and some of his warriors would be going on a trip. The warriors had sat around last night, smoking a pipe that was passed around the circle. It was his understanding that each warrior who smoked it would be going. If this is true, when they did leave, only a few would remain in the village.

He surprised José and many of the Indians, as he began to speak and understand their language. He had a long way to go, but his progress was noticeable. A very old warrior, Brown Bear, father of Wounded Bear, began to take an interest in Pedro and José. It was Pedro's understanding that the old warrior would be the one to teach them many of the necessary deeds of the Comanches. However, Pedro could not believe that it would be training toward being a warrior. It was just too soon, but José kept telling him it was. His argument was that it took a very long time to accomplish the difficult training required to become warriors. It will be interesting, thought Pedro.

Around noon that day, Wounded Bear and about fifteen of his warriors left the village. José had informed Pedro there was no way of knowing how soon they would return. The boys went into the woods to collect firewood and José asked Pedro, "Would you like to hear more about the habits of the Comanches?"

"Sure."

"When a warrior dies or is killed, it is the obligation of his brother, or some other relative, to marry and care for his wife and family."

"That's nice, real nice. They don't deserve the bad reputation they have."

José smiled. "Yeah? Wait'l you hear this. Sometimes one brother 'borrows' another brother's wife for a night."

"Hmmmmm that's not so nice, huh?" Now the two youths each grinned as they piled up the wood. "A coupla nights before you came, Wounded Bear asked for his younger brother's wife, Fawn. Little Bear could not say no but you could tell he was mad. He took Brush Fire for the same night, and it irritated our chief."

"Well, if it's the custom why did they get mad?"

José had to think about this. "Well, I guess sometimes good brothers do not use custom."

"Yeah, José, yeah. I see." Walking back to the village, each carrying a load of wood.

"Boy, our chief has a good eyeball. That Fawn is some looker, but Brush Fire is also nice yet older."

José gave Pedro a smirk. "You told me I don't miss nothin'. You really got an eye for women folk."

Pedro felt strange, and wondered if José was right. It had to be Running Fox's fault. Maybe she caused him to look at other women more, as she kept his blood boiling. He never answered José on that one.

Brown Bear began to teach them how to shoot the bow and arrow. It was an amazing thing to watch the accuracy that an older man like Brown Bear still possessed. In fact, it was a surprise to Pedro, when he was shown the accuracy that was expected of a warrior. José had been right again. It would take a great amount of time before they would ever come close enough to even be considered a warrior.

Several days later, with the main force of warriors still not back, Pedro took José down the stream to teach him the art of fishing. Surprisingly, as they arrived at the bank's edge, someone was following. Both thought maybe it might be Running Fox, but it was Little Elk. She had been very friendly toward Pedro, and José had observed it. Pedro took a deep breath when he saw her, for he knew this would give his friend more ammunition to tease. She just watched as Pedro caught a small fish.

Little Elk's blouse did not fit as loosely as many others, as her bountiful breasts were very prominent. Her buckskin skirt was attractive with an extra amount of fringe, and a very appealing beaded necklace made her one of the best dressed of the women.

"Me try?" asked the young woman in Comanche. Pedro nodded, handing her the branch, while José giggled. Turning pink, Pedro quickly made up another pole with a similar branch and tied on the line. When it was ready, "Here, you smart little one, do something and shut up."

Chief Wounded Bear and his warriors returned that evening

with a surprise for every one. Little Bear had a captive of his own now. A young blonde Anglo girl, probably thirteen or fourteen years old, and another warrior had a small boy, also an Anglo, about four years old. The loot included a group of about ten horses. All the warriors returned but one was slightly injured. A bullet had just grazed his shoulder. Pedro wondered how many people were killed. Surely, the girl and the boy's parents. He did not know if they were brother and sister yet, but would find out as soon as possible.

Since he was the only one that could speak English, Pedro imagined that he would be called in, as José had been, when he first arrived in camp. This time, Pedro was right. An hour after they arrived, Little Bear had sent for Pedro. It was the beautiful Fawn. They walked to the teepee together. "You speak our tongue some. It good." It was Comanche, and Pedro was proud he could understand.

Then he tried to answer her. "Yes, I try to speak Comanche." A little giggle made him realize he had not answered her well. She just reached over and squeezed his hand. It was only in friendship, but he was glad José had not seen it.

As they entered Little Bear's teepee, it was obvious that the Anglo girl was very nervous and upset. Her blonde hair was hanging wild, and her eyes were swollen. He decided that she could be attractive under normal conditions. Pedro almost laughed to himself, for here he was, evaluating a girl's beauty again. José was in the teepee, and he was glad his evaluation had been only in his mind.

Little Bear told José in Comanche, then it was relayed to Pedro, as to what to tell the girl. So that's why José was involved. They had no faith in his Comanche yet. "This is Little Bear, brother of the chief of this tribe of Comanches. He wants you to know that no one will harm you as long as you do the work given you each day. You are his property, as I am the property and captive of the chief of this tribe, Wounded Bear. They told me the same, and it has been true. I live in Wounded Bear's teepee, so if you do not understand something, come and speak with me."

José relayed what was said to Little Bear, who was pleased with it. Finally, she spoke, "My parents will be worried to death. I was tending the horses and they took me, along with the horses."

"Is the little boy your brother?"

"No, they already had him."

Pedro felt bad as he left the teepee for the young girl had tears rolling down her cheeks, and there was nothing he could do.

As he returned to the chief's teepee, Wounded Bear met him outside the entrance. "Cha ar ne ner too ah" (Good, my son) in Comanche. Then came the answer that shocked the chief.

"Cha ar ne ner ak pee." (Good, my father) in Comanche.

The chief was all smiles, and patted the youth on the back. The incident should have made him feel even better but the new captive girl had him shook up. Her parents were alive, but he would like to know more about the little boy.

There was a celebration that night that lasted until the morning hours. There was dancing and a large feast. The drum beat was always exhilarating to Pedro, and seeing Running Fox with a beautiful blouse, beads, and her face painted red and yellow brought out a feeling in the youth that he could not understand. Love? Maybe. He had never known what love really was. José and Pedro went to their separate teepees around the middle of the night. Both had eaten until they were almost sick. On the way back to their teepees, José had confided in Pedro about Running Fox.

"I was just swimming and taking a bath. She came out of the woods, undressed in some bushes, and came in the water but she never got close. She is beautiful without clothes."

Pedro tried to act unconcerned but it was a blow to his pride. That one night, she had undressed for him in the dark, and now she undresses for little José in the daylight.

"What happened next?" asked Pedro, trying not to act disappointed. José started to laugh, and at first, Pedro thought he was laughing at his reaction, but it was not the case.

"She looked at me and laughed as we came out of the water. She said that she did not know it happened to little boys.

The funny thing is she was almost right. It was the first time for me, really."

Pedro was laughing now. "Did you tell her that?"

"Certainly not," the smiling José answered. Then they parted and went to their own teepees. Pedro thought he was the first to go to bed that night. He was wrong as Little Elk met him as he entered. She smiled and stepped outside. The celebration was down at the other end of the village. Pedro assumed she was going back but again he was wrong. She came right back in, undressed and walked over to Pedro. He was straightening out his pallet and was shocked as she hugged him from behind. She was a slender young woman but her breasts were full and firm. They were pressed against his naked back.

"Please, we will both be killed."

She laughed and replied, "I just looked, no one is on the way here, so we have a little time. Please hug me just once."

Pedro was in a dilemma. He certainly wanted no trouble. Acting quickly, he turned around and hugged her tightly. It was a no win situation. If they were caught, it would be his scalp. If he did not hug her, she might be insulted, and tell Wounded Bear an untruth.

"Please, someone could come."

This did it, as she went back to Wounded Bear's pallet and covered up.

Then, with no one coming in yet, she whispered, "Meet me sometime in woods. I like you."

Pedro was lost for words, but he understood this Comanche. He did not know what to try to answer. Finally, "We could get caught."

Little Elk laughed at this. "Me teach you Comanche love." Then laughing she added, "You need love."

This completed the conversation as a few moments later, Chief Wounded Bear came in. Pedro shuddered as he realized what a few more moments could have cost them. He decided at that moment, they would never get together. But she knew the truth, he needed love.

CHAPTER 8

As days passed into weeks, and weeks into months, Pedro was surprised when he realized a year had passed since the Comanches had captured him.

Brown Bear was really pushing their training now. It seemed he took more interest in Pedro and obviously his friend resented it. José was aware of the reason for there were no thirteen or fourteen-year-old warriors.

Both of the boys were improved with the bow, and now they killed small animals regularly. They were taught to slip up on the horse corral from the downwind side. One day, they decided to steal Wounded Bear and Running Fox's beautiful paints from behind the teepee. It was a success and later Wounded Bear and Brown Bear had a good laugh together. It was noticeable that Wounded Bear really began to care for Pedro.

It was his conscience that was beginning to get to him. He had become very fond of the old warrior, Brown Bear. Many times when they were on their way toward some training session, the old Indian would put his arm around the taller Pedro, and they would talk and laugh together. Despite all of this, he knew that being a warrior meant killing, scalping, and stealing from others. It was not for him, and under no circumstances, could ever be.

The proudest day for both boys was when they were given horses. Both were nice looking, but neither had been broken. José's young colt was brown with a white blaze between his eyes. This young horse was on the calm side, and it proved to be a big help. Pedro's black horse was a different matter. A very spirited animal that would have presented a problem to almost anyone. However, Pedro had a big advantage over José. Not only was he older, bigger, and stronger, but he had ridden his own horse by the time he was five years old. Still the black beauty gave a strong account of himself, and many times Pedro had to get off the ground, before he finally mastered him.

Once they were riding well, the next training consisted of roping the other horses. They had been taught to rope while standing, but found it a little more difficult from a horse. Having already made their own bow and arrows, tomahawks, and other needed equipment, Brown Bear explained the leather loops needed for them to be able to ride on the side of the animal, and be able to shoot their bow and arrow from under the horse's neck. Then he explained how they could slip out of it, if the horse had been wounded, or fell while in battle. Once they had made the loops, it took some time for them to be able to do this and get any accuracy with the bow and arrow.

Then came the training session that proved to José that he was not ready to be a warrior. If a warrior was slain or wounded, his tribesmen never left him. They were afraid the enemy would mutilate or torture him. Two warriors would move in and help, or if necessary, lift him off the ground without stopping their horses. This was very difficult for

Pedro and absolutely impossible for José. Brown Bear brought in a different warrior almost daily to work with Pedro, and soon, it was accomplished. The seventeen-year-old young captive had come a long way. Brown Bear was very proud. He also encouraged the very disappointed José, who grudgingly understood.

The boys were like brothers, and confided in each other, openly discussing Running Fox. The nude swimming had stopped after three times. "That's strange," added Pedro. "The posing in the teepee stopped after three times." After a laugh, Pedro continued, "Maybe she was just proving a point."

José shrugged his shoulders. "I guess." He did not quite understand the statement but let it go.

Pedro never mentioned his incident with Little Elk. He felt this was dangerous, and the less said about it, the better. The youth thought of her often, and like any other red blooded youth of seventeen, it had bothered him. The danger outweighed the possible pleasure, and Pedro avoided her except in groups. He understood her actions more after a few months. She had to sleep with Brown Bear every fourth night, yet he never took her as a wife. The fact that she was a full blooded Comanche, while he had married the Apache captive, Short Duck, could not have helped her feelings. Besides that, Short Duck would soon have his child. Pedro felt sure Little Elk would like this, believing of course, this would move her into the role as one of his wives. He was only seventeen, and she had to be close to twenty-five, so her interest in him was for excitement.

The young lad worried about his future with the Comanches. For the first time, Brown Bear had told him in confidence, that soon he would get his chance. They would send scouts out to see how far the warriors and their helpers would have to go for the buffalo hunt. He assured Pedro that he would be asked, but not to tell José yet. The boy was just too young and not strong enough, but someday would be a great warrior. This was a strong reminder to Pedro, that planning an escape soon, was very important. He knew the life and understood the fabled

Comanche warriors. In camp, he had gained much respect for them. Out of the village, Pedro knew there was no way for him to be a part of their deeds. He understood these fierce fighting people believed that they were being pushed out of their land, that the buffalo were being killed off. In their Great Father's belief, they were right. No one could ever really make them understand anything else. He knew the Comanche could never be happy on a reservation. These fiery people would fight to the bitter end, and bitter it would be. There was little chance for them.

Then his thoughts drifted to Running Fox. No longer did she stare at him when he looked at her. He would catch her looking at him, but the moment he did, she would look away. Little Flower, a cute fifteen-year-old, had flirted openly for sometime now. For whatever reason, the beautiful daughter of Wounded Bear had changed.

North winds had recently brought in the first cold weather of the season. Everyone were now in their full winter clothing. Then, there was great excitement in the village, as one of the scouts rode in. His report to Chief Wounded Bear was astonishing. There was a small herd of buffalo not far from the village. It would only be a three day ride for the warriors, which meant about six or seven days for the helpers. Wounded Bear and his council needed to talk.

Usually, they would go north for weeks, meeting other Comanche tribes, and hunting together. This year might be different. If the buffalo were that close, and the herd was small, they needed to talk about hunting alone. If so, the celebration would be tonight as they would move out in the morning.

CHAPTER 9

That night while the celebrating was continuing, Pedro got a chance to speak with Amy, the blond Anglo girl. Except for the color of her hair, she looked more Comanche than he could believe. She was very tanned from all the outside work, her hair had been cut short, and with the same clothing as the other girls wore, the transition was complete. She spoke the Comanche language well and had adapted to their ways so closely that it actually amazed Pedro. She spoke of Little Bear in glowing terms, and although he did not ask her, it was easy to believe the rumor that soon she would become one of his wives. Pedro had to give her credit for keeping up with the little boy, Ross, who had been captured at the same time. His family was killed by the Comanches so both Amy and Pedro had soft spots in their hearts for him.

After his conversation with her, Pedro was disappointed. From a scared little teenager, she had grown in less than a year to a Comanche woman, who never even suggested that she would like to go back to her family. He had given her many opportunities to say it, but it was never even hinted.

While they were talking, Brush Fire had come over to inform Pedro that Chief Wounded Bear wanted to speak with him. Amy got excited, knowing that it was going to be an invitation for him to go on the buffalo hunt. She is more excited about it than I am, thought Pedro, knowing the hunt was making it closer to the time when he would have to go on a raid with them.

Pedro entered the tent and was surprised. Besides the chief, sitting in a circle with their legs crossed, were Brown Bear, Little Bear, and three other warriors. One of them was known as a great young warrior, Blue Tomahawk, whose reputation increased with each raid. Pedro sat with them and then noticed that Running Fox was sitting in the back of the teepee with Brush Fire.

"You have the makings of a good warrior," began Wounded Bear. "We want to test you on this buffalo hunt. You will ride with us as a warrior. If you are successful with a kill, you will soon be full Comanche warrior. After we condition meat and skins, we go to winter home. In secret canyon, where soldiers never go." At this remark, all the warriors laughed and agreed.

Pedro knew it was time to say something. "I will do my best to make tribe proud." All the warriors seemed pleased with his statement. They did not like a young man to brag before he accomplished anything.

Then Wounded Bear continued, "Once we arrive at winter home, it will be time for you to go and learn your power. Brown Bear has explained this. Take your buffalo hide, pipe, little water, and materials to build fires. On the way, you must stop many times, smoke pipe, and let the Great Spirit know your feelings. Many have had much success from high places, for it is closer to Great Spirit. You must not have food. Give Great Spirit four suns to get message to you. You will dream and learn of your power, and sometimes other messages. A warrior must carry what is necessary for power. Smoke the pipe and sleep facing the direction of rising sun."

Pedro, never good at concealing his feelings, was doing his best to look happy about it. "Thank you, Chief, I look to this. First, I must kill buffalo."

The chief smiled at him. "From what my father has said, you will not fail."

Pedro looked at Brown Bear. "I will not fail you, great teacher."

"Also, when you return with your power, we will give you a name that you will be proud of." The warriors all laughed.

Little Bear spoke up now. "Yes, Pedro is not a name for a warrior."

Pedro breathed easier as he left the teepee. Running Fox seemed to listen very closely. He wondered why, as she had never given him the time of day.

Pedro spent several hours getting everything ready for the hunt. José was going along with the women and a few older men. The children would all be left in the village with some older men and a few of the women.

Pedro checked his black horse, now named "Black Rock." On the way back to his teepee, from out of the darkness, came a voice, "Pedro, come here, please."

He recognized the voice. It was Little Flower. He turned and walked toward her in the darkness. She was in the heavy cover. When he reached the edge of the cover, she came out.

"I am so proud of you. I want to wish you good luck and may the Great Spirit be with you."

Pedro smiled at the cute little Indian girl. "Thank you, Little Flower. You are very sweet."

She put her arms around the much taller Pedro. "I just want to hold you for once. May I?"

Pedro held her and kissed her on the cheek. He did not know if she knew about kissing, but when she faced him and looked up, he kissed her pretty little lips.

"I liked that," she whispered. "I must go now. Please be careful on the hunt."

"Thank you, I will."

In a few hours, it was morning, and the entire village was buzzing with excitement. Little Bear, Blue Tomahawk, and three other warriors left early to locate the exact spot where the buffalo would be. Chief Wounded Bear and the rest of the warriors, including Pedro, would go with the helpers. Wounded Bear would not leave the women and older men to travel alone.

When they made camp that night, José was very excited for him. He is a wonderful friend, thought Pedro. There should be more people in this world like him. He did notice that strong stare from Running Fox. Like when he had first arrived, she did not look away when their eyes met. It was that same penetrating gaze that seemed to go through him. Little Flower was also there, and she smiled broadly when he looked in her direction.

Four nights later, Pedro got a chance to visit with Amy, and again, she spoke highly of Little Bear. Pedro decided to ask her if the rumor was true. She smiled at the question. "Yes, it is true. I am ready now but Little Bear insists I must become sixteen years old first."

"Does it bother you that you will be a second wife, and that Fawn will be your boss?"

"No, she is nice and looks forward to it. Besides, never in the white world could I have found a man like him." It was the first reference to the white race he had heard. If she is happy, I will say no more, thought Pedro.

The following morning, Blue Tomahawk and two warriors came into the camp. It was decided that with the buffalo closer than believed, the hunt would start in the morning. Little Bear had been appointed by Wounded Bear, as the leader of the hunt. Pedro was now very excited and was counting the hours for morning to come. Blue Tomahawk and Little Bear led the warriors out of the camp. Pedro was surprised how proud he was to be among them. This could be a great life without the killing and stealing from other people.

The warriors approached the herd from the downwind side. The cold wind was whipping through, leaving numb faces as it seemed to increase its intensity, while the dust swirled along invading the hunters eyes, nose, and throat.

Slowly, they tried to circle around the downwind side but something was wrong. The strong wind possibly had them nervous, for they started to move. Not stampeding yet, but moving. Little Bear gave the signal and the hunt was on.

Pedro moved "Black Rock" on the side of a huge bull. Although they were not stampeding yet, the noise was deafening. Pedro let his first arrow go and it looked like a great shot but the huge animal never even grunted. A second did no damage either but he was determined. A third arrow sank into the beast and he moaned and swerved sideways, right into the path of Pedro's mount. He pulled hard on the reins, trying to avoid the bull, but his horn scraped across Pedro's leg. The wound was just below the knee, across the muscle. Blood flowed out, and Pedro knew he was in trouble. He put another arrow into the wounded bull and the huge beast toppled over. Blue Tomahawk, off to the side of Pedro, had witnessed the incident, and tried to call Pedro out of the hunt. Unable to hear, with the thundering noise, Pedro was after a second bull. Before he could let another arrow go, Blue Tomahawk had closed in on him, ordering him out of the hunt. Pedro pulled up on his mount, and Blue Tomahawk ordered him to go get the wound taken care of.

Returning to the newly organized camp, he immediately dismounted, being in great pain with the blood flowing freely, he did not even bother to see who was working on him for some time. When he did notice, it was a shock. Running Fox seemed to be in charge with Fawn helping her. Then he spotted Brown Bear, who had a big smile for him.

"I knew you would not fail me. One warrior came in, told of your deeds. Killing one and chasing another while bleeding badly until Blue Tomahawk ordered you out."

Pedro smiled at his wonderful old teacher. A grim thought came over him. How would this grand old man feel when he finds out that I have deserted him? What a mess this is turning out to be.

When they had finished with Pedro's leg, Little Flower came over, but before she could say a word, Running Fox loudly told her, "Leave him alone. He needs rest now. Get away from him."

Little Flower was frightened by the tone of her voice and moved away. Pedro almost laughed to himself. She does care, she does care, he repeated to himself. When the warriors returned that evening, although he had killed only one bull, Pedro was the toast of the tribe. Everyone knew about the young captive and his deeds. Then came Pedro's proudest moment. Blue Tomahawk came up to were he lay.

"Here is arrow from big bull's heart. Your arrow."

His leg hurt badly, but his smile was big. "Thank you, I am proud."

Blue Tomahawk returned the smile. "We proud of you." Again the youth felt a pain in his chest. How could he run away and let these people down. The Anglos had not treated him as well. Then came another big thrill.

When he looked up a while later, Running Fox was approaching with food for him. First, her smile almost took his breath away, but when she sat by him and began feeding him, the youth was so excited he could hardly breathe. She never spoke, but as he finished eating, Pedro did, "Thank you, Running Fox." The smile that followed left his heartbeat far faster than normal.

Pedro had learned to ride and fish as a young lad. He could speak three languages. He had completed all the necessary physical accomplishments to qualify as a full Comanche warrior. Yet, there was one part of him that was just plain dumb. It would probably plague him all his life. He doubted he could ever learn about...*women*, as so far they had been the real mystery of his life. He wondered if Brown Bear could teach him about them.

CHAPTER 10

The buffalo hunt had lasted into the afternoon of the second day. It had been successful, and the mood was good throughout the camp. Following the hunt, the warriors skinned the animals, and cut them into large pieces. The women took over at that point. They sliced the meat, then placed it on specially prepared racks to dry. Their other job was the tanning of the hides, which also began at that time.

Pedro felt awkward as he was unable to walk on the second day. When he offered to help the women, they would not let him, and with this, came a message. He was already classed as a warrior in their minds. He was forced to tell the story of his kill to José several times. It was easy to see that his little buddy was very proud of him. As soon as his leg was better, Pedro knew it would be time for him to go on his trip, to hear the

Great Spirit's message that would tell of his power. Following this, he would go on a raid with them. There is no way, thought Pedro, escape has to be soon.

He could not even believe how nice everyone was to him. The warriors smiled at him, and the women and girls were entirely too friendly. Running Fox was the only exception, but even the gray-eyed beauty smiled at a distance. However, whenever Little Flower came around him, he could see the scorn in her face even at that distance.

Pedro did not want to try to escape while on his trip. He felt this would be in poor taste. He must leave, preferably, before this. What that meant was, soon he must take the chance, yet he still had no real plan.

A few days later, he was hobbling around on that leg fairly well. Then came the word that they would be on the way to the canyon in the morning. The youth was glad, as it was certainly a reprieve for him.

Moving was enjoyable for Pedro. The women never ceased to amaze him at their speed. In a matter of a few minutes, teepees were down, and being packed on the travois. All the spare horses were used, as they tied long poles to them on each side, separated in the back by heavy dried skins. These carried all the shorter poles, bed pallets, cooking utensils, clothing, their prized buffalo meat, and many other necessary items.

The trip took eight days, and the last few were boring to Pedro. It did not take long for him to realize that Wounded Bear was right. This was a beautiful canyon, and no doubt, well protected from the strong winter winds. He wondered if he could even find his way out of here, and that, he must do soon.

The next day, Wild Wolf, an older warrior who was considered the best scout, came into camp in a rush. After a short conversation with Chief Wounded Bear, all the warriors were quickly assembled. All hurried for their mounts as Wounded Bear called Pedro into the teepee. Pedro's heart dropped as he walked in. He had been wrong again. They were not going to take him on this raid.

"Stay in the village until we return. Then, you must go to

meet the Great Spirit. On the next raid after that, you will be allowed to go."

Pedro smiled at the chief. "I will do as you say." With this, he turned around and left the teepee, while his heart was still doing flip flops.

Later that afternoon, after almost all the warriors had left with Wounded Bear, Pedro was hunting with his bow. He was near the mouth of the canyon, in the heavy brush that was sprinkled with trees. A light snow had fallen all day, and it was a beautiful sight. Hearing a noise behind him, he quickly turned, and to his surprise, the beautiful Running Fox was walking directly toward him. No smile, just that same penetrating look, directly into his eyes. She walked to within a hand's distance of him. Then he stared back and it brought the slightest of a smile from her beautiful lips.

The smile disappeared, and after over a year, she finally spoke to him, "Soon, you will be a full Comanche warrior. Then, who will it be, Little Flower or me?"

Pedro could not believe his ears. Besides that, she was so close to him, that he could kiss her without moving a step. "You really surprise me. Little Flower has let me know long ago how she felt. You never speak with me."

Running Fox looked genuinely puzzled. "Maybe you do not understand. I am the chief's daughter. You have been only a captive. My father has never permitted me to associate with captives. I even undressed for you several times at night, when it was safe. I saw you watch me do it."

Pedro just had to tell her about José. It had been bothering him for a long time. He hoped it would not get José into trouble with her. "Yes, I watched you undress in the dark teepee. However, how much better could José see in the daylight, when you went swimming together nude? I thought he was also just a captive."

This brought one of her rare smiles. "I did it to make you jealous. I just knew he would tell you, and I hoped it would get you to approach me. I guess it did not work, for here I am approaching you."

When Pedro did not make a comment, she continued, "Did he say anything about my teasing him?"

He smiled at this. "Yes, he did."

"That part of it was to let him know that he is only a boy. I am eighteen, and I need a man, not a boy. A husband preferably, but with you, I would settle for less if that is what it takes."

This brought perspiration to Pedro's face even though it was snowing. Running Fox continued the conversation. "I have denied five warriors. My father will let me choose my own husband. Two of the refusals have come since you arrived. One, I would have accepted, had you not come into our village. It was Blue Tomahawk. Pedro, I need to know how you feel."

She was so beautiful that for the moment, he was still speechless. The fact that he was getting ready to run, certainly was helping to make it impossible for him to tell her how he really felt. He really loved her and wondered if maybe, she would run with him. Then he decided that was silly, there was no way that could happen.

"Beautiful daughter of the chief, come to me and hold me close." He put his hands on her shoulders and she moved in close and hugged him tightly.

"Good looking young man, sweet one, you do care for me."

"Yes, I do care. I am not sure about what love is, but I guess this must be it. Never being able to take my eyes off you, and always wanting to be near you. I never did realize that two people could fall in love without any conversation between them."

She held him tightly as he turned to kiss her on the cheek. Then their lips met, and while he did not know about Indian ways of kissing, she certainly was holding up her end of the tender encounter. She was almost as tall as he was, and even in this weather, he could feel the warmth of her body through their clothing. When neither could catch their breath, they parted their lips, but remained in the tight grasp of each other.

"Pedro, you are too honest for your own good. You have a problem, and it is not with us. You need your freedom to take care of this. Your face has given this away many times. You are not excited about being a warrior."

At this point, Pedro cut in. "I can explain that part, about being a warrior, I mean."

She continued to hold him, and he did not have the will power to stop holding her. "I'm listening."

"My problem with being a warrior goes back to my own early life and religion. I was raised in a Catholic orphanage, and our religion forbids killing and stealing. In your religion, the Great Spirit does not forbid this for it is necessary for your survival. Do you understand?"

Running Fox moved her face back a few inches but her body remained very close. "You did not tell me about your outside problem. Do not lie to me, for I am in love with you, and would never say anything to hurt you. Please tell me about it now."

He was in a very tight spot now. How did this beauty know about his outside problem? Could he admit to the chief's daughter that he was going to try to escape from their way of life?

"Sweet man, if you will admit it, I will help you make it possible, but there is a catch. I am not sure that is the correct word, but maybe you understand."

What an amazing young woman. Well, this may cost him his life, but he was going to tell her the whole revenge story.

"My gray eyed beauty, I am going to tell you the whole truth. You must believe every word and promise not to tell anyone."

With a grin, she asked, "Do you want to know what the catch is first?"

"Knowing what you do about me, it would not be anything I could not handle. I will tell you my lifetime problem first."

He was desperate, and knew she would not be unreasonable in her request. Then he proceeded to tell the entire story of his life, his mother's rape and murder, what he knew about the five men, his life in the orphanage, and how he was looking for the men, when captured by her people. After finishing, before she could say anything, he kissed her with an even more passionate kiss than before.

As they continued to cling to each other, she whispered, "Something is telling me the catch will be a pleasure for you. Do you know what it is?"

The sexy grin on her face, along with the way she pushed against him, gave him the answer.

"Yes, but it sure will not be fair to you."

Her smile partially disappeared. "I have thought about that. You are talking about a possible child. That would be good in a way. I would always have a part of you with me. It would require me to get a husband soon, so no one would ever know."

Pedro was very serious now. "If you get caught, you would be in real trouble."

She hugged him even tighter than he believed possible. "I will take the chance. How about you? If you get caught escaping, it would mean death, and you know it." A series of small kisses followed.

"Running Fox, why would you help me escape when your first question was about my feelings for Little Flower and you? I do not really understand."

She turned him loose, and stepped back, hitting herself on the forehead. "I love you. What ever it takes to make you happy, I will do. Is that so hard to understand?"

Pedro reached out and pulled her close again. He kissed her lips, her cheeks, and all over her neck.

"Pedro, please, I have never made love before. It is too cold here and there is no other place now. Give me a day or two, you know I will work out a way. I cannot stand any more of your kisses for now, as my desire is too strong."

He released her and stepped back. Then she pulled him part of the way back. "Not that far away, please." Both of them laughed at this.

"You may not approve of my method of helping you to escape. We should talk about it."

He looked at her puzzled. "Your time to do the talking, pretty one."

"Well, to start, my father is no fool. Do you remember the day he told you about the buffalo hunt?"

"Sure, you were in the back of the teepee with your mother."

"That is right. Your expression was terrible, not one of

happiness. I knew it and so did he. As we traveled toward the buffalo hunt, we rode and talked for almost two of those days. We agreed that something on the outside was bothering you. It was not just wanting to get away. To you, it was far more serious than that. I admitted to him that I was in love with you. It was no surprise, for he already knew. I know my looking at you has probably let everyone know, that is, except you." Then they both laughed heartily together.

Pedro stuttered as he tried to speak, "Did...did he know about my escape plans? Did you tell him?"

"He has it figured you will escape when you go to the Great Spirit to learn of your power."

Pedro quickly cut in, "He is wrong. I was going to do it before or after. Not during one of your religious beliefs."

"If you will let me tell him of your plans and why, I believe you will be released to go. He loves you as a son yet he wants me to marry a true Comanche since I am the Chief's daughter. You see, I will wait a year if I am not going to have a child. If you return, he will not stand in our way. If you do not leave, we also will get his blessing. His promise of letting me marry the man of my choice will always be there. Can I tell him of your revenge plans? There is one question he will ask. If you cannot kill, how will you get your revenge?" The brain in this Comanche young woman was really something. She had covered it all in just a few quotes.

"Yes, you may talk with him about it. It is difficult to answer your last question. For over nine years, I have tried to answer that one. When the time comes, the decision may not be mine. I hope you understand."

She smiled and reached over to kiss him again. She had been totally satisfied with his answers. He was honest, good-looking, brave, and when he held her close, her heart beat so fast it scared her. "I do not know when they will return, but we must make love before they do. Maybe, more than once, agreed?" After being in her arms for such a long time, Pedro weakly agreed.

CHAPTER 11

The following night was a very difficult one for young Pedro. With Wounded Bear away, he knew it would be soon that Running Fox and he would be together. Although he realized that it was unfair to her, he was excited about it. In their conversation, when she told him that it would be her first time, he should have admitted that it would also be the first for him. He would have, and meant to, but it had slipped his mind. No wonder, with that beauty kissing, hugging and squeezing him. It would be another new experience for him and there had been plenty of them lately.

He was the first one in bed that night. He needed to think, and that seemed to be a good place. It was very cold, and a fire was burning. To his surprise, it was not one of Wounded Bear's wives, who came into sleep on his pallet. Instead, it was

Fawn, Little Bear's wife. She looked unhappy, and Pedro wondered what the problem was. Little Bear was one of the few warriors left in the village. Pedro was wondering why, when she suddenly spoke up.

"I know Brush Fire should be here tonight, but my wonderful husband has taken her to his bed. I know that Comanche women are supposed to understand this, but I do not, and never will. Comanche warriors are not one-women men. The white man has only one wife. I do not know if he is loyal, but I do not believe he is disloyal in front of his wife. They tell me that I am lucky having been the only one for such a long time. Soon, he will marry the white girl, Amy, and he will spend time with her. Meanwhile, he is always borrowing other warriors' wives."

Then she opened the flap on the teepee door and looked out. Returning, she removed all her clothes and scared him by walking over to his pallet. "Have a good look, and remember, once you are a warrior, you may borrow me any night." She was a gorgeous woman, with perfect breasts and shapely legs, and Pedro was never so nervous.

Then she continued, "I would crawl in with you now, except that if Running Fox came in, my eyes would be clawed out. She really has it bad for you." With this, she returned to the pallet, slipped into some clothing, and relaxed. Pedro remained quiet. Boy, was Fawn upset. She would probably regret saying all that in the morning. Soon Running Fox came in, followed by Little Elk. Then he relaxed and tried to go to sleep.

The following day, it rained without stopping. It was still very cold so it was a miserable day. Despite all her efforts, there was just no place for them to get together. However, they had hopes that the men would be gone at least another day or two.

The following afternoon, Running Fox's heart dropped when she saw the men returning. There had been no place to meet, and now, she could see the black paint on the warriors' faces. It meant at least one warrior had been killed. As it turned out, two warriors were dead, and one of them was the fabled young warrior, Blue Tomahawk. This hurt Running Fox, for she had even admitted to Pedro, he could have been the one except for him.

Wounded Bear rested after arriving. Then he noticed the firewood was low. "Call José, Pedro. Tell him to go get wood."

"He is at the other end of the village, helping an old woman do a chore. I will go."

As he left the teepee, his beautiful Running Fox smiled sweetly at him. He had no doubts now. He would try for revenge for one year, and if successful or not, he would try to slip back into the village and take her to the white man's world, as she called it. He could never find anyone who loved him as she did. Even Fawn, in her bad mood, had mentioned it. Pedro already knew it.

The rain had turned to snow as Pedro carried a heavy bag to bring back the wood. It would be wet, so he would try to find the driest pieces around. About five hundred feet from the village, he set the bag down, and started to look around. After a few minutes, he decided that it was a good place despite the distance, and would not take long to get enough for the chief.

Then he heard the shooting. This was followed by the thundering of many horses' hooves. It was dark, but Pedro could make out the uniforms of the soldiers. Then the screaming, crying, and shouting. There were many soldiers, far too many for the small band of Comanches, and there was no doubt about it being a complete surprise. He wanted to help, but there was nothing he could do. No weapon of any type on him, he was totally terrified for his love and her people. Then he could see the teepees aflame.

Almost hysterical, he moved closer in an effort to see his love. He wanted to ask her to come with him to collect the wood, but knowing Wounded Bear was not in a good mood, he decided not to ask. Now, he could see a group of women with their hands up in the air. It was a surrender. He could not even see a single warrior fighting or even standing. They had been routed.

Straining his eyes, he could see Little Elk. Running Fox was not among them. If she was, he could not see her. Then he spotted Amy. Continuing to look, he recognized another one, the beautiful Fawn. There were only about fifteen women and four or five children. Yes, one of them was little Ross. This meant that about thirty or so women were missing, and sadly, probably dead. There was not a single warrior or older man alive, or so it looked to him now.

He knew that Running Fox was smart, and may have slipped out the back of the teepee. The fact that he could not see Brush Fire either, was encouraging to him. If Running Fox was alive, he would not leave without her. This may have been a good hiding place, but it was not easy to escape from. The high canyon walls limited escape routes.

A group of about twenty soldiers were digging a hole. Maybe, it was to bury the dead Comanches. Pedro had always heard that soldiers never buried dead Indians. One deep hole for all the dead was not any better. If he did not find Running Fox, he would dig them all up. Soon, he knew the hole was for the dead Indians.

They piled them in there, some of the soldiers laughing, as they tossed in the bodies. It was a sickening sight to Pedro, who had crawled closer, so that maybe he could recognize some of the dead. He did recognize Little Bear, and then one that almost broke his heart, José, his young buddy, was dead. When the hole was full, they made no effort to cover them. More of the dead were piled on top of them. Another heart breaker, his old warrior friend, Brown Bear.

An hour or so before daylight, the soldiers began to move out. Although they took all the horses, the women and children were made to walk. Sadness hit him as he saw Running Fox's beautiful paint. Once more he looked at the women, trying to be sure about his true love. Running Fox, Brush Fire, Little Flower, Short Duck, and Red Bird were missing. Chief Wounded Bear was also missing, so Pedro could not help but wonder about this. Maybe Wounded Bear had somehow helped Brush Fire, Running Fox, and some others escape.

Daylight came, and Pedro moved up and down the cover, confirming the soldiers were all gone. Then he thought, what would they be guarding? All the teepees were burned to the ground. All the captives were taken, every horse was gone, what else was there?

He moved out of the cover and entered the terrible sight of the totally destroyed village. They had made a half effort at covering the dead. Dirt had been thrown on top of the pile of Indians. An arm was sticking out, legs were sticking out, even the heads of some were exposed. It was a sight he could never forget. Walking around the pile, he found some bodies almost totally exposed. One was the body of Chief Wounded Bear.

He checked several bodies around him and none were of his family. Then he found several tomahawks, and a bow. A few feet over were several arrows, then more in a pile. He decided to take one tomahawk and the bow and arrows. Placing the weapons near his old teepee, the smile that Running Fox had given him, came to him as a vision. He felt she was close to him. Going around the back of the teepee, he saw nothing, but as he turned around, it looked like a body lying in the light cover. Almost afraid to go to it, he finally did. It was not Running Fox, but it was Brush Fire. She had been shot in the back, apparently almost escaping. This was bad but it raised his hopes. Maybe his Running Fox had escaped.

He decided to walk on into the trees. There was no trace of anyone here. Then he saw some drops of blood on a bare spot. He walked on and came upon more blood. This time, only a trace, but it was there. Walking on, he could see a body in the heavy cover. Pedro was afraid to go look. He stopped completely, totally afraid. With fear in his heart, he suddenly walked to the body. It was already cold when he turned it over. He did not have to look. It was his beautiful gray-eyed love, Running Fox. Pedro dropped to his knees, and cried until his heart almost stopped.

Two hours later, when he was completely cried out, Pedro decided to bury the family together. It could not be an Indian burial, for the white man would find this, and probably destroy it. He carried Chief Wounded Bear, Brush Fire, and his lovely Running Fox farther into the woods. Having found a partially broken shovel near the big hole of dead Indians, he dug graves for the three of them. Running Fox was buried last, and before doing this, he had hugged her and then kissed her cold lips. When the job was completed, he just sat there.

Soon it was nightfall, and he remembered that he had not eaten or even had any water all day. Somehow, he was not hungry so he would wait until tomorrow. Actually, there was nothing to eat. Except for an old half burned buffalo hide, he would have frozen to death that night.

Pedro had used his bow to acquire his lunch, then waited until late that afternoon before leaving. He did not know if the soldiers would return. If there were other survivors, it was doubtful they would come back here. He could be the lone survivor. It was luck or was it? Maybe the Good Lord has other plans for him.

He was hoping to escape, and now was free. However, there was no happiness as he walked back to the graves. He prayed for each of the three, then a single love message to Running Fox. Soon Pedro left the burned village with a flame in his heart.

CHAPTER 12

The following two weeks were difficult for young Pedro. There were problems with his returning to the towns. First, he needed to change his looks. With his hair long and his Indian clothing, he looked more Comanche than Mexican or Anglo. Without a mirror, it was not easy, but he trimmed his hair with his sharp knife. It did not feel like it was cut with any class, but would help some. The clothing was a different matter. Although he wanted to harm no one to accomplish this, for the first time, he might have to steal or borrow what was needed.

The second problem was to find his way back to San Antonio. Brown Bear's training would be a big help. He had taught the boys to use the sun in accomplishing this. However, there was still a very difficult task.

Third, he had to hide from everyone. He saw only one band

of Indians, and after hiding, had walked all night to avoid what had happened before. Until he could replace his clothing, Mexican and Anglos were also avoided.

The tomahawk was of little value but the bow and arrows kept him in food. Having nothing to fish with, he looked at the streams with desire as he passed them.

Finally, he felt that maybe his luck was holding out. Two little boys, playing nearby, had pointed down the road when asked if San Antonio was close. They probably live in the small house down the trail and off the road, reasoned Pedro. He moved on rapidly to avoid any contact with their family. At this moment, he said a prayer for Brown Bear. He would use some of his training for the rest of his life.

Having cut off the burned part of the buffalo hide, its warmth was a life saver at night. Even though the weather had warmed up, it was chilly when the sun went down. He felt blessed as it had not rained on his long trip from the burned village. Pedro was glad he was so tired at night. It was hard enough not to think of Running Fox in the daytime but was impossible when wrapped in his buffalo hide during the night. The youth really believed that no one would or could ever take her place. Pedro realized she would want him to live his life, but even the revenge was minor compared to his present loss. He had always heard that time is a great healer. Boy, he hoped this would be true. Not that he wanted to forget her, but his sadness was actually getting the best of him.

Knowing he was on the edge of San Antonio, Pedro still wore the Indian type clothing. Oh, he might survive, but the youth preferred not to wear it in town. He had spent more time on his hair, and hoped it looked better. A loud splash and some yelling reached his ears. The noises were coming from a group of trees not far off the road. They were boys' voices, and maybe this might be the chance he had hoped for. Slipping through the cover, Pedro approached the pond. Moving as silently as any Indian could, he saw the three boys playing in the water. Then he spotted their clothing. It was close, but a stick was needed to reach it without being seen. Moving quietly, he found a thin one made for the job. Keeping himself out of sight, Pedro slowly pulled part of the clothing to him. One pair of pants, two shirts, and some underwear were in his grasp. Then he pushed the underwear and one shirt back. Satisfied with his loot, the youth made his way out slowly. This was a new experience for him.

Soon he was on his way again, but now stayed off the road. Close enough to see it, but far enough away to be able to hide. When darkness came, Pedro realized he would be in San Antonio tomorrow. Today was his first experience at stealing, and he did not like it.

The night was a miserable one for Pedro, as he slept very little. When he finally removed Running Fox from his thoughts, poor little José had moved into them. The realization that the little lad would have been the survivor instead of him, had come to his mind many times. José had volunteered to help the old woman, and this had put him at the other end of the village, so Pedro offered to do his chore. Fate is very strange, thought the youth. When morning came, he started down the road watching the sunrise as it was his plan to go south of the town, so he could hide his bow and arrows. He hoped to be able to leave this city soon, if he could make enough money to purchase his needs. When he did leave, it would be to the south. He smiled for the first time in over two weeks as his thoughts had gone to Ricardo, María, Sister Theresa, and the others.

San Antonio was a very busy city. Many wagon trains were organized and departed from here. People were very enthusiastic about moving to the west. Pedro hoped that the black and Mexican people were being treated better than previously. He realized that many blacks and Mexicans were anything but good, but he could not see the innocent ones being punished because they were of the same race.

After ten days of working odd jobs, Pedro had accumulated enough money to purchase what he needed. Finding a small general store, he bought a large piece of old canvas, an old back pack, a western hat, some string for fishing, a few hooks, some cork, an old wire grill and other necessities for cooking. With a little money left, he spotted some beef jerky. Then he had enough for a few hard biscuits. Broke but satisfied, he left San Antonio.

After finding the bow and arrows, Pedro was undecided about keeping them. Having done away with the tomahawk several days before, this was a tougher decision for the bow had produced food regularly. Wrapped in the buffalo hide, it was difficult to carry, but he decided to keep it for a few more days.

Over a week out of San Antonio, he saw a sign pointing left. It read "Rainy Roundup." He liked the unusual name and wondered what size town it might be. On a hunch, he turned down the road toward it. About the same time that he could see the buildings in the distance, Pedro crossed a very nice stream, To the right, the water went into a thick tree line. It was the most cover that he had seen for some time. Pedro had felt that he needed a rest and this might be the answer. If he could set up a camp here, maybe he could find a few odd jobs. It was now over three weeks since the Comanches were slaughtered, and he had traveled hard, before and after working in San Antonio. Pedro was thin, tired, and his body ached everywhere. The revenge thing still bothered him, but Running Fox still controlled his thoughts.

The stream widened as it entered the woods. He was very happy with the appearance of this place. Then came the spot he had been looking for. The stream was wide and there was no heavy cover for about fifty feet. About thirty feet back, the cover was much heavier. He immediately set up his canvas, with the aid of some branches. The buffalo hide was put inside, and would be his bed. It would be hard to see unless someone walked well into the heavy cover. Later, before dark, he found a nice turn in the stream, where there was grass in the edge of the water. He would try this spot tomorrow, as it looked like an ideal place for fishing.

It was the best sleep for him since the catastrophe. Under the canvas, it felt like he was sleeping in the best hotel in town. Wrapping some leaves and small limbs in his towel, he even had a first class pillow. The following morning, he angled through the trees in the direction of the town. He came out on a small road and the town was just ahead. No more than a mile, thought Pedro, who was enthusiastic for the first time in a while. Then as he was passing a nice ranch on his left, a horse and buggy was coming down the trail from it. As the buggy turned toward town, it soon passed Pedro. The buggy came to a halt and a young blonde woman looked back at him.

"Need a ride?"

Pedro was shocked but eagerly ran to the buggy. "Yes, thank you."

As he got in, the buggy moved toward town. "New around these parts?"

"Yes, I am. Think there might be some part time jobs around town?"

She flashed a pretty smile. "There is always an odd job around. Might have some at the ranch in the near future. I'm Julie McKeever. My husband and I own the JT Ranch over there." She was pointing, although it was obvious where she had just come from.

"I'm Pedro. If any job develops, I should be easy to find around town. I really need the work."

"Great! Meanwhile, I would try the bank. I do not know how it looks now, but last week it needed lots of cleaning. Then you might try the Town Saloon. Tom Baxter is the owner. There are others, but those are probably both good bets."

They were now in the middle of the town. Pedro was pleased as it was a fairly nice size one. She stopped the buggy in front of the "Rainy Roundup Bank." Pedro jumped down.

"Thanks for the lift. Hope you have to look me up."

She gave him another smile, and drove the buggy away. Although wearing trousers, she was still very feminine, thought Pedro. Mrs. McKeever was probably in her middle twenties, and although not a beauty, was certainly attractive. As Running Fox came to his mind, Pedro realized that after her, there would be very few that he would consider beautiful.

Julie McKeever's suggestions were both good ones. Pedro was hired to scrub the bank every other day. Tom Baxter, despite some cruel looking eyes, had hired him to clean up the saloon every morning. He was nice to Pedro, who was pleased that he always got a free sandwich there before he left. Occasionally, he did other jobs including running errands.

One week later, Tom Baxter offered him a steady job. He would continue the morning job, but now, would return at night. His job would be to keep all the tables clear of bottles and glasses. He did not want to be a clean up boy much longer, but it gave him the opportunity to keep his eyes open for those five men. It was bothering him more lately, so he knew that he could not give the hunt up.

Ten days later, Baxter found out that Pedro was living in the open. At the back of the saloon building, near the door, was a small room. The room needed cleaning badly, but there was a single bed with a decent mattress. He accepted the offer, for he did not like the lonely walk back to the woods late at night. He would keep his canvas tent and setup in the woods, so his afternoons could be spent there.

From the back door of the saloon building, it was about forty feet to the back door of the saloon. In this area were extra tables, chairs, and many other items that Pedro considered to be junk. Baxter's private office extended into this area with the entrance being at the end of the bar. The back door to the saloon was on the side where the customers sat. Many of the supplies were kept on a doubled deck frame rack that extended through most of the back area.

Pedro was to be his night guard, and was told to notify the sheriff if necessary. The one restriction Baxter had placed on him was about his office. It was strictly private, and he was not to enter it without permission. This did not bother the youth, as he felt it was a good deal for him. Several days later, Pedro realized the job was not all that he thought it would be. He knew that being a clean up boy was not really a job that would ever gain him any respect. He objected to the customers who called him "greaser" or "boy." The Comanche Indians had shown him respect even as a captive. He wondered what they would think, if they knew he had successfully completed all the training required to be a full Comanche warrior. He did not believe they would be calling him any names to his face. Pedro knew if he started a fight with a customer, Mr. Baxter would probably fire him. Then he thought about a gun. He had seen several gun fights, and the fast draw did not look that difficult to him. Pedro did not want to kill anyone, but at this time in his life, he was tired of taking insults. It had become obvious that the death of Running Fox had hardened him.

One day, he decided to go check on a gun. A lady, at the general store across the street from the saloon, had guns but knew nothing about them. He found a smaller store with more guns. After pricing them, Pedro decided it was out of his reach for the present. The owner, Bert Allen, was very nice and explained a lot to him. He would go back later.

As Pedro approached his camp through the heavy cover, he heard splashing water. He had just stepped into the open when he saw her.

CHAPTER 13

She was skinny, long legged, and her breasts were almost flat. The nude girl had short hair, and appeared to be about twelve, maybe thirteen years old. Pedro immediately turned his back on her. "Sorry, you surprised me."

The girl responded to that with a giggle. "When you catch me like this two more times, we will be even."

Pedro did not know what to say. Finally, "Put your clothes on so we can talk."

Again he could hear her giggling. "O.K., Mr. nice guy, I'm dressing."

A few moments she spoke again, laughing as she did, "It's safe for you to turn around, sir."

She was dressed like a boy, and really looked like one. "Forget the sir part, my name is Pedro."

She had a cute grin on her face, and he had to admit to himself, she was cute and quite a character. "Hi Pedro, I'm Jane. Plain Jane is what they call me at school. I guess you already know that with what you just saw."

Pedro knew she could dish it out, but could she take it? "Have the others at school seen you as I just did?"

The grin on her face was gone. "Course not. My mother is the only one besides you, really."

Pedro was smiling now. "That remark about me needing to see you two more times for us to be even. Explain it to me now."

The grin returned to her face broader than ever. Her eyes were sparkling. "I used to come here to swim all the time. Lately, I have been helping my mother in the café. The last three times, you were in the water, so I stayed in the bushes."

He looked at her sternly. "So you hid in the bushes until I came out. Then you watched me dress, right?"

The grin was smaller, but still there. "Yeah, I was so impressed."

Pedro looked at her with disbelief. "Was it the first time for you? Is that what you mean?"

"Gosh, no! I sleep in the same room with my sixteen-year-old brother. He parades around the room with nothing on all the time. I was impressed with you. Oh, you know what I mean."

This girl was something else, thought Pedro. "Young lady, I'm a stranger. You need to be careful. Do you understand? And that brother of yours needs his butt kicked. Does your mother know?"

For the first time she appeared very serious. "I'm sorry about my nasty remark. My brother is very mean. I'm scared of him. If I told my mother, he would hurt me. She has no control over him or my dad, who drinks all the time."

Pedro's feelings softened toward her, he had seen the fear in her eyes. "If he touches you, I'll whip his butt. How about your dad? Do either put their hands on you?"

The gleam came back to her eyes. "My brother is tough. Really think you could?"

"Yes, and?"

"Well, my dad walks around naked when he's drunk. My brother tells me when I'm prettier, he'll get me." After a pause. "My dad's O.K. when he's sober. He hits mom when he's drunk, but he never bothers me."

Despite his troubles, the youth was feeling for this girl. "Jane, you should tell your mother what your brother said. Tell me if he bothers you."

Her eyes were gleaming. "Gee, you are serious. You would do that for me? O.K., I promise."

Both were seated, and Pedro relaxed back on one arm. "Your mother has a café in town?"

Jane raised her knees and cupped her hands around them. "Yes, we own the Roundup General Store and the little café next door. It's open for suppers only."

Pedro flashed a big smile now. "I work across the street. Mornings and evenings in the Town Saloon. Cleaning up, not great but I need to eat. I was in, looking at guns today."

Her eyes were sad. "I hate guns. My brother thinks he's a fast gun. Boy, he's a long way off. He practices though." Her warm smiled returned as he decided she could be a good friend. He needed a friend.

"You must be new in town. I have not even seen you around, except out here."

"You're right, just a couple of weeks. I need to catch a fish or two for supper. Would you like to watch?"

"Love to," was her eager reply. Then he showed her his canvas tent as he went after his fishing pole. She was impressed with everything, and very surprised when she found out where he was living. It did not take him long to catch two fish at his favorite spot down the stream. Meanwhile, she had asked questions about everything he did. Before leaving, she wanted to know if she could come back tomorrow afternoon, and fish with him. His earlier observation had been right. He had made a friend, and probably a good one.

By the time she arrived the following afternoon, Pedro had her fishing pole ready. He had never seen a girl so excited about fishing. Quickly, she caught the first fish, and Pedro never could catch up. She caught five, and his total for the afternoon was only two. While she watched him the day before, he had told her all about his being the "champion fisherman of all Mexico." Now he realized what a jewel she really was. Instead of bragging, she never even mentioned that she caught more.

She continued asking him questions about the sport. He invited her to eat with him, and together, they cooked the fish on Pedro's grill. They had to hurry so she could get home before dark. Before she left, Pedro confessed, "You are the only one ever to outfish me, really."

She laughed. "I was lucky. Can I come again?"

"Sure, anytime, but no more peeping." Giggling, she quickly hugged his neck, and ran off. Pedro had never considered a young girl as a friend, but now he really had one. Then he laughed aloud as the thought of what a character she was. He had heard her whistling a tune long before she had arrived that day. When she left just now, it appeared she could run as fast as a deer. Never had he known anyone like her. A genuine tomboy. In two days, she was like his sister. Her brother, Kelly, had best keep his filthy paws off her. Nothing could bring out the Comanche in him quicker.

CHAPTER 14

A few nights later, Curly Duncan, a young rancher, came into the saloon. He liked Pedro, and was one of the rare ones that was nice to him. He was carrying a package, and handed it to him. "Thanks, but what is it?"

Duncan, a nice looking but overweight young fellow, was very successful in the cattle business.

"Go put this in your room. Later, when you get time, come over and we'll talk." The young rancher had looked around closely, confirming that Tom Baxter was not around.

A half hour later, with Duncan siting alone, Pedro approached him. In a low tone that was almost a whisper, the young rancher spoke, "I bought me a new pistol from Bert Allen. While I was there, he mentioned you had been in. That package contains my old pistol. It's in good shape, I just wanted a new one. Treat it with respect, and don't get any ideas that might get you killed. Meanwhile, I prefer that Baxter not know I gave it to you. We are not what you call close friends, as you have probably noticed."

Pedro smiled as he leaned over. "Yes, I noticed it a coupla times. Thanks, I really wanted one. No one will know you gave it to me. They may never see it. If the bartender or anyone else asks, I'll say it was underwear."

"Great, and by the way, I know Baxter has been good to you, but take my word, it would be a mistake to really trust him."

Pedro remembered those cruel eyes the first time they met. "I appreciate that. Thanks again."

Pedro soon made a makeshift gun holster. Using a piece of board for the back of it, he cut and fit a piece of soft canvas for the front. There was no doubt, it was tough to draw from this crude holster. His feelings were if he could learn from this, than when he got the real thing, it would be easier to really get faster. He knew Jane's feelings about her brother's gun. This would be his only secret from her, although he had never mentioned the revenge thing. Eventually, he would show her the gun, however unless there was a reason, he doubted she would ever know of his desire for revenge.

Jane came to see and fish with him three times a week. They agreed if she did not come on her day, she would try to come the very next day. They became very good friends, and soon they even quit counting who caught the most. There was no question, she fished very well. He decided it probably saved him embarrassment when they quit counting.

It became apparent to her that Pedro was not getting a balanced diet. Ideas began to whirl around in that busy mind of hers. Then one night, Pedro received a real pleasant surprise.

Jane had told him to be at the back door of the saloon at nine o'clock. When he opened the door, there she stood with a tray full of hot food. One meat, two vegetables, potatoes, cornbread, and pie. A feast, if he ever saw one. She was all smiles, and for the first time, it appeared to be more than a friendly smile. She had celebrated her fourteenth birthday a week before. They were friends, so Pedro had thought, now he wondered if he had overdone his friendliness. He would never hurt her but wondered and realized that maybe they had spent too much time together these last three months.

"I hope you enjoy it. Put the tray on that box, and I will get it later."

Pedro finally found his voice. "Jane, I don't want you to go to all this trouble."

With that gleaming look in her eyes, and that cute grin, "What trouble?"

"Let me pay for it , please."

"No, these are leftovers. We close at nine. Mother knows about you. I'll tell you about that later. Bye." She was gone in a flash.

Pedro shook his head and then placed his food back of the door that opened into the saloon. This way he could eat while working.

To keep her from bringing him food every night, Pedro started eating in the café before going to work. He did this several times a week. When he didn't, she was there with the tray at nine o'clock.

He would never forget Jane's face when she introduced him to her mother. That blush told him what was obvious. She had feelings for him and it concerned him how strong they were.

Pedro began to practice everyday with the gun on his fast draw, but could not afford to shoot for accuracy that often. He was encouraged with his accuracy but not too happy with his speed on the draw. Although he made an excuse to himself that it was the holster, deep down he was worried about it. Having been successful at almost everything he had tried, this was too important for any type of failure.

Numerous strangers and regular town people came into the saloon but still not one clue on those five men. He decided to stay a few more months, so that he might be better with the gun before leaving town. Then there was Jane. He was not in love with her, but somehow she had become the best friend he had ever had. He realized how she felt, but being only fourteen, she could find someone else in time.

Pedro would climb up on the rack, close to Baxter's office, to get napkins and other supplies. There was a crack in the wood where the side met the top of his office. Several times, without even trying, he could see the owner sitting at his desk. This time he heard a sob. Wondering who was crying, he glanced into Baxter's office, and was surprised to see Julie McKeever sitting there and crying. Pedro had spoken with her several times since that first day, but she never came through with the part time job offer. He had found out just recently. Her husband was a cripple and now had some type of disease. The rumor was that she was in financial trouble.

He could hear every word of the conversation.

"I'm sorry I don't have the money yet. I do have some coming soon. Would you give me a chance and wait?" Baxter came around the desk, that cruel look never more obvious despite a smile.

"Baby, we can handle this now. Just pull off all those clothes and lay on my desk. I've wanted you for a long time. I'll give you a receipt for a month's payment before we do it. How about it, Babe?" She looked dazed, and he continued as he dropped his trousers, and pulled down his underwear exposing his aroused shaft. "See how bad I want you. Undress while I write the receipt. You can catch up the other month the same way later." He turned to write the receipt as she stood up to undress.

As she began, Pedro felt a cold sweat and a stirring feeling in his groin. He realized it was wrong to peep but he was fascinated. He had never done it and now he was going to at least watch the event. As her beautiful breasts were exposed, Pedro could feel an instant arousal. At this second, he thought of Running Fox and his disappointment of what was never to be.

She was totally naked now, and as she lay across the emptied top of the desk, he noticed Baxter was also nude. She had stopped crying and looked perfectly calm, almost as if nothing was going to happen. Baxter checked the lock on the door, and then something did happen. He moved into her, and quickly she wrapped her firm legs around his back. She was coming off the desk to meet his thrusts, and nobody could tell Pedro she was not enjoying it. Then heavy breathing and extra movement signaled the end.

"Really good, Baby. Come back soon for the other month."

"I'm not too proud, but I'll be back."

"Don't give me that proud business, you loved it too."

Looking sadly toward him, "Yeah, guess I did. Its been a long time for me."

Pedro slipped down quietly and went to his room, sweating and excited. I am old enough, but still just an inexperienced kid, thought the youth.

Several months later, while cleaning tables on his job in the saloon, Pedro was completely shocked at what he saw. Three men had come into the saloon, stood at the bar for a while, then took seats at an empty table. He was busy, and really did not pay any attention to them, until he heard one of them call one of the others Toro. His head did an about face. Trying not to stare, he easily recognized the big Toro. who had raped and killed his mother. There was no doubt in his mind. Then came another surprise. One of the men had top of his left ear missing. This one had to be Luke, but he could not recognize the other man. Knowing they had never seen him, he purposely worked around that table, until he heard the other name. Well, well, thought Pedro, as the other man was addressed as Gabby. He immediately hoped they lived in this vicinity.

He had been trying to plan a way to tell Jane that he was leaving town, but as of now, he had no plans to leave. After they left that night, he had asked the bartender about them. His excuse was he thought he knew the big man. That was no lie, he knew him too damn well. He told Pedro that the big man was named Toro, and that he was the foreman of a ranch, owned by the other two. He had even volunteered that it was about fifty miles southwest of here, and that they came to town usually every couple of months.

Pedro thought about them most of the night, and when he finally fell asleep, he had a strange dream that left him in a cold sweat that he could not explain. Earlier, he had thought how fast he could draw with his new holster bought a month before. He had witnessed two gun fights since being in town, and none of them looked to be as fast as he was. That had made him feel good last night but after the dream, a strange feeling had blanked out any good feeling about what he wanted to do. Maybe killing them was not the way, but certainly the courts could not help since the crime was in Mexico, and years had passed by.

On his way to his camp the following day, he went into the church to say some prayers. It was only his fourth or fifth time since coming to this town eight or nine months before. Pedro was ashamed of himself, and continued to wonder about the strange dream, one that he couldn't remember yet brought on these feelings.

Outside of town, he saw the buggy coming toward him. It was Julie McKeever, and she had a big smile for him. "Hi, Pedro. Remember when you first came to town, and I told you about some part time work?"

"Yes, I can work afternoons usually."

"Good, I need some fences mended. Have had hard times, but now I can afford two part days a week. Are you interested?"

He looked at the smiling blonde woman. "Sure, when do we start?"

"Tomorrow is Thursday. How about Tuesdays and Thursdays?" Then with a laugh, she added, "Till my money runs out."

Pedro returned her smile. "Great, tomorrow at the ranch?"

"No, I'll have the supplies in the buggy. Pick you up along here at this same time and drop you off where I need the work done."

"See you tomorrow then."

As he walked off, she drove on toward town. Pedro could

not help to wonder if she was going to pay off another note. A smile came to his lips, as he thought about working for her. He secretly wished she would pay him off the same way.

The good thoughts didn't last but a few minutes, as his problem of revenge came back. Almost eighteen now, he had dreamed of finding those men since the murder of his mother when he was eight years old. Ten years had passed, and now he knew where three of the five killers were. He had lived at the orphanage, slept in the open, lived with Comanches, and now in the back of a saloon. During his entire life, revenge for her death, had been the main ambition of his life. The very first night he found three of them, he had a weird dream that left him in a cold sweat. Puzzled, and not sure, he believed a battle within his own conscience was going to decide which road to take. It was time to hurry, for today was Jane's day, and he needed a bath before the little cute tomboy arrived.

By the time he arrived at the camp, he had decided to wait until those killers returned to town. He needed to settle things within his own mind and make his plan. Revenge was a necessity, whether he decided to kill them or not. Meanwhile, just in case, he would work with that gun until it became a part of him. Law and order was still not proven as far as he was concerned. Until it was, the gun would be an important part of his life.

CHAPTER 15

Pedro hurriedly removed his clothing and ran into the water. He wanted to be finished before she arrived. His mind had been running wild since he had seen the three men last evening. The cold water worked on his thoughts some as he shivered upon entering it.

Still undecided, he really wanted to tell Jane about the revenge thing, since seeing those men had changed a lot of his plans. Several weeks before, Jane had confided in him, that her brother had packed his things and left. He had said very little except that it was for good. It was her understanding that Kelly was to be one of a group of hired gunmen. However, this told them very little and nothing else had been heard since he left. Finally, she had a room to herself, and certainly had shed no tears.

Pedro liked her mother, Agnes Skaag, an attractive slender

brunette, who worked very hard. She had been very nice to him, always remembering to thank him for the fish whenever Jane brought the extra ones home. He liked the idea that she trusted him to be with Jane. As for her father, George, that was a different matter. The man was friendly when he was sober but from what Pedro could see, it was not often enough.

First he heard some noise in the bushes, then her voice, "Pedro, stay in the water."

Then she came out into the open. "Wait until I turn my back after you finish your bath. That is, unless you want the score to be four to one." Then came one of her typical giggles. Pedro gave her a stern look that lasted all of five seconds, then it gave way to a big smile. She was a tease, and quite a character, and he thought more of her every day. What a change she had made in the nine months or so they had been friends. Her hair was now almost shoulder length, light brown and wavy. She usually wore a tight blouse and tight britches. She was not big chested yet, but certainly not flat like at first. Those tight britches showed that her legs had filled out some and she had the cutest fanny. Not yet fifteen, Pedro wondered how pretty she would be by the time she was sixteen. He did not know exactly how he felt about her. Maybe she was just a friend, but if so, why did he think of her so often?

"Turn around, I'm coming out." He came out, dried off, and slipped into his trousers. "You can turn around now."

She turned with a giggle and a grin. "That was really tempting. It was almost four to one."

"You're still bad. I thought you had changed for the better, but now I'm not sure."

"I love to tease you because you're so serious. Lighten up, my love, and enjoy life. You know I am kidding." That cute pug nose and grin made it impossible to really fuss at her.

"I really have some serious things to talk to you about. You think you could settle down and listen?"

With another of those grins, she continued the game, "Boy, you look more muscular every time I see you without a shirt." Then she whistled at him.

Pedro walked over and picked up his clean shirt. Then as he put it on, "O.K, so I won't tell you anything today."

"I'm sorry, really. Sometime I get carried away with you. Let's get serious. Tell me whatever." She sat on the ground and relaxed.

"Jane, for you to understand, I need to tell you almost my life history. Promise, this will be our secret, It could cost us both our lives if not." Pedro put his forefinger up to his lips and then put it on her lips. As he moved it away, she lightly grabbed his wrist and kissed his finger.

He smiled and began his story. Jane was completely awed by the story, saddened by the way his mother had been killed, and was taken in by the tale of his capture by the Comanches, and his life with them. Her expression of jealousy was very obvious when he told her of Running Fox, her beauty and the entire truth. She again was saddened by the death of the entire tribe, but her face remained red with jealousy from that point on. When he told her about the three men, she shocked him. The big Mexican, Toro, and his two friends knew her family, and usually came into the café and ate whenever they were in town.

"Maybe I should not have told you about them."

Trying to overcome the Running Fox story, she put her hands on his shoulders. "Listen, lover boy, I am more than glad you told me. Surely you understand that friends like that need to be watched. In fact, who needs them?"

He was so glad with her reply, he unconsciously reached over and hugged her. She immediately returned the hug, and it was Pedro who had to break it up.

"What are you going to do about it?"

He knew, at this point, she needed to know it all. Taking the gun and holster out of his back pack, he showed it to her, and then admitted he had hidden it from her because of her attitude toward her brother and his gun.

"You know something, Pedro, between this Indian beauty and your hiding things from me, I'm not sure we are as close as I had thought." Pedro looked at her with sad eyes. This time, he purposely pulled her close and held her. She relaxed and let him hold her but did not attempt to hold him. "Honey, let me tell you the rest before we settle this."

As she moved away, she had a small grin for him. "Well, that is something. It's the first time you called me that."

He smiled sweetly at the young girl. "Being raised in the orphanage, my love for God is strong. How can I get revenge without killing them?"

Saying "Please," she pulled him toward her, and motioned for him to lay in her arms. He did as requested, then relaxed.

"I am sorry you have such a problem, especially since you have no family of your own. You do have Mom and I, we can help. Now, love, may I kiss you?"

"Boys are supposed to ask that. Remember all the explanations of what is right and what is wrong."

She had that devilish grin. "Yeah, I remember all those instructions you gave me. You never explained what the girl does, when the guy never does anything except talk. Several times, when I brought the tray, I kissed your cheek. Even then, I ran off to keep from hearing a lecture. Soooo, now...," then she lowered her head and kissed him on the lips, holding it until he gradually moved her away.

"Why are you breaking all our rules when I have so many problems?"

"That's easy. Just trying to cheer you up. Maybe I am the better friend. Telling me all that stuff about the Indian girl, and hiding the gun from me." Then she gave him a strong stare. "You're lucky I kissed you instead of walking away."

He sat up and stared at her. She was not grinning. "I guess I deserved that. It was hard to tell you about the Indian girl, but having never lied to you, it just came out. The gun was different as I did not want you to be unhappy with me." Then as he smiled, so did she. "I enjoyed the kiss, but we have to be careful. Know what I mean?"

Then she surprised him, "I understand that if you don't kiss me often enough, I will do the kissing. With all the worries you have, it might help." Then with a grin, she continued, "We will work out some way to get those men, I promise." Boy, he did not know where to go from here. He would never take advantage of her, but this looked like the beginning of some difficult times with her. If Julie McKeever ever made a pass at him, he would take her up in a minute. However, Jane was too young, and beside that, how come his feelings about her confused him so? How could he concentrate on revenge? Then he decided to tell her about Julie McKeever.

"Julie McKeever finally asked me to help her with the fences. On Tuesday and Thursday afternoons, starting tomorrow."

"I have been coming on Monday, Wednesday, and Friday, so that is good for us. That is, if you still want to see me, I was just having my say. If you want to kiss me fine, if not, hey, I might find another friend."

He studied her face for a moment. Obviously he had hurt her several times today. "I take that back. I'm sorry I hurt you today." Then for the very first time, he kissed her with emotion and feeling. When it ended, she had a glow in her eyes that he had never seen before.

"Now we know I don't need another friend. Huh?" He loved her smile, but it was another worry. She was far too young and those type of kisses could only be occasional. He did not trust her, but even more, Pedro did not trust himself.

Then he got his pistol, and she watched the practice. She was impressed and swore that he was faster than her brother. He did not believe it, and told her she was partial. She never agreed with that, and kept insisting it was the truth. She bragged on his accuracy, insisting it was ten times better than her brother. Pedro knew that was an exaggeration.

They were to eat in the café that evening, but they fished anyway in order to bring the catch to her mother.

Toro and his friends were there again that night, and finally before leaving, spent some time in with Tom Baxter. Pedro would have liked to have heard that conversation but he was unable to leave the tables at that time.

As they walked out, Pedro almost got sick in the stomach just looking at Toro. He vowed to himself, somehow that man would not leave here next time.

CHAPTER 16

The following day, Julie McKeever picked up Pedro on the road, and they drove several miles toward the back part of the ranch. They stopped and she showed him several places along the fence, where repairs were needed.

She was back in about an hour. The timing was good, as he was just finishing up the work. Then she drove into a woody section of the property, where there was several days work needed. Again she departed, leaving him with his work. It was much cooler here in the shade. It would have been a better place to start in the heat of the day, instead of where she took him first.

When Tuesday came, she picked him up at the same place, and left him in the wooded section. When she returned several hours later, Pedro was surprised to see her get down from the buggy, and unload a large picnic basket and several other bags.

"I don't like to overwork my help, especially when they are as handsome as you are." The remark took Pedro by surprise. He immediately thought about her relationship with Baxter.

"Well, the work isn't too hard, but if it's food and something cold to drink, I'm ready."

She grinned. "That comes as no surprise. Young men usually are ready…for food, that is." Pedro was more uncertain than ever about her now. Her smile about that last remark told him that he could be right.

In the picnic basket, there was food for a small army. thought Pedro. They ate fried chicken, red beans, potatoes, cornbread, and chocolate cake. Just as they finished, she sprawled out on the ground. "Relax, Pedro, you have worked enough for one day." He could feel perspiration more now than when he was working on the fence. She wore a light blouse and even tighter britches. Julie told him all about her crippled husband, his disease, and the fact that he could not live much longer. Pedro knew all this from gossip, but wondered what this might be leading up to. Of course, she did not know he had heard about it, so maybe it was all innocent. He had relaxed, and also laid down.

Then she asked, "Is that cute Jane Skaag your girl friend?" He wanted to answer truthfully, but really wasn't sure what that would be.

"Yeah, its getting to be that way. Started out as just good friends, but the situation is changing as she gets older."

She turned sideways and looked across the blanket of food, smiling at him. "You are soooo old yourself. Neither of you are dry behind the ears yet."

Pedro raised up, leaning on his arm. "I'm eighteen, and have been on my own since I was fourteen. I certainly hope so." Then he rubbed behind one of his ears.

She laughed aloud. "Now dry your hand."

He tossed a chicken bone at her, and she laughed even more. "Pedro, it feels really good to have someone to talk to. Especially if the person can be trusted."

He began to wonder if Julie McKeever wasn't a much nicer woman than he originally thought. Maybe she did that to Baxter out of desperation and still enjoyed it. "I can be trusted if you need a favor. Just ask."

She gave him a reassuring smile and look. "Thanks, Pedro, I'll remember that." Then she jumped up and started to clean up the picnic food and letter.

Pedro folded the blanket and helped tidy up the ground area. "I have some money coming on the first of the month, so we will settle up then. Is that O.K.?"

"Sure, anytime," Julie looked at him with sad eyes. "I have had some bad times because of money. You probably know that, everyone else does."

"I may be only eighteen, but it has not been an easy eighteen, believe me. I understand."

With tears in her eyes, she walked over to Pedro, and placed her head on his shoulder. He put his arms around her and the embrace lasted for several minutes. Pedro could feel her warm body tightly against his, and his thoughts had gone to Running Fox, and their tender encounter in the snow. He was embarrassed as they parted, and through tearful eyes, she had a grin for him. She took him to the road, knowing his camp had to be near.

As he jumped off, he waved. "See you Thursday."

"Great, and Pedro, I take it all back. You are dry behind the ears." With this, she took off in the buggy. Now he was really embarrassed. He would see her Thursday, if he could face her by then.

After arriving at the camp, he decided to bathe immediately, and go to eat at the café. Jane's bright eyes and cute grin greeted him as he walked in. The aroma of this place compared to where he worked was a contrast. Agnes Skaag's cooking brought very pleasant thoughts even before the food arrived. As usual, regardless of his order, his plate was overfilled. If he left any extra payment, at nine o'clock sharp, there would be a knock on the back door and the extra money would be on a box.

After dinner, Pedro went to work. Business was usually

slow until Saturday night, and tonight was no exception. Soon, his friend, Curly Duncan came in. It was seldom that they had a chance to talk. "You mentioned Saturday night that you had worked for Julie McKeever last Thursday. Have you been there since?"

Pedro wondered at his interest in her. "Yeah, today and every Tuesday and Thursday for awhile. She is a nice lady."

Curly smiled at Pedro. "Very nice, but a lady, I'm not sure." His first thought was that Curly knew about Baxter.

"I do not follow you, friend."

Curly gave him a rather doubting look. "I guess that remark surprised you. You are a good kid, and I trust you, so confiding my feelings should be safe. Her husband is not long for this world. I have it bad for her, and you know what I mean."

Pedro stared in amazement as the rancher continued, "Sometimes when you sit on the side and watch, you see things that make you sorry you ever bothered to look. Maybe I am a bastard for waiting for her husband to die, but damn, I found out something that really has me torn up."

Pedro was afraid to ask what he found out, especially since he felt he had watched it. Being deceitful was not to his liking, but he never could admit this. "Curly, we are friends, but you don't need to tell me your private feelings or personal business." He slapped Pedro on the back.

"You are going to listen if I have to tie you up. Your boss, Tom Baxter, holds the notes on Julie McKeever's ranch." Looking around, verifying no one could hear, he continued in a whisper, "She has money trouble as you probably know. Well, the bartender told a buddy of mine that during the last two months, she has screwed Baxter twice. Once for each note, and I have not slept since. I hate him anyway so now I'd like to kill him. Meanwhile, my feelings for her have hit rock bottom, though it's going to be tough to forget her."

Pedro looked at the sad cowboy. Curly had told him before that he was lucky with money but unlucky with women. Twenty nine years old and still single was not his dream. He wanted a nice wife and a family. The only decent looking woman, who was ever friendly with him, turned out to be a whore. "Maybe there are two sides to this. If she can't pay her notes, and knowing Baxter, she is probably desperate. Have you thought about that? Having a very sick husband, and no help, that has to be rough on her."

Curly quickly replied, "Hell, I would pay the notes and not ask for anything."

"Sure you would, but she certainly doesn't know."

Curly studied for a moment as the sadness remained. "Never thought of her being desperate. God, I hope so. Maybe you could do me a favor. Feel her out, find out what you can, would you?"

"Sure will."

"Good."

At this moment, Pedro decided to do more than Curly asked. Julie would probably be happy to hear that Curly would loan her money with no strings attached.

Then Tom Baxter came in and the conversation ceased. Pedro went about his job. He wondered why Curly Duncan hated Baxter but knew there could be a world of reasons. If he knew why, and accepted the reason, then he would tell him about his problem with Toro, Luke, and Gabby. What worried him was, where were the other two. He didn't believe Curly was involved as he would have been fairly young, but now that he had found three of them, he could take no chances. Pedro was very suspicious that Baxter was one of the masked men. He had him pegged as the one whose name he never heard. Curly Duncan was above this bunch, and maybe he could help with some good advice. If he could help Curly with Julie, then he would ask about Baxter. It was not much of a gamble, and it could help him.

CHAPTER 17

Thursday afternoon came quicker than Pedro really wanted it to. However, she greeted him with a sweet smile, and soon they were in the wooded area again. There was practically no conversation as Pedro unloaded the new wire and the necessary tools. As Julie left in the buggy, she called out, "See you in a couple of hours with some supper."

"Thanks." Pedro answered back, wondering if she could hear it. He felt good and worked very aggressively on the fence. The afternoon before had gone very well with Jane. She did not tease him, as they talked mostly about his problem coming up with the three killers. While she was there, they fished and then Pedro practiced with the gun. It seemed to him that he was faster than ever. Jane confirmed this, but of course, he knew she was too partial to give an honest opinion. Neither had come up with any idea about how he could get his revenge without killing. This is what really kept Jane out of the teasing mood for she was scared to death about the whole idea. They had agreed to talk more on Friday.

As they were leaving, she hugged his neck and held him close. He did not resist for he also felt the same need. While he was in the café that evening, she started up the teasing game again, whispering in his ear, "I missed the golden opportunity today, for I believe you would have returned my kiss as strong as you returned my hug. Don't you deny it either." Then as she moved away with that cute grin, all he could do was smile back, for he knew she was probably right.

He could not believe it when suddenly Julie approached him in the buggy. However, looking at the amount of work that he had finished, it must have been at least two hours.

"Chow time, young man," was her greeting. Pedro finished up that piece of wire as she prepared the picnic area.

"It will not be a feast, as you called it the other night, but I believe it will be satisfactory." Then she put out the home made bread, sliced chicken breast, tomatoes, and lettuce. From another sack came the dessert, rich looking chocolate cookies.

"It looks like a feast to me." The picnic setting was on a smaller blanket so they sat closer together than the other day.

She talked while preparing the sandwiches, "I believe that you are the only real friend I have. If you are wondering what my definition of a real friend is, here goes. A person that will do you favors and not expect something in return. That is a short description, but it says it all. For a favor, some people put their hand out and others go even further. Being a young woman, you probably know where they want to put their hand. On my butt, and I want you to know that I am damn tired of it. If it was just a case of feeling it, that would not be too bad, but you know they want it all, and you are old enough to know what I'm talking about."

Then her serious expression t turned to a smile. "Now that I know behind your ears are dry, I am talking to you in an adult way."

Pedro gulped and weakly smiled. He knew this was his opportunity to put in a plug for Curly. He hoped he wasn't too shook up to take advantage of this opening. "Julie, I know someone who would help you and expect nothing in return. Do you know Curly Duncan?"

She looked both surprised and shocked. "Barely. We were introduced once, and have spoken since but why in the world, or better yet, what makes you think he would want to help me?"

"He did not tell me why but I think I know the answer. You might be surprised, and then again, maybe not. He has feelings for you."

Julie looked at him in disbelief. "If I had a fiddle, I'd play you a tune." Pedro was beginning to think how difficult convincing her was going to be.

"Pedro, tell me the real story about this. How did it come up, and just exactly how did he word it?" He knew there was no way he could answer that. All his life he had a problem of being unable to say anything not truthful and look convincing. Running Fox and Chief Wounded Bear had seen right through him. Now, he would make a run at her. Maybe, she was gullible enough to believe him.

"Well, I told him in the saloon that I was working for you, and his eyes glowed so bright that it was almost funny. He asked if I knew about your financial problems. I told him I had heard about it, but not from you. Julie, he told me that Tom Baxter holds the notes on your ranch. Is that right?"

Her face turned whiter by the second. "Yes, he's right, so?"

Pedro gulped again, and wondered how he was doing. "He hates Tom Baxter, and doesn't trust him. How do you feel about Baxter?"

Now she hesitated and obviously was puzzled about what to say next. Maybe he was getting through to her, but he waited with anxiety as to what she would say next. "I agree with him. Tom Baxter is a bastard. Excuse my English." Now Pedro did not know what to say next. "Truthfully, Pedro, he is a bastard but if he wasn't, I would have lost this place to him. If I knew this was in complete confidence, and I mean strictly between you and me, then I would tell you everything. This would not be for Mr. Duncan's ears."

"You have my word. I'll tell Curly what you want him to hear. I can promise you, he means well." They were finished with the food, and now she lay on the ground relaxed. Pedro continued to sit near her.

"First, the real truth. Then we will decide what you can and cannot tell your friend."

Pedro nodded his approval.

"With my husband so ill, it has been rough. I have only one old cowhand left. He takes care of the few cattle you see. It is expensive to not let them feed out on the range behind there, but it takes more help to let them roam. I bring in hay and other food to them, for these are the backbone of my ranch. I have a few bulls on the other side of the ranch house, and we breed them to these cows in this field. This little thin wire fence will hold them only if I feed them well. Most of the rest of the fence is wood, and as you can see, it is fairly rotten. Anyway, I recently sold the last of the cattle that I intend to part with. The money is due here soon. It will pay my notes for the next two months, and take care of a few of my other bills for food and other things. Now to Mr. Baxter."

At this, she paused to look at Pedro. It was a look that almost told him that she was getting ready to tell him the truth. Maybe it was his imagination, but it appeared to be a look of shame.

"Two months ago, I asked him to let me be late for my payment. He agreed but wanted me to come in before the next payment was due. Still without money, I went into his office, and cried to him. He knew I had money coming but would not listen. It was no problem, so he told me, then added all I had to do was to screw him and get a receipt for the monthly note marked paid in full. I was so scared of losing my ranch I agreed. Truthfully, having none for over a year, I enjoyed it. Then two weeks later, despite a haunting conscience, I went back for seconds, to clear up the other month just starting. This time I felt dirty, like a whore or something even worse. I can't do it again, Pedro, not even if I have to move my sick husband out, and give him the ranch. I will have the money, as I told you for the next two months. Now, tell me what you think of your friendly little whore?"

Then she broke down and cried, with Pedro sliding over to her, trying to console her. She sat up, and with her head on his shoulder, cried until he could feel the dampness of her tears on his shoulder. The blonde woman appealed to him, and with those very ample breasts pushing against his chest, Pedro was soon very excited. It was the wrong time, and was the last thing he wanted. As he squirmed around, changing positions, it was obvious she knew it, but neither made a remark about it. "I understand it. You were desperate. I guess it seemed the easy way out at first."

Julie dropped her eyes, staring at the blanket. "Thanks for wording it so nicely."

"How about I tell Curly you will meet with him about your problems?"

"O.K., let's do that. Something tells me he knows about Baxter and me, but if he mentions anything like that, I will simply walk."

Pedro knew she meant every word. He could also tell by the fire in her eyes that her actions with Baxter were finished.

Then he decided to tell her more. "Julie, you have been so honest, even telling me a very personal experience. I want you to know more about Curly Duncan. In a few words, lucky with money, unlucky with women. His feelings for you are real, but he would never say anything since you are married. I honestly believe that he is a fine man."

"Sounds like he might be the opposite of Baxter. I hope so, because I'm gonna need help in time." Then they picked up the basket and blanket and placed them in the buggy.

When they arrived at the road, Pedro jumped out and waved. Before driving away, she came up with a shocker, "Pedro, one of these afternoons when things are not so serious, as one friend to another, I am going to take care of your problem so completely, your ears will be dry forever."

CHAPTER 18

Several days later, while Pedro was working in the saloon that morning, the town doctor brought him a note from Julie McKeever. He knew it was important, for never before had he received a note from her or anybody else. Putting down his mop, he opened it and quickly read its contents. Her husband was very ill and she had to remain at his side. He was not to come back to work until she contacted him again. The money that she owed for his work was also in the envelope. Returning to his mopping, Pedro became deep in thought. He was sorry for her husband even though he had never seen him. The youth was ashamed of his first thought when he completed reading the note. It was a disappointed one because of her last promise to him. Hating to admit it even to himself, he could not get his mind off what was going to happen. Well, I guess Jane and I will both be green horns when we get married. At that point, he caught on to what he had just thought. When did I decide that? he asked himself.

Laughing out loud, he looked around to see if anybody had heard him. People will think I'm nuts and wonder about me. I guess the fact is, I do love Jane, and that has to be what love really is. When you feel like you can't ever imagine yourself without someone, that has to be it. He remembered that he was going to leave Running Fox, even though he thought it was love. Pedro was glad that the revenge thing was coming to a head, for he never could leave Jane. She had stolen his heart, along with his title as the "champion fisherman of Mexico."

Two weeks later, Pedro heard the news of the death of Julie's husband. In this time, he had not heard a word from her, but the doctor had told him that she had not left his side. He was to meet Jane today, so now he had more news for her. Of course, the big news was going to shock her out of her britches. He was in love with her, and she would know it today.

As he approached the camp, Pedro could hear her whistling. That girl could whistle a tune better than anyone he had ever heard. He started whistling the same tune, and she came running at top speed. He would even be afraid to run her a race. All in all, she was still a tomboy, and he loved it.

"Hi, honey" she greeted him as she jumped into his arms. Pedro had to catch her in self defense, and the next thing he knew, she had kissed him. Letting her slide down until her feet touched the ground, he surprised her by hugging and then kissing her solidly. "Wow, what's up, good lookin?" grinning as she spoke.

Pedro released her, took her by the hand, and together they walked to the camp opening that was near his tent. "Well, I have two pieces of news for you. One not pleasant, but the other, something tells me that you might like."

"Great, but I also have some news and I'm afraid mine is not very good. In fact, it has my mother crying about it."

"What is it, Jane?"

"Well, Mom got a letter from my brother, Kelly, telling her

that he now has two notches on his gun. He had two fast draw gunfights, and killed both men. One of them was experienced. He is now known as 'Kelly Boy.' Can you imagine, killing those men and bragging about it like he was a hero or something. Mom says he works for some big shot rancher, and does whatever is asked of him. She never wants to see him again. Do you think she means it?"

Pedro put his arm around her. "I'm sorry, Jane. I just don't know. Being his mother, she probably did not mean it, but your dad has given her a lifetime of trouble. So who knows?"

"Yeah, tell me your news."

"Julie McKeever's husband died last night." She looked sad. "I knew him before he got sick. He was a nice guy. From what I hear, he has done a lot of suffering."

Then Pedro brought out a genuine smile. "Now for the news that I hope you like. I have discovered something. I love you." Jane was in pure shock. She just stood there with her mouth open. "You did hear me. I love you. How do you feel about me?"

Then she reacted. First, a big smile, then she jumped right in the middle of him, with both arms around his neck, and then came the kiss. It was a loving, passionate kiss that left Pedro's knees weak. The kiss also brought out his usual problem, and she quickly realized it.

"I guess you are the one who needs a lecture today." Her devilish grin left Pedro completely speechless.

Finally, "You never answered me, do you or don't you?"

She moved in close and put her arms around him, hugging him very tightly, as he tried unsuccessfully to move away. "Yes, yes, yes, I love you! I have since the day you caught me nude coming out of the water. You have made me the happiest girl in the whole world."

"Well, that is just it. You are only fifteen and still a girl."

The big smile left her, but she still had a cute grin. "Something tells me you didn't think that a few minutes ago after that kiss."

Pedro was pink now and getting pinker by the minute. "I

only said that because I want to be fair to you. Here is the deal, and please take this seriously."

She cut in on him now. "O.K., let's get serious, but don't forget, before you leave you are going to get a lecture. Remember how many you gave me?"

Pedro smiled at her and held his precious one, lightly kissing her cheek and then she moved her lips in place. Another of those kisses followed. Neither tried to pull away as love had moved in on them. Finally, she had her face against his chest as he looked down at her.

"Before you give me the terms of this deal, I accept." She was grinning now and he was next to heaven.

"There is one part of it that I am concerned about. Anyway, here is the deal. I love you and want to marry you but you cannot say yes until your sixteenth birthday. You are not old enough, or maybe the word is mature enough, and the year would give you a chance to really consider it. Besides that, your mother would appreciate this. Another thing, you deserve better than having a clean up boy for a husband. I need to find a better job."

Jane let go and walked away. Pedro knew the part that had agitated her. She walked about fifty yards before turning back to him. When she was close, "I have already accepted it so the deal stands."

Suddenly, she jumped at the now seated Pedro. She wrapped one arm under his arm, and her other arm had him by the neck. As she kissed him, she forced him down on his back, leaving her directly on top. She kissed him until her wind played out, and had to come up for air. Pedro had just relaxed and enjoyed it. He was too pleased to resist, knowing he would never take advantage of his precious love. Finally, she rolled off and lay beside him. Then the teasing started again.

"Your mouth says I am too young and immature, but your body is saying something else." Then a giggle and again she had him embarrassed.

"O.K., young man, let me tell you a few choice words that are on my mind. I may tease you, but don't you ever forget that

I know what I'm doing. I will wait ten years to marry you because you are my heart, so don't give me that stuff about needing a year to decide."

Pedro gulped and realized he had a tiger by the tail and wasn't sure how to get out of the situation. Finally, "I am sorry as to how I worded it. When a young fellow asks a pretty girl to marry him, naturally he is nervous, and never says it right. Let's put it this way. I accept your yes now, so we will just wait until after your sixteenth birthday to get married. However, please tell your mother how I worded it the first time. Meanwhile, I will have to hustle up another job. Now, are you happy, love?"

She leaned up on one elbow and looked at him. "That sounds better and I will tell mother exactly how you said it at first. Darn it, she will agree with you. Did I say darn? I meant damn it."

Before he could answer, she responded again. "Pedro, we could use you at the café and general store. In fact, she could use both of us. I will talk to her about that. Meanwhile, there is something that you have not mentioned today yet, and it is important to our future. What is going to happen when that Toro and his friends come back to town?"

"We could talk to your mother about that. We could enlarge the store and maybe open the café all day. I promise that I will be a help and not a burden. As for Toro, I cannot make you any promise. It will be a matter of what happens when I face him again. The last time I looked at him, my stomach became upset. If it happens again, I just don't know." Now he reached over and pecked her on the lips.

"Pedro, I love you so much. But that little mush is not going to keep you from your lecture. Here it comes, Buddy. I peeped and watched you dress three times, but that was a first for me today. I didn't even know what it was at first. You should not give fifteen year old girls bad ideas by letting that happen. You ought to be ashamed of yourself." Then she could go no further, and started to giggle.

At that minute, he loved her so much that it would be

impossible to even guess at the amount of love he really had for her. "I guess I'm sorry but something tells me you're not."

She laughed out loud at this. "Even if I was proud, I wouldn't tell you. Anyway, the lecture was only for the first time, since the last time I purposely wanted to see if I could make it happen again."

Pedro tried to look at her sternly but was not too successful. "I think we better go fishing now. I don't feel too safe around you." They both had a laugh as they got up to get their poles.

CHAPTER 19

From the minute he arrived at the saloon that night, Pedro had reveled in his thoughts about his proposal to Jane. He was never happier in his entire life, but one black cloud still hung over his head. Toro and the others would always be there unless he could come up with the answer.

A minute later, he was totally shocked as Toro, Gabby, and Luke came in. They immediately sat at a table, and right away, Luke got up to go to the bar for drinks. Pedro could not even glance at them. His first thought was about his gun. It appeared killing them might be his only solution. No, not the same day he had proposed to Jane. They would be in town for a few days, and he needed more time.

An hour later, the saloon became crowded. Curly Duncan had come in, and immediately spoke of Julie's husband's death. At this point, Pedro was sorry he had not confided in Curly in regards to his revenge problem.

"What's wrong, Pedro?"

"Nothing."

The youth was so upset he even forgot to mention his news about Jane. They were laughing and talking, really enjoying life while his wonderful mother lay in her cold grave. It was getting the best of Pedro, but he had decided to wait at least another night.

With a big tray of glasses and empty bottles, he started toward the back part of the bar. He saw Toro look back, and as he passed their table, Toro's foot came out and Pedro tumbled to the floor with the tray full of glass. The three had a big laugh as Pedro tried to rise without cutting himself again. The youth's neck was bleeding freely.

"Next time look where in hell you walk, bastard," mouthed off the big Mexican, as Pedro wiped the blood from his neck.

"Yeah," chimed in Luke.

Pedro was furious, for he had seen Toro's foot come out. Ten years of waiting, looking, and hoping to find this man, this scum, and here he sits cursing and laughing at me. He made no effort to pick up the glass.

As he walked toward the back door, he heard Toro again, "Don't leave yet, you still have this mess to clean up."

More laughter followed as Pedro walked to his room, put a tight handkerchief over the cut, strapped on his holster, checked his pistol, and put on his black hat. He had wore it whenever he practiced and everything needed to be the same. He was calm now, his mind made up. All the years of frustration was at hand now, at his fingertips. The youth was cold as ice, forgetting all his religious training, as he decided his mother would rest easier tonight.

When he came out of the back door of the saloon, it took a few seconds before he was even recognized. When he was, a pin dropped on the floor would have sounded loud. Toro turned white and the big smile had disappeared. Tom Baxter tried to get in his way.

"Move out the way, Mr. Baxter. This is my problem to settle now."

"You cannot start anything in here…"

Before he could finish, Pedro brushed him aside. "Toro, it's lesson time for you."

Toro cut in on him, "Put that gun up before I make you eat it."

Pedro stared him down. "I saw you look back, then stick your foot out."

Again Toro cut in, "You're a liar."

Then Pedro dropped the bombshell. "Get your fat ass up and come outside. Let's see if you are as brave fighting a fair gun fight as raping and killing a helpless woman!"

Now both Luke and Gabby were white faced. Tom Baxter had a look that could hardly be described. Maybe a look of terror. Pedro, never turning his back on them, backed toward the door. Toro finished his drink, and slowly got up. Curly Duncan spoke up, "Your two buddies of his—remember, I will be watching. Don't make any moves you'll be sorry for." Pedro heard him and Curly Duncan would be his friend for life.

As they faced off, Pedro looked across the street to see if Jane was there, but only her mother was watching. He was glad, as he preferred she not watch what was going to happen.

"Anytime, fat man," needled Pedro. Toro noticed how Pedro had his gun tied down. Just like a professional, thought the scared man. He knew he was fair with a gun, and maybe this kid was all mouth. Suddenly, he went for his gun.

Pedro drew and fired before Toro could even get his gun up. The big Mexican shook as his gun fell to the ground, and suddenly he collapsed. Only one shot had been fired, and the front of Toro's shirt was already full of blood. The town doctor pronounced him dead right away. The Sheriff told Pedro he wanted to talk to him in the morning.

Jane's mother came over and took off Pedro's bloody handkerchief. "Come on over and let me take care of that."

Before he could walk off, Tom Baxter told Pedro not to come back tonight, but they needed to talk in the morning.

This meant Pedro was not to sleep in the back room that night. He decided Baxter would fire him in the morning. Pedro did not know it, but he was the talk of the saloon as everyone went back in. They all were amazed at his speed and accuracy with that gun.

A business man with a western hat and boots was one of the most interested of the spectators. He walked over and sat with Curly Duncan, who he realized had to be a friend of that kid. "Name's Drew Hampton."

Duncan looked the man over carefully. He was a polished gentleman if he ever saw one. "I'm Curly Duncan. What can I do for you?"

The stranger leaned back in his chair. "I am very interested in that kid. Tell me about him. How well do you know him and how trustworthy is he?"

Curly liked what he saw in the man, but sometimes looks could be deceiving. "I like him well enough to risk my life tonight. What does that tell you?"

Hampton smiled and it was easy to see how he felt. "I need a bodyguard to accompany me around this part of the country. I sell jewelry, and audit books for banks. Sometimes I have to carry large sums of money. Need someone that is totally trustworthy. I can pay well, but again, I have to be careful."

Curly was smiling now. "Truthfully, months ago I gave him that gun. He could not afford it. Before tonight, I had no idea he even knew how to hold it. But, boy, now I know. Pedro is one of the finest kids I have ever met. Hiring him would be one of the smartest moves you could make."

Drew Hampton smiled at Curly. "Tomorrow I want to speak to him. Be in town until about Tuesday. Tell him for me."

"You bet I will. And, believe me, don't mention it to Baxter. He might try to mess up the deal."

Hampton's expression changed. "I did not like what I saw of the man tonight. Thanks, Duncan."

Pedro confided in Jane's mother about Toro. She seemed very interested in when his mother's murder had taken place and where. She took care of his wound, then told him how happy she was for the true love between them.

"You are both young, especially Jane, but by the time she is sixteen, I believe she will be ready to make the big move. We have all the work you will ever need here, if you so decide."

Agnes Skaag was a sweet and wonderful woman. If Jane takes after her mother, Pedro knew he would always have a truly devoted wife. Jane's father, George, had been totally worthless to his wife for no telling how many years. Pedro looked at the attractive slender brunette, and decided that is probably what Jane will look like at just under forty. He would be thrilled if she could look as good at that age. "Thank you, we will discuss that later."

"Would you like to sleep here tonight? I heard Baxter tell you not to come back tonight."

Before Pedro could answer, he saw Curly Duncan at the door. Agnes opened it and he came in. "How about sleeping at my ranch tonight? I believe it would be better than sleeping in town or at your camp."

Pedro looked at Agnes, and she immediately agreed. "Great, Curly, and thanks."

With a grin, Curly came with a surprising comment, "You are known as Pedro by some, and by just plain kid by others, maybe after tonight we ought to call you 'Pedro the Kid.'"

Agnes let him know what she thought about that remark. "No, Curly, Pedro is not a gunman, now or ever. Please don't tag him with that name. I have a son, whom I have disowned, because he is an out and out killer. Pedro is not that kind of kid."

He smiled as Curly began to stutter, "I...I'm sorry. It was only a poor joke, I guess. Please accept my apology."

Before she could say anything else, Pedro spoke up, "Curly, I didn't get to tell you tonight, I asked Jane to think about marrying me, but I won't accept an answer until her sixteenth birthday."

Curly was all smiles. "I accept your apology. Maybe that is why I was so influenced by your remark."

"I love Pedro as much as I would my own son. I would never say or do anything to hurt him."

"Then we feel the same. but I am worried about those two buddies of Toro."

"You know them?"

"Yes, they have been coming in the café for about six years, I would guess. Gabby and Luke have a ranch about 40 or 50 miles away. They are not gunmen, but I wouldn't trust either one. They were good friends of Toro."

"I'm going to tell Curly everything. Should have told him before."

"Yes, Pedro, and be sure to tell the sheriff your concern tomorrow."

"If that will make you feel better, I will, but please don't worry. When Jane hears about all this in the morning, I am glad you will be here to do the explaining." Agnes laughed for the first time that evening.

"I can handle her."

Then they said their goodnights and Curly took Pedro to the town horse barn and rented one for him. When they left for the ranch, Pedro looked up at the sky. He said a silent prayer, asking for forgiveness. Pedro waited until they arrived at the ranch to fill Curly in on the revenge motive. Then he told him the story of his life. Curly was fascinated with the part about the Comanches. Duncan told him about Drew Hampton, and Pedro was excited and happy over the possible offer. He could hardly wait until tomorrow.

CHAPTER 20

The following morning, Pedro saddled the rented horse and rode into town alone. Curly was very disappointed that he had a cattle drive starting so he was unable to accompany him.

Arriving in town, Pedro immediately dropped off his rented horse at the barn. He realized that today would be the funeral for Julie's husband. Although he had wanted to attend, right now his important mission was to find Drew Hampton and check out his job chances. Curly had been really impressed by the classic gentleman.

His first stop after leaving the barn was the general store, despite knowing that Jane would be in school. As he walked in, he was surprised to see George Skaag behind the counter. It was the first time that Pedro had ever seen the man look totally sober.

"Howdy, Mr. Skaag, how are you?"

The man knew who Pedro was, but there was no smile. "Got yourself into trouble last night, so I heard."

Pedro studied his expression for a moment. Skaag was obviously avoiding a meeting of their eyes. "Yeah, it was bad, I know." Skaag didn't say anything so Pedro continued, "On my way to see Sheriff Harlow now. Is Mrs. Skaag here?"

His eyes finally met Pedro's. "No, she had to go to the bank. Should be back soon."

"Tell her I'll be back later. See you." With this, Pedro was on his way to the sheriff's office.

Arriving there, Pedro found the sheriff sitting on his desk, talking to one of his deputies. The jail's office was larger than he imagined it would be. On the back wall were about fifteen shotguns and rifles. A barred door in the middle, obviously leading to the cells. Photographs lined the walls and there were several chairs spaced around, being well aged with wear.

"Come in, kid, glad you dropped by." Jack Harlow was a capable sheriff, respected by almost everyone. Now in his early fifties and his brown hair speckled with gray, he had earned the reputation by years of fair and dedicated service. Harlow needed to do this in order to wipe out his early reputation as a noted bounty hunter.

"You asked me to come in, so I hope you only want to hear my side."

The sheriff smiled at the kid. "Oh, I know your side of it. Four out of five saw him trip you and two even saw him look back at you before you reached his table. I saw the gunfight—it was fair so there are no charges. One question, though. You brought up a rape and murder charge against him. Would you like to talk about it?" The deputy had left so they were alone.

Pedro hesitated, for he had no idea this would be the question. Then he decided it was best to tell Jack Harlow the whole story. "Maybe I would have been smarter if I had kept my mouth shut about that, but I wanted him to know that justice was finally going to make him pay the price."

Harlow looked at Pedro with a definite serious expression.

"Tell me everything. Something tells me Gabby and Luke are also involved."

Once more, Pedro found himself telling his life story. It had been a habit lately. First, Jane, then Mrs. Skaag, Curly, and now the sheriff.

When he had finished, the sheriff just sat and looked at him. "Would you have challenged him to the gun fight if it was only the trip?"

Pedro did not hesitate with that answer. "Killed him? No, but I would have whipped his ass."

The sheriff smiled. "I'll bet you could have, too. You are in danger here. Although the murder was in Mexico, Luke and Gabby are not going to want you around. Do you have any idea who the other two were?"

Pedro smiled at the sheriff. "I may know about one, but can't say anything now."

"What are your plans? Think old Baxter will let you work for him?"

"I am meeting with a man named Drew Hampton. Do you know of him?"

This brought a real smile to Harlow's face. "A real gentleman. Could not be a nicer man."

"He asked Curly Duncan to tell me to look him up today. Seems he needs a bodyguard to travel with him."

"Great, but I would not tell Baxter."

This brought the biggest smile of the morning to Pedro's young face. "I'm going to talk to Baxter now. Then I will look up Mr. Hampton. I'm sure Baxter will fire me. If not, I'll put him off and quit later."

The sheriff hesitated for a few moments. "Pedro, be real careful. Those two are dangerous in town or even out of town."

"Thanks, sir, I will."

"I'll try to keep an eye on them, but I can't promise anything. Good luck with Hampton."

"If I get the job, we leave Tuesday. Meanwhile, I'll be watching."

"Good, now about that gun. You impressed a lot of old-timers with your speed. Don't let it go to your head. There's always somebody faster. Be careful and good luck."

Pedro knew of Jack Harlow's reputation so he valued his opinion. He had no idea of being a professional gunman. He would, however, take the job as a bodyguard. He needed the money to be able to help him with his coming marriage. They shook hands and Pedro walked toward the saloon.

Sam, the bartender, was cleaning the tables when he walked in. "Want me to tell Baxter you're here? He's got company in there now."

"I need to check on my belongings in the back. Let him get through with his company. I think he's going to fire me anyway, Sam."

Sam gave him a sympathetic glance. "I'm afraid you're right."

Pedro walked into the back and checked his room. He had only a few personal belongings and decided to leave them until he finished his conversation with Baxter. On the way back to the front, he heard some loud conversation coming from Baxter's office. Quickly, he decided it was worth the chance to look in at his secret spot. Climbing up the rack, he listened as he peeped in. The shock hit Pedro right between his eyes. Arguing with Baxter were Gabby and Luke, and it was Baxter who appeared to be the most upset.

"Don't you ever call me 'Silver' again, understand?"

Luke answered quickly. "I never called you that in public. Besides, I don't like your attitude. You are just as guilty in those killings as we were."

Baxter's face was red now. "It is not my fault that you wasn't smart enough to wear a mask. Anyway, that kid probably will leave as soon as I fire him. I wonder who he really is and what he knows. We may have to take care of him later."

Gabby broke in, "I don't know what you mean by later, I plan to do something earlier than that."

Baxter calmed down and so did the others. "Listen, let me fire him. I have the perfect excuse. Then we will see what he does. Don't rush into anything. I don't think we have to panic. All of our problems were in Mexico. Let us see what today's firing brings out."

Pedro could see this conversation was about over, so he came down and walked out into the saloon. He had been right about Tom Baxter's cruel eyes. Now, he knew the fourth killer and somehow he had felt it all along. Pedro sat at one of the tables, talking to the bartender, as the three men came out a few minutes later. Luke and Gabby did not even look at him, walking out with their eyes glued on the doorway.

Baxter walked up to him. "Come on in, kid. Let's talk." With this, he turned back to his office. Pedro got up and followed, knowing exactly what was coming.

After they were both seated, Baxter began, "I don't see any reason to drag this out. You cannot kill my customer over an accident or whatever and expect to keep working here."

Pedro was silent for a moment. "I guess being tripped, cut, cursed and insulted was more than even a clean up boy could take." It was a stare that Baxter was getting and the comment was not in an apologetic tone.

"I have been damn good to you, kid, not only giving you a job but also an inside room to sleep in. You were living in the woods, or have you forgotten?"

Pedro continued the stare. This man had been one of the killers of his mother. The job and the sleeping room meant absolutely nothing to him at this time.

Then Baxter continued, "There is no need to continue this conversation. You are fired, but I do want to know what you meant by that remark about Toro being involved in rape and murder. That is a serious charge to make with no obvious proof."

The icy stare continued. "Since I'm fired, there is no need for more talk. I don't see a badge that gives you a right to ask me anything." With this, Pedro got up and walked out. The only thing he regretted was that Baxter hadn't reached for a gun. His conscience hurt for having such a thought but it was the truth. He decided to try to find Hampton in the bank.

Pedro realized that he had left those few belongings in the back room, so he turned and went back to the saloon.

"Sam, I forgot my few belongings in the back. Can I go get them?"

The bartender thought a moment. "Wait here, Pedro, I better go get them for you."

"Good, they are in a little pile on the bed." As soon as the bartender went into the back, Baxter came out. "What the hell are you still doing in my place?"

Pedro faced him and again the icy stare came out. "I have some things in the back. Sam went to get them."

Baxter never answered. He just stood and waited for the bartender to return. When he did, Pedro took his belongings and looked toward Sam. "Thanks, Sam."

Entering the bank, Pedro looked around. He saw no one of Hampton's description. Then he asked the clerk, who promptly requested Pedro take a seat. Soon a man fitting the description came out of the back room. He walked straight to where Pedro was seated.

Extending his hand, and with a nice smile, "I'm Drew Hampton, and I know who you are, Pedro." They shook hands and the man sat next to him.

"I need a bodyguard, and you have the qualifications. It would require a lot of traveling, mostly in stagecoaches, and would pay well. Are you interested?"

Pedro was all smiles. It would be the first decent job ever.

"Very," was his one word answer.

They proceeded to have a long talk. Pedro was flabbergasted at the proposition. The money was very good, and an almost equal amount would be placed in a bank account that would remain until Pedro really needed it. All expenses including food, a room, and even some new clothing would be furnished. The one thing stressed by Hampton was total trust and honesty. Pedro would be required to spend all day on the job. He was to stay out of trouble and avoid saloons, where most of the trouble usually started. By the time they parted that day, it was a done deal. They would leave on the stagecoach

Tuesday morning. Hampton would rent Pedro a room next to his in the hotel until they left town. They would meet again tomorrow morning in the hotel café for breakfast to wind up all the details. It was eleven o'clock now and Pedro went back to the Skaag's General Store. Agnes was very excited about Pedro's job, although the type work certainly scared her.

"You mean you leave on this coming Tuesday morning?"

"Right. Would you ask Jane to meet me at the camp?"

Agnes Skaag smiled. "Who's going to tell the little tiger, you or me?"

Pedro gave her a big grin, and for the first time, leaned over and kissed her on the cheek. "I appreciate the offer, but that is definitely my job. Don't you agree?"

Again she smiled and now touched her cheek where he had just kissed it. "I agree, Pedro, and thanks for the show of affection. I have learned to love you as a mother should love her own son. I hope it means you are beginning to feel like my son."

"Yes, I do feel that way." As Pedro walked out, a feeling in his heart gave him warmth that he had not felt in years.

CHAPTER 21

At noon, Pedro was walking down the road that passed in front of the McKeever's ranch. He had been humming a tune. A few moments later, he heard a buggy behind him, coming from the direction of town. Turning to look, it was Julie with two other people crowded into the one seater. He stopped as they pulled up beside him. "Please accept my apology for not attending the funeral. After last night, I had some business in town."

"Pedro, I want you to meet Mr. and Mrs. Robert Landsdown. We're having lunch at the ranch. Would you join us? I know about last night, thank goodness you're O.K. How about lunch?" They were a nice couple about fifty or so years old.

"Yes, thanks. Nice to meet you folks."

"Nice meeting you, Pedro," chimed the friendly gentleman.

Pedro put his foot on the step, and they rode to the ranch

house. When they arrived, Mrs. Landsdown reached behind the seat and pulled out a good sized basket of food. Then they all went into the house. As it turned out, Pedro had lucked into a feast, that included fried chicken, potatoes, several vegetables, home made bread and two pies.

While they were eating, Julie brought up the night before. "Is it true that Baxter fired you?"

Pedro smiled as he answered, "Yes, it is. I was offered and accepted a better job just after he fired me. Never told him that I knew I was getting it. It is a traveling bodyguard one, be working for Drew Hampton."

At this, Robert Landsdown spoke up, "Oh, yes, I know him well. He sells expensive jewelry and audits books for almost all the banks in the entire area. You will be gone most of the time." Julie's face had no smile nor even a pleasant look.

"Yes, that's true, I leave Tuesday morning."

"I'm glad for you, but I hate to see you leave. Who's going to fix my fences?" Julie followed the question with a forced sounding laugh.

"Julie told us that you had been very kind to her. My husband and I appreciate that. We live across Rainy Roundup on a little place of our own, and we really love this young lady. We plan to see a lot more of her now that she is alone." Julie's pleasant expression had returned.

"I really have learned to like this town, but after last night, it is best I leave for a while. I know you heard what happened."

"Yes," spoke up Landsdown, "but Julie told us he must have had it coming."

Pedro did not elaborate. He nodded his head in agreement. A half hour after lunch, Pedro excused himself to leave. "Going to drive Pedro down to the road. Be right back."

Julie and Pedro got into the buggy, drove to the road where Pedro stepped out. "Have you heard from Curly?"

Julie smiled at him before answering, "Don't be pushing your buddy on me. Since you are leaving town Tuesday, I want you here on this road about ten or so on Monday morning. I owe you."

Pedro looked at her with surprise. "You don't owe me anything. You just buried your husband today. I'll be back."

Her smile vanished, but the scorched look in her eyes remained. Then in a low voice, almost a whisper, "My husband has been dead for a long time. You know I'm no angel. I know you want me. I need you. Your little girl friend won't know. Please." She did not wait for an answer. The buggy took off at a rapid pace.

Pedro, knowing how much he loved Jane, still knew he would be on that road. Julie admitted she was no angel. Maybe he needed to admit something similar about himself.

Arriving at the camp, Pedro got a lump in his throat as he looked around. After Monday, it would probably be a long time before he even saw this place again. He had decided to leave his little tent and fishing poles. It would be nice if Jane could bring one of her girl friends sometime. Then again his conscience hurt. Sure, he was thinking of a girl friend for her, while he had plans to be with Julie on Monday. It just wasn't right but he doubted that road could be avoided. He was almost nineteen years old and there was considerable doubt that he could wait another year. His mind kept telling him that being with Julie did not mean he loved Jane any less. If that was true, why did he feel so lousy about it?

He took the fishing poles out of the tent, dug up a few worms, and walked down to the fishing area. Soon he cleared his mind of all thoughts as he concentrated on fishing. He knew she would be along soon, and knowing he had to tell her he was leaving town, Pedro felt more nervous than when he had faced the fat Toro. He had checked, looking in all directions, to be sure he was not followed. However, there was always a possibility that they might follow Jane Everyone in town knew they were close. Pedro promptly caught two nice size fish. He laughed to himself as he decided that if Jane was fishing with him, she probably would have caught both of them.

Soon he could hear her whistling, so he moved out of the edge of the water, and started back to the camp. They arrived together and quickly she ran to him and put her arms around her love. Tears flowed from her eyes. "I could choke myself for going to bed early last night. All that excitement and baby Jane slept through the whole thing. Are you O.K., love, and how is the cut on your neck?"

Pedro kissed her tearful eyes, and smiled as their noses were almost touching. "It just happened. I had put if off, but I lost my cool when he tripped and then cursed me."

She looked up in admiration. "I would say he tripped and cursed the wrong person." Pedro placed his hands on her cheeks and kissed her tenderly on those luscious lips. "Mom says you brought up the rape and murder. Are you in danger?"

"Maybe that was a mistake, but I wanted him to know. I will wait for them to make a move. I found out this morning that Baxter was one of the five. He fired me but doesn't know I found out."

She looked at him and Pedro could not figure out her expression in regards to what she was thinking. "That is bad. He is much more dangerous than the other two. Tom Baxter would never try to kill you himself, for he is too smart for that, but goodness knows what he might do. Pedro, I am scared to death for you. I wish you had not made that remark." Then she hugged him tightly.

"I have some more important news for you. You will not like this at first but maybe it is for the best for now." Putting her face up toward him, with the most serious look he had ever seen her with, she asked, "I am afraid to hear it." Then she squeezed him. "Please kiss me before you tell me anything else."

Kiss her, he did, with all the passion and love he possessed. It was almost as if their lips were glued together. When the kiss was over, they just stood and held each other. Then she spoke in a whisper, "Your desire is stronger than I realized. It would be wrong, but I would let you."

Pedro tried to back his body away but she pressed forward. "What a fool I was to say you needed to mature. You are, and by saying it would be wrong, you just proved it to me. We will wait, for I know you are perfect, and neither could take the chance that you might get pregnant with what I am about to tell you."

This really scared her and she moved away and sat down. "I don't like the sound of this. Please tell me and get it over with."

Pedro gulped as he tried to get it out. "I have the biggest chance of my life. I am going to work for Mr. Drew Hampton, as his personal bodyguard. It is the break that you and I needed. My pay is great, and he is putting almost the equal amount in the bank each pay day. This would be mine whenever I need it. He travels all over, Texas, Oklahoma, and even Kansas. We go by stagecoach most of the time. He wants me to stay out of trouble. Not to go into any saloons. You must meet him tomorrow, he is a wonderful man, and it really is a great opportunity for us." Jane just sat still and speechless. "With what just happened, it might be safer if I left town on Tuesday. That is when I have to leave. I know it will be hard for both of us, but nothing will change. We will plan our wedding when you are sixteen. If those scum leave me alone, I might just settle with the killing of Toro. He was the one I saw on top of my mother. Say something, honey, please."

She looked into his eyes and seemed to force a small smile. "I like only the part that it might be safer for you. Pedro, if anything happens to you, my life will stop. Do you understand?"

Pedro sat by her and she put her head on his shoulder. "Can we trust this fellow, Hampton I believed you called him.?"

Pedro smiled at this. "He was concerned if he could trust me. I will know in advance where we will be so we will both be able to write."

"How long will you work for him? We could hardly get married if you have that job. Don't you agree?"

"Yes, I promise when we marry after you are sixteen, that will be the end of this job. Cross my heart."

Now the famous Jane grin was back. "O.K., love, now are you ready for your lecture?"

They both broke into a hearty laugh and then Pedro filled her in on all the facts about the job. They fished for a while. Of course, she caught three to his two. So now they had a total of seven fish, which they brought with them so Jane's mother could use them in the café. They sang and whistled all the way into town.

A few feet from the café, she whispered, "Mom wants you to go to church with us Sunday, and then eat dinner in the house since the café will be closed. And by the way, love, you think I could slip in the hotel room tonight?" They were laughing as they entered the café.

CHAPTER 22

The breakfast and meeting between Drew Hampton and Pedro had gone off without any problem. Both were very happy with the arrangements between them. By the time they had finished breakfast, Pedro knew that he would learn a whole lot from this man in the near future.

When Hampton got up from the table, he commented, "Let us go over to the general store and pick out some clothes for you." Then with a smile added, "Isn't that who you prefer to give the business to? Besides that, I might get to meet this young lady, Jane."

Pedro nodded in agreement as he could not hold back a big smile. Entering the store, it was Agnes Skaag standing near the doorway.

"Mrs. Skaag, please meet my new boss, Drew Hampton."

She smiled brightly. "Pleased to meet you, sir. Pedro has told me a lot about you."

Pedro noticed a brightness in his eyes that he had not seen before. "It is my pleasure, I assure you, Mrs. Skaag. I do not know what Pedro said, but I believe I am the lucky one in this new arrangement."

Agnes Skaag looked over at Pedro. "Let's don't give him the big head, but he is a fine young man. If you do not believe me, my daughter will fill you in with a few thousand words about him in less than five minutes."

All three had a laugh just as Jane entered. Boy, Pedro almost choked. She was not wearing the usual tight britches, but instead wore a beautiful light blue dress, that brought out the blue in her eyes, and she looked to be eighteen instead of fifteen. She is gorgeous, thought Pedro. Then she held out her hand to Hampton.

"I am Jane Skaag, sir, and am honored to meet you."

While Pedro stood speechless, Hampton spoke up, "Pedro certainly did not exaggerate your beauty. It is a real pleasure after hearing so much about you."

Now she lost a little of her cool and turned a little pink. "I hope he spoke well of me. Did he tell you that sometimes he gives me lectures?" She had regained her cool quickly and gave Pedro a big grin.

"No, he never told me that. After meeting you, I would not have believed it anyway."

A few moments later, Hampton told Mrs. Skaag to find the nicest black shirt, pants, boots, and hat in the store for Pedro. While going through the clothes, Pedro admired a checked black and white shirt so a moment later, Hampton bought that too. Then they purchased underwear, socks, handkerchiefs, and even a string tie. Then came the real surprise.

"That pistol and holster I asked you to save—let Pedro look at it." Even Agnes Skaag was surprised. He had asked her to save the beautiful pistol and holster but she had no idea it was for Pedro. When she took it out of the box, Pedro's eyes were gleaming. Everyone seemed happy except Jane.

To her, a pistol was associated with death, and she wanted no part of her Pedro and the possibility of death. She was totally against the job as a bodyguard, but would not let anyone know. She preferred he leave town for the present because of the problem, but was afraid this type job was leaving him open to his enemies. He was obviously thrilled so she would do nothing to make him feel bad for now. Really, she did not know what she could do.

A half hour later, Hampton helped Pedro carry all the boxes to his hotel room. Pedro left everything in the room except his new gun and holster. He strapped it on and promptly got the feel of it. Hampton told him that when they got to Kansas City, he would acquire more clothes for him, as well as a better suitcase. His boss had not been too happy with the looks of the suitcase but it was the only type available.

"Pedro, your young lady is precious. It is very easy to understand why you feel as you do about her." Then with a grin, he added, "She takes after her mother. Boy, what a good looking woman."

"Yeah, and they don't make them any harder working or nicer than she is. Have you met her husband?"

Hampton looked at Pedro with disgust. "No, but if what I heard is true, I don't want to."

"It's probably all true, unfortunately."

Hampton shook his head, and Pedro could see a lot of sadness in his eyes. There was obviously a lot about this man that he did not know about. "Too bad a no good character is lucky enough to get a good woman like that. I was married once when much younger and she was probably on a par with George Skaag. When she wasn't drunk, she was in a game losing my money or laid up with some saloon bum."

Pedro could see a tear or two slide down his emotional face. He only knew two words to say, "I'm sorry, Mr. Hampton."

He looked at the kid and tried to force a smile. "Thanks, Pedro. I got over her a long time ago. It is just that when someone like Agnes Skaag comes along, it seems they are always in the same boat that took me down the river." It was obvious that if a good woman came along, Drew Hampton would be real easy to haul in. However, being no fool, he would have to know about her from a reliable source.

Pedro decided to tell Hampton his life story. He had told him a little but now came forward with balance of it. Like everyone else, he became fascinated with the story of the Comanches.

He told Pedro it only took him a few minutes to completely distrust Tom Baxter but that he doubted any action by him would be coming forth. He was the type who would probably wait you out. He offered no opinion about the other two. When the conversation was over on this subject, Pedro hoped he would not have to tell his life story again for some time to come.

A few minutes later, Hampton told Pedro to take off and spend time with Jane and take care of any business. He wanted him to sleep in his hotel room and to be careful in the daytime. Just be ready to leave on Tuesday morning.

CHAPTER 23

Sunday morning came, and Pedro walked to the general store to meet Jane and her mother. From there, they proceeded down the street to the church. At the last minute, Pedro thought about his gun, so he went to the pastor's house next door and left it.

Pedro knew he had a lot of things to pray for, but first on his mind was to ask forgiveness for the killing. Despite his sincerity in praying for this, somehow he felt further away from God than ever before. Pedro was confused, for usually he felt in his heart that being close to Jesus was a natural thing for him. It had been that way all his life. From being confused, it soon changed to something entirely different, for he now knew it was fear. Fear, a word he knew little about but now could feel. Was it Jesus who was putting fear into him, or was it his own overworked conscience. For over ten long years, he had this battle of his mind. All this time, there appeared to be no other way but to do it with a gun. He wanted to kill Toro, yes, but he had talked himself out of it that night. The man had forced his hand, but yet he knew a fist fight would have been sufficient. Yes, for the tripping, but deep in his heart, he knew it was for revenge. Pedro had almost become ill in his stomach when they had such a good time before in the saloon. His thought of his mother's cold grave and these scum having such fun was really more than he could stand. At this moment, Pedro realized he had a lot of prayers to say before he could ever hope to be close to the Lord again, and even that was doubtful. There may not be enough prayers in his lifetime for forgiveness.

When Pedro picked up his gun, it was difficult for him to put it on. He knew what was capable of happening, it was a necessity or he may not live long enough to say any prayers.

The three walked down the street together. Jane was in the middle and she held the arm of each of them. "Gee, how lucky can a girl be? Sitting in church between my two favorite people in the world, I was so proud I was afraid my buttons might pop on my blouse."

Agnes and Pedro both laughed at her. "I asked you not to wear that blouse anyway. You only wore it because it fits tight," teased her mother.

"Yeah" laughed Pedro "I believe that." Jane had that grin that he admired so very much.

"I am sure that Pedro is well aware of your becoming a young lady instead of being just a girl."

"Sure I am, you don't have to put your charms on display."

Jane was turning a little pink now. "I promise to change as soon as I get home. If you have a extra large size in the store, I'll put it on."

She let loose of their arms and walked a little in front of them. "The number one teaser doesn't do to well when the shoe is on the other foot." Jane looked back at him, grinned, slugged him on the arm, and moved back between them. All three had a good laugh as they arrived at the store.

As they entered, George Skaag was standing behind the counter, near the kitchen door. "I see you folks all made it back from church." He looked totally sober to Pedro. They all went in and sat around the kitchen table, and drank coffee. It was revealed that a letter from Kelly had been delivered Saturday. While he never asked how the family was, the young man told of his third killing in a gun fight. It was hard to believe that this Kelly and Jane could be brother and sister, thought Pedro.

"A man has to be careful who he calls out," needled Skaag at Pedro. "Two of the three had experience in gun fights before they tangled with my son."

Pedro looked at George Skaag with a lot of surprise. He was not sure how to take what had just been said. It was easy to see that Agnes and Jane were on edge. "I don't quite follow you, Mr. Skaag. I don't know your son, but I can tell you about my feelings on gun fighting. I hope I am never in another one as long as I live." This brought smiles from Agnes and Jane.

George did not say anything for a moment, then, "You mean you are going to rest on your conquest of one slow, fat Mexican and retire from gun fighting. You just took a job as a bodyguard. What you're saying doesn't ring true. Does your new boss know how you feel?" George Skaag was smiling now.

Agnes broke into the conversation. "If this is your idea of teasing, it sure is in bad taste. I don't appreciate it, I know Jane doesn't, and sure as hell Pedro doesn't."

Then Pedro spoke up, "For your information, Drew Hampton does not like gunfights any better than I do. I will defend him with my life but I hope I never have to pull that gun out."

Skaag smiled broadly now. "Calm down, Agnes. I was just feeling the boy out. I really don't want my daughter married to a professional gunslinger. Truthfully, your response was good. I hope it was sincere. The only thing that bothers me is why you called that poor Mexican out. You knew he didn't have a chance."

At this point, Agnes Skaag got up as if leaving the kitchen, but as she got behind her husband, she shook her head from side to side and put her finger up to her lips.

Pedro saw this and then continued, "I guess that job finally got the best of me. As a clean up boy, you have to take a lot of insults from people. I saw him look at me, then the leg came out. Should have whipped him but when he laughed and cursed me, my cool was gone. Never thought about how good with a gun he might be. It made no difference."

Skaag stared at Pedro for a minute. Pedro was waiting for the question about his remark. It never came. "Well, it is done now. Tell me more about your future plans for my daughter."

The other three breathed a sigh of relief. "I love her very much, and have asked her to marry me. She must wait until her sixteenth birthday to decide. We will discuss it if she agrees."

Jane broke in, "It will be yes, yes, and yes." Even George broke into laughter with the others.

"Don't know what I will do for a living, but can promise, it won't be with a gun."

"Glad to hear that, but remember one thing, now that you have the beginning of a reputation, it may not be so easy to quit."

Agnes Skaag ordered them all out of the kitchen so she could get the dinner ready. Later after a delicious meal, with everyone full, they just sat around and talked.

Then Skaag asked Pedro, "Tell me more about yourself, young man. What part of Mexico did you come from and what happened to your family?"

Agnes knocked over a cup of coffee on the table at that moment. During the confusion of wiping it up, she looked at Pedro, gave him a little shake of the head, then apologized to the family for being clumsy.

"Mr. Skaag, I was born in a small village far south of Monterrey. When I was three years old, my mother and father were killed in a rock slide in the mountains. The neighbors took me in and I spent a few years with them before they finally put me in an orphanage. I ran away from there, and have been in this country for about five years. I have worked very hard, and only started with the gun because of being pushed around too much."

It was about as good a job at lying that Pedro had ever done. His insides were all in a knot, for it seemed too obvious to him that Agnes Skaag was protecting him from letting her husband find out the truth of where he had really came from. There was only one answer to this. George Skaag, Jane's father, was the missing fifth killer of his mother. My God, what a new horrible problem. Maybe Agnes was sure and maybe just guessing. He remembered how she had questioned him about the location and time when he first told her the facts. Pedro quickly assumed that George had been running with this bunch of scum, and that Agnes never knew or wanted to know what he had been involved in.

"I see." Then after a pause, "I think I understand you a little better now. Your life has been tough. I wish you and my daughter well."

Pedro looked at Agnes, but she looked away. Even Jane's eyes did not meet his at this time. He could understand Agnes being unsure of anything at this time, and it was very likely Jane had witnessed her mother's actions so she was probably as heartsick as he was. Pedro knew he could never kill Jane's father unless it came to a matter of life or death.

A little later, Pedro thanked the family for the wonderful day. They had attended church, ate a wonderful meal, and visited. Jane walked out of the general store with him.

"Pedro, meet me at our place at the usual time tomorrow. Before I forget, you need to know this. It hurts to say it, but I want you to get some experience in making love before we get married. It wouldn't be good for two total greenhorns to try to make love. Don't go overboard, just pick out some fat unattractive woman who works at one of those houses. She could show you all the ropes. I would be jealous if she were pretty. If that happens, don't tell me about it. Promise?"

Now his plans for tomorrow were hurting his conscience more than ever despite the fact that he sorta had her approval. "I promise. If she is nice looking, I won't tell you. Be there waiting for you, love."

Looking both directions, they quickly stole a kiss. Then as he got a few steps from her, suddenly Jane screamed out, "Look out!" Her warning had come a split second before a shot rang out.

Pedro dropped to the ground, just off the boarded walk, and instantly pulled his gun and fired at a man standing on top of the saloon. His accuracy took its toll, as he came rolling off the slanted roof and fell to the ground.

As Pedro rose to his feet, another shot rang out. Jane saw her love drop to the ground. As she screamed again, Agnes and George Skaag were both coming through the door. Jack Harlow, out for a stroll on Sunday, had seen it all from down the block. He ran into the alley between the saloon and the next store.

As the man on the roof slid down to the ground on a pole, he saw the sheriff running toward him. He fired at Harlow as he mounted up on one of two horses positioned there. As he tried to ride away, Harlow's aim was accurate and the man tumbled off the horse.

Pedro was sitting up now, as Jane, showing no regard to what her family might think, clung to him. There was a trickle of blood coming from his temple area, but was really only a scratch. Agnes checked it out, and asked George to go for the doctor.

Soon Harlow returned from behind the saloon. He walked over to Pedro, who was just rising to his feet. "You are a very lucky young man. I saw it all."

Pedro smiled at the sheriff. "Did the other one get away?"

Harlow looked back with a small satisfying grin. "After that shot you made, I would have been too embarrassed to walk over here if I had missed my shot."

The doctor confirmed what Agnes already knew. It was only a scratch, but emphasized that Pedro had missed death by only a fraction of an inch. The glancing blow had stunned him for the moment.

Pedro was not at all surprised as they identified the two dead men. His victim on the roof had been Luke, and the man killed by the sheriff was Gabby. That leaves only two, reasoned Pedro, and his belief was that the most dangerous one, Tom Baxter, was still alive. If George Skaag was the other one, he would never try to prove it. He did not know for sure it was he, but at this moment, Pedro hoped he never would.

As people began to congregate, Agnes suggested that Pedro come back into their home. The sheriff also came inside and during the following conversation repeated his earlier assessment that it was good Pedro was leaving town for the present. George Skaag appeared very solemn and only added one comment. It was a reminder to Pedro, that sometimes it is not easy to quit with a gun once you start using it. No one answered his comment, although Pedro did nod his head.

Before retiring that night in the hotel, Drew Hampton and his young bodyguard had a long talk. Hampton felt the same as the sheriff, and believed also that it was over unless he pursued the issue.

"I know Tom Baxter well. In fact, we have done business before. The other night another side of him came out, showing his true colors. However, he is a successful business man, and believing you are unaware he is involved, will do nothing. The death of his three friends closes the door on the revenge thing unless you decide to open it." Pedro did not answer for a few moments.

Finally, Hampton asked, "Does silence mean you are not ready to give it up?"

"Not at all. You understand there is another one besides Baxter. I'll wait for now, but Baxter will make his move, sooner or later. He doesn't have the guts to do it himself, but his expression told me that you are both wrong."

Hampton facial expression turned to a more worried one. "The sheriff and I don't want to influence you wrongly."

"I know that, sir. It is my decision to wait for now."

Hampton relaxed some. "Good, for it has to be your choice."

CHAPTER 24

Monday morning brought more nervous tension into Pedro's young life. He was admittedly excited as he walked down the road in front of Julie's ranch. In an attempt to soothe his own nervousness, he tried to reason that any other young man about to have his first encounter with a woman would be just as nervous. Yes, he thought, this is natural.

Before he could reach the road leading to her ranch, the buggy was on the way. As she stopped the buggy for him to get in, she did not look the least bit nervous. She wore her usual tight britches, but the blouse was very skimpy and even unbuttoned. Pedro could tell she had nothing on underneath the light green soft type material. Her blonde hair was flowing in the wind, and her pretty smile added to her beauty. He had never decided who had the bluest eyes between Jane and her and this was not the time to think of his true love.

As the buggy took off, Julie was the first to speak, "It is ten-thirty. You surprised me for I thought you would be on the road before ten." With this she flashed a smile that had lust written all over it.

Pedro gulped out, "I'm sorry to be late."

"Don't be so nervous. I am not going to hurt you. Not only will you enjoy it but I hope you will always remember today." He finally forced out a smile, as he noticed she headed for the woods. This was good for he wanted no part of going into her home.

"We need total privacy, and if the buggy's out in front of the house, we may not get it. No one could ever find us here."

As they stopped, it was obvious that she had been correct. They were totally isolated, and Pedro was glad for this. Julie McKeever sure did not qualify under Jane's terms. She was one of those that Jane never wanted to hear about. Now he needed to try to relax so he could enjoy this. She was certainly happy about it, why shouldn't he be? She unloaded a lunch basket. "This is for later."

Then with a laugh, she grabbed two big blankets out. "These are for now!"

Laying out the blankets, one on top of the other, she sat on them and began to pull off her boots. Pedro followed her and also took his off. She had that pretty smile as she took off the blouse. There was nothing underneath it but a beautiful pair of mounds of flesh. Despite the fact that he had seen them before, they looked much more beautiful to him at this moment. Maybe it was because he was so close to them, for the rose colored nipples were much more noticeable, and the tips were pushing out.

Pedro took off his shirt as she slid off her britches. This had to be the surprise of the day, as there was no clothing under them. Again, he had seen it before, but now it all looked better. She stood up and posed for him, turning around as she continued her torched look. Her blonde pubic hair, well shaped legs that appeared to be fairly muscular for a woman, a real good looking rear end and small waist line with a flat stomach. No question, she was a damn good looking young woman. He felt real good about having his first encounter with her. Another relief was the fact that she had told him she was not able to have children. An earlier miscarriage had ended all hopes of her ever becoming a mother.

"Don't be bashful. Take off the rest of your clothes." Pedro was still standing, so he slid off his pants and finished by taking off his underwear.

"Wow, come here"

He lay beside her as she leaned over and they kissed. Then she kissed his neck and the side of his face as her hands roamed over his body. When one of her hands grasped him, she moaned, "Hmmmmmmmmmmmm." Then she sat up.

"Pedro, I am not a statue. I am real flesh and blood, and that includes my titties, legs, butt and whatever." This brought him out of his stupor as his hands roved over her body. Her breasts were very firm and as his hands moved around the nipples, she again moaned. The kissing became intense and soon they were all wrapped up together on the blanket.

"Don't make me wait any longer," she whispered.

He again did what she asked. As he entered her, she shook all over with passion. Pedro thought he was being aggressive enough but she was more so. Then suddenly she rolled him over, and straddling him, really worked him over. She moved up, down, and around on him furiously and then began to quiver all over.

At this same time, Pedro knew it was over for him too as his feelings seemed to explode within his body. It was everything he thought it would be and more. He only had one reservation about it with Julie. He wondered if she was over aggressive or if all the women were like her. Whatever he felt at this moment as she slid off him, that she was right about him never forgetting today.

It was only a short while before they made love again. Then, in the nude, they had lunch.

Lying back afterwards, she pointed at herself with a smile.

"You have already had dessert twice. Here I am if you want it again."

Again, Pedro accepted her offer. It was near two o'clock when she dropped him off on the road. She had asked him to send her a note occasionally with his future address so she could write him the news. He saw no harm in that and agreed. Pedro asked her to talk with Curly, and she had promised him she would.

In regards to their relationship, she understood about Jane. Her sincere promise was to never tell about today and also not to interfere with them in anyway ever. Then, with her prettiest smile of the day, told him that she would always be as available to him as she was today, married or not. That remark didn't exactly raise his opinion of her. Then, his morale builder of the day was her statement, "Some cowboys are super in the saddle, while you are super in the sack."

Pedro could hardly look at Jane in the eyes when she arrived and she soon questioned him about his attitude. Pedro was beginning to lie better, and was able to convince her that it was just because of his leaving. He was not proud of himself for lying to her on his last afternoon, but he could not tell her the truth. She had asked him to learn about it, and today he had a pretty damn good lesson. They fished for the last time for a while. Jane again caught the biggest and the most. The final count was four to two. They decided to cook the big one and take the others to her mother.

"Nice fish, huh?" needled Jane. She never had bragged on anything so he realized that she was only trying to keep the pleasant part of today going.

"It doesn't seem I will ever win back my "champion of Mexico" claim again." Then he leaned over and pecked her on the cheek as their mouths were full of fish.

"Well," Jane began as she swallowed some fish, "You have taught me how so we both know I am just lucky. Besides that, I prefer to tease on other subjects, and lover boy, you know what I mean." Then she returned the kiss, only it was not on his cheek but right on the lips. They put up the fishing poles, fixing up everything in the right place, knowing it would be sometime before they would be together again. When the work was finished, they put the other fish on a stringer, but neither wanted to leave. It would be dark soon, but they decided there was still a few minutes left. With his conscience still bothering him, he sat with his arm around her.

"You are leaving in the morning, yet we have kissed less than we have in a long time. I am not in a teasing mood, but dern it, kiss me for the next fifteen minutes and then we can leave."

Pedro looked at her. There was no question in his mind that he was completely in love with her. What happened this morning was strictly physical love making. There had been no "I love you" statements. She was no more in love with him than he was with her. Pedro knew it hurt so much because he loved Jane more than anyone since his mother, and that was a completely different kind of love. He would not leave here with her unhappy.

His arm moved around her as he whispered, "Please forgive me for being so solemn." Then she forgot everything as he kissed her long and passionately. They laid back and hugged each other in between kisses. It was a torrid pace, and neither realized it or cared. Pedro could feel her firm breasts pressing against him, and realized the little devil had nothing on under that tight blouse. It took great will power not to reach and feel of them.

She could feel him against her, and was forced to use all her will power not to reach and touch him. As they finished the next long kiss, Pedro was shocked to realize that he had both hands on her cute fanny and was pulling her toward him. This brought him back to reality, and he moved away.

"We need to stop this now, honey, my desire will not let this go on without going too far. Do you agree?"

Sitting up, with a disgusted yet dreamy look, Jane answered, "Yeah, dern it, damn it. You are very right, and I thank you for it. I confess I was ready to do what we agreed not to. You had me, babe, for I was getting ready to unbutton my blouse and jerk my britches off." She gave him the sweetest smile that he had ever seen in his entire lifetime. His desire to kiss her at that moment was too strong.

Moving over closer to her, with a smile of his own, he whispered, "We stopped at the right time, but darling, may I kiss you just once more. Never have you given me a sweeter more loving smile than just now." It was a long and tender kiss but both appeared on guard.

Then they took the fish and started for town. They walked with an arm around the other. They stopped three times to kiss so it was just dark as they neared the café. Only a few feet from the door, Pedro leaned over and casually told her, "With nothing on under that blouse, you almost did me in." She laughed more than he did, and looked pink when they entered the café.

CHAPTER 25

The following morning, Pedro put on his new clothing and felt very proud. He came down to breakfast, and was surprised that Hampton was even earlier than he.

"Good morning, sir"

"Those clothes look great on you. Sit down and let's put on the feed bag."

Pedro laughed and sat down. After ordering their meal, the conversation changed to business.

"This will be a short trip. San Antonio, where we will be about a week or possibly more. From there we go north, to Austin, Waco, Dallas, Fort Worth, and others. Later Ft. Griffin and Fort Sill, and north through lots of places to Kansas City."

"Fort Sill, isn't that where the Kiowas and Comanches Reservation is located?"

"Yes it is. Does the Comanche part of that interest you?"

Pedro smiled at him. "Sure, I would like to visit, and maybe see some of my old friends."

"We will see that you get that chance. Be glad to help."

"Thanks, and by the way, when will we be going to the valley near Mexico?"

"It will be quite a while."

"When we get there, I have a special place to go."

With a big smile, Hampton answered, "Yes, I know. To try to see your friends living in the orphanage or nearby in Monterrey."

"You know enough about my past to read me like a book." They both laughed as breakfast was served.

Pedro was surprised to see Jane and Agnes as they prepared to board the stagecoach. Jane came running up and promptly put her arms around him. Agnes was smiling and shaking her head as she came up.

"Mother is letting me go to school late so that I could see you off."

"Pedro, I wouldn't say I was exactly letting her go late." They all laughed at this, but Jane didn't care. She was there, clad in a pretty light green and white dress with her long wavy hair blowing in the breeze.

"Glad you're here, honey." Then he kissed her and everyone whistled and laughed. Agnes moved closer and Pedro kissed her cheek and gave her a strong hug. The stagecoach driver broke up all the good-byes.

"Everybody on board."

Pedro was the last of the three to get in. Before doing so, he stole another kiss from Jane. Waving as the four horses took off, Pedro knew he saw tears coming from his honey's eyes. The next face Pedro saw was that of Tom Baxter, who was standing out front of his saloon. Someday, thought Pedro, he will make his move. I hope I can be ready.

The third man riding in the coach was a burly looking rancher named Ben Bowman. He was little company as he soon fell asleep. However, not so with his boss, as Hampton began to explain to Pedro all about money and banks. All of the banks that Hampton audited were private banks. He was surprised to hear that the city of Galveston had the most of these banks in this entire area. The different kinds of money included demand notes, legal tender, compound interest treasury notes, and the most plentiful of all were the national bank notes. Pedro realized this job was going to give him a chance to learn about what was really going on in the world besides the inside of a saloon.

The next few weeks were uneventful in regards to Pedro and his job as a bodyguard. However, Drew Hampton and he grew closer each day and soon they were more father and son than being only boss and bodyguard. So far, two of Jane's letters had caught up with him. He read each one a dozen times, and wrote her about four times a week.

As the stagecoach left a small town northwest of Austin, there were two other passengers besides them. One was a thin old fellow, who owned a small ranch. His name was John Lincoln and he was a very friendly gentleman. The other passenger was not nearly as friendly but much better to look at. She was Suzanne Van Clyde, a blonde beauty who was the wife of Lieutenant Marcus Van Clyde. She was on her way to visit him, and he would be in Waco waiting for her.

It was a small and rough road and Mrs. Van Clyde let everyone know how uncomfortable she was. In fact, the other three passengers, including Pedro, were tired of hearing about it.

"It is rough, and I believe that gun you carry could be dangerous with all this bumping around."

Pedro looked at the young woman, but before he could say anything, Hampton spoke up, "Mrs. Van Clyde, in this country it would be much more dangerous for all of us if this young man wasn't along with that gun. There is no danger from the bumping."

She did not back down one bit. "Too many people are killed or wounded with so-called safe guns. Just arrange your sitting so it does not point at me."

Pedro never answered her but he changed his position as

much as possible. Later that afternoon, after a stop at the station where lunch was served and fresh horses replaced the tired ones, the stagecoach made its way through a hilly countryside that had lots of cover. As the coach slowed considerably at a very rough spot, two men appeared from the heavy cover, holding guns on both the driver and guard besides the passengers.

The guard dropped his rifle, and was told to hand down the strong box that they knew had money and valuables. The other, a tough looking man probably in his thirties, ordered everyone out as he moved back away, removing his pistol from the window, and smiling , "Keep your hands up as you come out, especially the young man with the peestol."

Pedro made sure he was the last one out, as he had just moments before slipped his old pistol out of a small package sitting next to him. The gun was quickly placed on the back side of his hip in his pants held tightly by his gun belt.

As he stepped down, away from the others, he was told to carefully unbuckle his gun belt. A glance at the other man showed him what he wanted to see. Doing what he was told, Pedro than raised his left hand and with lightning speed his right hand pulled the gun from the side and immediately shot the bandit in the shoulder, with the gun falling to the ground from the numbed hand. The other bandit had put away his gun as he reached for the money box.

"Drop the box, and let your holster down easy."

The wounded outlaw cursed the other one. "You stupid bastard, you jist too greedy to geet your hands on thee dollars."

It was Pedro's time to laugh. "We all make mistakes. You weren't looking close. I tried to just wound you, and almost missed."

"If you meesed, señor, your ass would be feenished."

Now the smile left Pedro and a fiery look replaced it. "I should have killed you, scum."

"I am a man, that blonde woman could told you that een the morning." With the stagecoach guard helping, Pedro used the extra rope carried in the coach's repair box, to tie both outlaws hands behind their back. Then they put them on top of the coach and tied their feet. Another rope secured them from rolling off.

The driver, guard, Hampton, and Lincoln all gave Pedro praise but the blonde woman remained silent. As they were entering the coach, the bound outlaw yelled, "Too bad the young señor ees so fast weeth the gun, señorita, you would never forgeet me."

They arrived in another small town and immediately turned the outlaws over to the sheriff. They were to spend the night there and proceed on in the morning.

Later that evening, Hampton and Pedro were ordering their meal when Suzanne Van Clyde walked in. She was on the way to another table when Hampton went over to her, asking if she would join them. Surprisingly, she agreed.

As they ate, there was a lot of conversation between Hampton and the pretty young woman. She smiled and actually appeared to be a nice person. However, she never included Pedro in her part of the conversation. Several times, Hampton tried to bring him into it, but her answers always excluded him. Pedro believed that once she sat down, she never even glanced at him. Only a few moments after finishing his meal, Pedro excused himself, sitting on a couch far enough away that he did not have to listen. He preferred to go to bed but as Hampton's guard, it was not possible.

The following morning all four of the passengers ate in the hotel together. As they were finishing, the sheriff walked in and handed Pedro an envelope. The stagecoach driver and guard had told the sheriff the entire story, thereby making the reward money his. Pedro thanked him and placed the envelope in his pocket without opening it.

The day was very quiet in comparison, and even the roads were a lot smoother. They ate in one of the stagecoach stations while changing horses. Everyone was enjoying the day except there was no conversation between Suzanne and Pedro. It was very hot and they changed horses again, and just after dark they rolled into Waco.

Before they could get out of the coach, there was a nice looking lieutenant smiling at Suzanne. When she reached him, he was so jubilant, she was picked up and turned around in a circle as they kissed. When he finally let her down, she introduced the driver, guard, Lincoln, Drew Hampton, and finally it was Pedro's time.

"And this is our hero, Pedro. He unbelievably shot the outlaw to just wound him, tied them both up, and was given a reward by the sheriff. That is not all, the outlaw told all of us that he was going to take me captive, and fussed at Pedro for upsetting his plans that he had for me. I don't think you will mind if I give him my little reward."

Pedro was already in shock by what she had told her husband but then she walked up to him, kissing him very solidly on the mouth! It was the most embarrassed he had ever been. The Lieutenant laughed with all the rest as it was obvious how pink Pedro had turned. No wonder some fellows say you can never figure out a woman. She had ignored him for two days, and then in front of her husband, kisses him right on the mouth. He would have enjoyed her being civil to him all that time instead of just the kiss.

CHAPTER 26

The next six weeks were uneventful as there were no problems on the road or when they were in town. Pedro stayed away from saloons and had decided that his boss had been right. It appeared to be easy to stay out of trouble providing a man did not frequent places where the wrong type of people spent their time.

He was very excited about his finances. Most of his salary was being saved, and Hampton was now matching this and saving it for him. Then there was the reward he had received. Two hundred dollars, which he handed over to Hampton, to bank for him. Pedro had figured out what he wanted to do when he married Jane. Mainly, he wanted to raise horses, but he also would have a few cattle. Hampton liked the idea, and now he hoped that so would Jane.

Letters were at every hotel from Jane. Bless her heart, thought Pedro, she was really loyal in writing to him so often. Inside, he hoped he deserved it. The time spent with Julie McKeever was still among his thoughts.

Then came a letter from her. It had been forwarded several times and was almost a month old when he received it. Pedro was so happy with the contents that he read it three times in a row. Julie McKeever and Curly Duncan were going together. It did not help his conscience any, but he was glad for them both. With Curly gone on the cattle drive, he never got to tell him good-bye but he had written.

Pedro found his old notes from the orphanage, and finally got off letters to Ricardo and Sister Theresa. It had been just two weeks since he mailed them, so he had not heard anything from them as yet. As long as that revenge thing was a secret, he had never written from Rainy Roundup for fear the wrong person might see a return letter. He knew he was over cautious but had decided it was best at that time. Now he figured he had let his friends down, and regretted his failure to write while living there.

Leaving the general area of Dallas and Fort Worth, Pedro was happy as they would soon be at Fort Sill, and Hampton had promised him time off at Lawton or at the Fort. He would look for Fawn and Little Elk, and inquire about Amy and little Ross. However, they had to go to Ft. Griffin first.

There were a total of six passengers on the coach. A rancher and his wife, Bill and Betty Jackson, on their way to visit their son at the fort. They were a very nice couple in their early fifties, and soon Pedro talked with them about his possible future with horses and cattle. The man was very cooperative and gave Pedro a lot of hints and information. Another passenger was a skinny little fellow named Sammy Skeeter, a traveling salesman. Pedro laughed to himself at that name. Skeeter was close to mosquito, as he was not much bigger, thought the kid. The other passenger was nothing to laugh at but she was something to look at. Pedro tried to keep his eyes off her, but it was difficult. It was the first time Pedro believed he had laid eyes on Running Fox's equal as far as beauty was concerned.

With her long black hair and gray eyes along with a somewhat dark complexion, she could pass for a sister of the beautiful Running Fox. What made the whole thing almost bizarre, was the fact that she hardly took her eyes off him. It was the same type stare and Pedro could not sit still. He knew the others recognized that she was looking at him, but they had no idea how it was affecting him inside. She was the wife of an army officer, a Major Stephen Saunders. She introduced herself as Leigh Saunders, but never mentioned her husband until asked about who she was going to see.

It was the nicest group that Hampton and Pedro had been in the coach with. Skeeter was very amusing, and Leigh Saunders kidded with him and also with Pedro. When they stopped at the station house to change horses and eat lunch, Leigh walked with Skeeter, while Pedro and Hampton walked to stretch their legs nearby.

Hampton needled at Pedro, "Boy, I bet Jane would scratch those pretty eyes out if she could see her looking at you. I don't believe she knows her husband is alive. Don't believe I know what your best qualifications are. It would be close between your pistol and bodyguard abilities but maybe your attractiveness to beautiful women also is close." Then he laughed heartily at his own joke.

Pedro looked at him with a pink face and a grin. He could not think of anything to say. Later that afternoon as the stagecoach came through a shallow stream, Pedro was awakened from his thoughts of how many fish were in that pretty water, by the howling and hoof beats of something he quickly recognized. Comanches!

Looking out the window, he realized how close they were, yet something caused an almost fatal hesitation. The two women were told to get on the floor. The other three men, as none had guns, also were told to lean over and stay down. The closest warrior was just a kid. An arrow stuck near Pedro where Hampton had sat. This is what it took to bring him out of his feeling of not wanting to kill a Comanche and a young kid at that. Pedro's shot was barely quick enough to keep another arrow out of the coach. The young warrior fell while pulling back on his bow. A groan was heard from above and Pedro realized at least one of their men had been hurt or possibly killed. Immediately looking out the other side window, another young warrior was closing in on the bumping stagecoach.

This time with no hesitation, Pedro took him out, and at that moment spotted the one he wanted. This was a real warrior, muscular arms and shoulders with long braided hair, a single feather in his head band, silver medals hanging from his ears, and a very beautiful paint horse. He was riding too far to the side for Pedro's pistol, but he decided to try his luck, and after two shots Pedro knew he was right at first.

Then the warrior moved in closer, and Pedro fired again. With a yell he turned away, obviously shot badly. The other two remaining warriors followed the wounded one, and the crisis was over. He may not have been a chief but he was certainly the leader of this raid. Pedro never enjoyed killing but this one hurt more than the others. The Comanche Indian still had a warm spot in his heart, but what he just did was a necessity for the life of his boss, the others, and himself.

As Pedro told them it was safe to come up, the stagecoach came to a halt. He quickly jumped out to check on the driver and the guard. It was the guard who had been hit by the arrow. They helped him down, and Pedro ripped off his shirt. It had penetrated the outside of his upper right arm and the tip had gone through the flesh.

With all the men watching, Pedro cut off the tip and pulled out the arrow. "I need a drink," gasped the guard, and Skeeter came up with the bottle.

Then the guard turned to Pedro, "Did you make those shots or were all of you fellows shooting?"

Hampton proudly spoke up with a smile, "Now you people should realize why he is my bodyguard."

The driver then added, "He really made that raid a nightmare for them Indians."

Mrs. Jackson, still nervous, finally found her voice, "I am glad that I didn't see none of it. Leigh and I were on the floor where we belonged."

"Well, I would liked to have seen him shoot one anyway," added the black haired beauty.

Almost two hours later, they arrived at the station house, and everyone was glad that a day that had started so fine had not ended in a disaster. Pedro was the toast of the supper when it was finally served.

When supper was completed, they assigned a room to the Jacksons and a room to Leigh Saunders. All the others were to sleep on the bunk beds in the huge open room where they had eaten. Pedro excused himself to take a walk for he knew he had to unwind before he could sleep. As he opened the door, Leigh spoke out to him, "Could a lady walk and unwind with you?"

"Sure," a surprised Pedro answered, with a glance toward Hampton. He had replaced Jane as the teaser. It was cool and nice outside, with the stars shining bright.

They walked side by side without touching, until she reached for his hand. Pedro was nervous, as her warm hand held tightly to his. Her similarity to Running Fox was unbelievable. "I am so glad that you were on that coach. I am afraid to death of Indians and actually, any kind of violence. You were so calm it was really amazing."

Pedro could not tell her he hated to kill those young Indians, and privately hoped they all survived. "Has your husband had any fights with Indians?"

She laughed, hesitated, then, "Let me answer that by saying again how glad I am that you were along." Pedro decided not to ask about Major Saunders again.

"I hope you and that girlfriend of yours have a happy life."
"Thank you," answered Pedro, knowing better than to ask anymore about her husband. Suzanne Van Clyde really seemed to care about her lieutenant. Not this one, thought Pedro. She was as tall as Running Fox, and in the semi-darkness, he just could not believe the similarity. Leigh had the same ample breasts, small waist line, and his imagination figured out the rest.

"I have never been as scared as I was today. My insides are still shaking."

As Pedro looked at her, she was staring at him again. "I need a favor, Pedro. Would you hold me for a few moments? I guess I need reassurance or something."

She moved into his arms and tightly held him and a few moments later, he did the same. She was almost as tall as he was, and soon she moved her face from his shoulder, and only had to look up a few inches to meet his eyes. Without another word, a long passionate kiss followed that left Pedro very confused and upset. It was her idea to hold him but the kiss was as much his fault as it was hers. All the strong feelings he has for Jane and yet this was part his fault. It hurt because he really wanted to kiss her. Could he blame it on his old sweetheart, Running Fox? They wanted to make love but her life was cut short. Since meeting her on the coach, he had hardly thought of Jane that day. Only Running Fox and how this beauty compared to her.

"Did my kiss numb you or what?" laughed Leigh. Pedro realized that his thoughts had left her just looking at him.

"I'm sorry, I guess maybe it came as a surprise."

She was still smiling. "How could it? I could not take my eyes off you today. I have a real problem, and must discuss it with someone. You are my selection to be the listener. I will arrange it with hopes you will not let me down."

Pedro was not sure what she was talking about. "Sure, if it can be arranged."

"We better go in. Thanks for the kiss. I enjoyed it and I know that you did." With a smile, she led the way to the door, with Pedro following like a little puppy. It was one of his most restless nights of his life.

Maybe he ought to give up this job and go to Jane. Then he thought about Julie McKeever and decided things could happen even if he were in Rainy Roundup. Several times, Drew Hampton had paid young women to spend the night, and each time, had offered to pay for one for him. He had refused and felt good about it, but tonight he didn't feel too good. In fact, he was afraid of this meeting with her because he doubted any man could not be tempted by that beauty. Then it occurred to him that he had killed two and probably three Indians today, and all he could think of was Leigh Saunders. Father Frankie and Sister Theresa could not be very proud of him.

CHAPTER 27

The following morning after breakfast, the stagecoach moved on toward Fort Griffin. Everybody was in a talkative mood with the exception of Pedro, who felt uncomfortable and washed out after a poor night's rest. Drew Hampton knew all of Pedro's moods by now, and realized that something had happened outside.

The black haired beauty addressed Hampton, "My husband would be delighted to meet a man of your qualifications, Mr. Hampton. Would you be free to eat with us at the fort. We could send for you, and of course, Pedro is also invited."

Hampton looked over at Pedro. "Would you join me? It would be a good opportunity to see a part of the fort, and also the food would probably be very good, in addition to the wonderful company of our hosts."

Pedro looked at Hampton, and answered as he glanced at Leigh. "Yes, it sounds fine."

"Good," added Leigh, "then it is settled. We will send for you at six in the evening on Saturday."

Then Hampton asked, "Do you need to clear it with the Major first?"

"No, it will be fine."

Around noon, the coach pulled into the small town just fifteen miles from the fort. Two soldiers were waiting for Leigh Saunders, but neither was the Major. She waved as she left in the buggy, speaking out, "See you Saturday, be ready."

Pedro was glad she was gone for the present. She had continued to look at him all that morning, and he was very uneasy. Was he losing his mind or how could she really look that much like Running Fox? He could not get that kiss out of his thoughts. Her darting tongue had made it the kiss of his young life.

After arriving, Hampton had checked on when they could get a coach to Fort Sill. With it off the old Butterfield Overland route road, they would have to wait until Tuesday. Pedro was surprised that Hampton was satisfied with that. He had thought they would have to wait longer. Although his work there would be finished by tomorrow, and at the latest on Saturday morning, a couple of days rest would do them both some good. Riding those coaches was rough, and the body got really beat up at times. He told Pedro that once they left Fort Sill, they would have to go to Sherman to pick up the old coach road, and from there it would be Indian country as they crossed the lower eastern part of Oklahoma, and up the western side of Arkansas to Fort Smith.

On Saturday evening, the buggy was early, but they were ready. One enlisted man had come for them, and he was very quiet but polite. Major Saunders met them as they arrived at the door of the office. He was about the height of Pedro, but thinner and not nearly so muscular. He had wavy sandy hair and was light complected considering where he was stationed. Since they were early, he suggested a tour of the main part of the fort. So far, Leigh was no where to be seen. Following the tour, they went into the private room that had been set for them. With only places for four, it would be an intimate dinner, with Pedro hoping that she would keep those piercing eyes off him. They sat around in some comfortable chairs away from the table and were served a glass of wine, along with some good yellow cheese. This was a favorite of Pedro, as Hampton had helped him with his knowledge of the finer types of cheese as well as other foods. Just as they were being served some chicken livers on little sticks, Leigh Saunders made her appearance. Pedro almost choked as he took his first look. It was Running Fox in a very refined evening dress that dipped very low from the shoulders down to the tops of her very ample breasts. He tried not to stare but wondered if he had been successful. The dress was solid black, and fit very tight until it reached her hips, then it flared out. There were a few shiny beads that resembled diamonds, along with a few little bows here and there. If she was trying to impress them, she was certainly successful.

A few minutes after she came in, dinner was served. It was very elaborate and Pedro knew the regular soldiers did not eat anything near this kind of food. In fact, he had serious doubts that even officers often ate what they had that evening. The main course was chicken, but oh what chicken! Pedro did not know it could ever taste that good. Vegetables were also delicious, as there were two different casseroles of them, and he did not know exactly what he was eating. The conversation was the banking business almost exclusively. Leigh had been right about her husband. He was fascinated with Drew Hampton. They followed dinner with a very special apple pie and coffee.

When the brandy was served and Pedro refused any, Leigh spoke up, "While they drink brandy and discuss the banking world, why don't I show you my horse?"

Before Pedro could accept, the Major agreed, "Yes, Pedro,

she has the prettiest paint you ever saw. I bought him from an Indian Chief, and had to give too much for it."

This put Pedro at ease and they left for the horse barn. In the hallway, with no one around, she whispered, "We will talk in the barn." They had to cross part of the open space to reach the horses, and Pedro knew all those soldiers eyes were not on him. She was far overdressed to be going into the horse barn. He wondered how many of these men had dreams about this woman, and also if she was ever as friendly with any of them as she was with him.

Inside, they were alone as they approached the stall of her paint. Most of the horses were outside in the open corral but some had private stalls. Pedro's heart raced as he looked over the beautiful paint. He was so shocked that he could hardly believe his eyes. It was the same color, brown and white, marked exactly the same, and left Pedro wondering if it could be Running Fox's horse. This was a possibility but he could not be sure but this whole thing was getting the best of him. He could not believe all this. The paint nudged Pedro and was very friendly as Leigh laughed.

Then she whispered although no one was near, "My husband leaves in the morning for at least five days. I would like to come to your hotel room for a private talk about ten o'clock. A driver will bring me in and then return about one o'clock. Can you spend the time with me or will your job interfere? It is very important to me and my future."

Pedro could not say no. He really was not sure of what was really going to happen or be said. It has to be important, he thought, as he answered, "We won't be working or going anywhere tomorrow. My boss has already told me that he won't get out of bed before noon. The stagecoach riding really takes it out of a person."

With a dazzling smile, she thanked him. "We can go back now. I will be on time tomorrow."

On the way back to the dinner party, Pedro wondered if

Running Fox was haunting him. That paint, her looks, her staring at him. Coincidence? He wondered. Pedro had been at ease all night as she seldom looked at him. He must be real jealous, and man, I don't blame him. A Lieutenant Powers was visiting with Hampton and the Major when they returned. Shortly after that, the Lieutenant excused himself. An hour later, Hampton and Pedro were on their way back to the hotel.

On the way to the room, Pedro told Hampton about Leigh coming in the morning. Although he tried to impress the fact that she could be in trouble, Hampton smiled at him, "I'm sure that you will be able to take care of her problem. She may have others but you and I both know that you can cure one of them."

Hampton's smile grew bigger as Pedro's face got pinker. The youth was totally lost for words as each entered their rooms.

CHAPTER 28

It was another restless night for the young bodyguard. These entire happenings were too real, as no coincidence could have so many angles. Her looks, the piercing eyes, and that exact horse were all to much for him. She was a living Running Fox. He buried her but now he wondered about this whole thing. He had wanted to tell Hampton about it, as he had already told him the story of the Indian girl, but he felt it would only make his boss laugh at him. No one would ever believe it so he would keep it to himself.

At nine forty-five, a light tap on the door told him she had arrived. Opening the door, it was Leigh as he expected. Dressed in a light blue and white dress, that was a simple one compared to the night before. She was still nevertheless a breathtaking beauty, with her long black hair, flowing over her shoulders, sparkling steel gray eyes that seemed to pierce and burn. She came in all smiles, and gently put out her hand, and Pedro responded by lightly taking it. "Please sit down." It was the first words spoke. She sat, and since it was the lone chair, he edged onto the bed.

"Pedro, I need to confide in someone, and I believe you may be the one."

Still puzzled by what this was all about, he answered, "I hope so. I do not have to meet my boss until much later, about four."

She gave him a sensuous look along with a smile, "Good, since I told them not to come after me until three o'clock."

"I'm listening."

She dropped her smile and looked almost sad as she began, "When I was seventeen years old, I fell in love with my music teacher. He was twenty-seven. We had plenty of chances to be alone, and soon we were making love often. When I graduated from high school, we planned to marry but when I told my family, that is when the trouble began. My family is very wealthy and influential. My lover was a poor voice teacher so they assumed he was after their damn money. We both loved to ride horses, and one day while riding, he somehow took a fall. His head hit a large stone," and at this point she started to cry. Pedro walked over and tried to comfort her.

Then she continued, "Anyway, he died in my arms. I believe my folks were silently happy. I felt my life was over. A year later, I entered college, and met Stephen. My folks knew his family, and invited them over one evening. They were crazy about him. His family had money, and he was a Captain in the Army. After a few dates, one night while the families were together again, he proposed. I asked for time, not wanting to hurt his feelings. However, in due time, I gave in to family pressure, and married him as he was being promoted and moving to the west. I never even got to finish my first year of college. Now, for the personal part: in six months he has only tried to make love to me three times."

Pedro cut in at this point. "A beautiful woman like you and

he only tried to? I'm afraid I don't understand."

"I was completely puzzled at first too. I loved it with my teacher, and I wanted him. Then about two months ago, I came in unexpected and caught Lieutenant Powers and my husband in a very compromising position. They are lovers."

Pedro was too stunned to say anything.

"I understand it, Pedro. Some people are born with feelings for their own sex. If he just would have not married me for the wrong reason. Now I know his commanding officer had insisted he get married, along with the promotion, before moving out here."

Now Pedro found his voice. "Who told you all this?"

"He did, after I caught him. I am leaving him next month and returning to my home town in Philadelphia. Then I will begin divorce proceedings. He will not fight the divorce as long as I keep quiet about him."

"Why is he so jealous of you?"

Leigh smiled at this. "He could care less about who gets to me. His only objection would be the other men would find out and laugh behind his back. He and his friend hide their feelings well."

All of this was a shock to the young bodyguard. He realized he had a lot to learn about life.

"Pedro, I just had to unload this on someone."

He really felt for her. What a horrible thing to happen to such a beautiful young woman. "What can I do for you? Can I help in any possible way?"

She settled down a little now. "Tell Mr. Hampton this story, and ask him to use his influence to route me the safest way to Philadelphia. I would not trust Stephen, and these locals here don't really know anything even if they work for the stagecoach people. Have him write it all out and then I will buy the ticket myself. Ask him to write me at this address, and I will surely get it. Somehow, I preferred to confide in you, instead of him. Do you understand?"

With a smile, Pedro added, "It is as good as done, but we sure have a lot of time left. Is there more?"

Getting out of her chair, she walked over to the bed and handed him the address. He carefully placed it in his wallet as he noticed her sitting and then lying back on the bed. "Pedro, everybody on that coach knew I wanted you. Since Roy was killed, there has been no one else. I cannot explain my fascination for you. There are lots of nice looking young soldiers here but none have excited me." By now, the youth's mouth was opened in awe. "You are handsome, but I can't explain why my eyes seemed glued to you. No one has ever affected me this quick, not even Roy."

This whole episode was also amazing to Pedro. He could not tell her about his Indian sweetheart, despite a desire to. She would think he was crazy, but somehow there had to be a connection. "I know you have a girl that you are going to marry. You will never hear from me again after today, I promise."

Pedro laid down beside her. In a matter of seconds, that darting tongue was working inside his mouth again. They undressed between kisses, and when they were finally nude, Pedro knew she was the exact equal of Running Fox in every detail. Although he had never seen his Indian girl in good light and this close, he had looked and strained his eyes enough to know. Then she told him to relax as her darting tongue moved from her warm mouth, covering his entire body down to his toes. The youth never felt this way in his entire lifetime. This was an experience he could never forget. Julie had promised he could never forget his day with her. As of this second, he couldn't even remember her last name.

Relaxing on her back, the black haired beauty pointed to her firm breasts. Pedro began to fondle them but she put her hand behind his head and pulled him down to them. It was another first for the young bodyguard. Jane asked him to learn, and from the way this was going, he might learn it all now.

First, he kissed the firm silken mounds of flesh, then with his tongue began to tantalize the rose colored circles around the swollen tips. She moaned in slow gasps, and the youth knew he must be doing something right. Then he moved to her neck and ears, with the moaning becoming louder, she reached for his arousal, stroking it gently and whispering, "Give him to me now, please."

As he slowly entered her, she inhaled with a slight sound of "Ohhhh," exhaling and pulling him closer. She wrapped those smooth firm legs around him, as he began to aggressively move over her. Leigh whispered, "Slow down, honey, we got nothing but time."

Her hips were moving so smoothly that he could not believe it. It was like he was gliding with her, and yet he was hardly moving himself. His mind flashed back to the wonderful ballerina that he had watched as a small boy. At times her long legs would wrap totally around him, then smoothly release him, guiding the movement with her skillful knees.

Gradually, she increased the tempo yet all the smoothness was still there. Her moist interior clung to his manhood, and at times seemed to squeeze him, causing the youth to almost lose his mind with the amazing wondrous feelings. His experience with Julie had been like riding a wild mustang, but this was more of a venture of floating on top of an ultra smooth wave.

Unbelievably, they exploded together, Pedro feeling an ecstasy that he never knew existed. She had tightened those legs around him, pulling him so close it seemed to drain all the strength from his muscular body. He just lay there, feeling he did not have the strength to move.

She cooed in a whisper, "Buddy boy, that was the best."

He finally found the energy to roll off her onto the bed. From her breathing it was obvious she was equally exhausted. As they relaxed, Pedro thought of her husband. Strange, how he could sleep next to her for six months and never make love to her. I guess people are just born with different feelings. Then he thought of Jane. Although, I did not pick the one she wanted me to, I did learn. This is the last time, he swore. He meant after today, for in a few minutes, she was working on him and he was responding.

"Believe me, your little bride is going to be happy with you," smiled the long haired beauty as they proceeded to make love again.

Later they talked about themselves. They were both nineteen years old, with Leigh only one month older. She would be here for one more month, and although it would be boring, she would remain true to him to assure their agreement on the divorce. She knew she could get away with today, but on the post, the chance was not as good and certainly not as tempting.

Pedro confided in her that his girl had asked him to make love, so that they would not both be total greenhorns. Then about Julie, and his experience with her. "Your girl must be a real gem and have some confidence in you. Not one in a thousand would tell her boyfriend anything like that. First, they would be jealous, and second, they would be afraid of losing their boyfriend."

Pedro smiled as he thought of Jane. "Julie and you are the ones she doesn't want to know about."

Leigh laughed as she once again began to kiss Pedro with that darting tongue doing its work. He tried to make more conversation, "Are there many who are aggressive like Julie was with me?" She barely let him get the words out, as she kissed him again. She wanted him now, and he only hoped it possible. He wanted her one more last time. Now, he would never feel that he had not made love to Running Fox. It was a dream come true.

At two o'clock, they got out of the bed. Pedro asked her to pose for him before she put her clothes on. With that sensuous look, she did just that. Her beautiful legs were long, tapered and very firm. Her breasts were perfectly shaped and stood straight out. Her waist was small and flowed into those perfect hips. Finally, he told her that she should put her clothes on now, and she gave him that sensuous smile again, laughing as she added, "What's the matter, good looking, wasn't three times enough?"

Pedro gave her a very serious look. "I don't believe I could ever get enough of you, please put your clothes on." She laughed as she purposely slowly dressed, flirting with every movement of her body.

Before leaving the room, Pedro gave her a list of the hotels where they would be. He wanted to know about her trip and also that she had arrived safely at home. She promised as she kissed him good-bye with that darting tongue. It was the most fabulous love tool he had encountered.

CHAPTER 29

At four o'clock, Pedro was waiting in the hotel restaurant when Hampton came down from this room. "Can you believe I almost fell asleep again before I came down. I must have really needed the rest."

Pedro was having a hard time looking at him, and it did not take his boss long to figure that one out. "I hope you got your rest before ten." Hampton grinned as he made the statement. "Pedro, I love you as my own son. I promise not to mention it again if you tell me one thing." Now he looked at him. "Just one, please."

The youth, smiling as he said it, "Just this one."

"Is she as entertaining as she looks?"

Pedro looked away to answer. "Better than that. She is unbelievable."

Hampton felt it was an unfair question. "I should not have asked that. I'm sorry. It is a secret that will always be between us."

Pedro looked at him seriously. "I did not mind. She even told me that everyone in the coach knew she wanted me." Then Pedro took out his wallet and handed the address to him. Following this, the story of her husband and the Lieutenant, and of the agreement and the divorce. When he finished, Drew Hampton was the one almost in shock. When he could find his voice again, Hampton assured him he would work on it tomorrow as they did not leave until Tuesday. Pedro reminded him that this entire story had to be forgotten, or it could ruin Leigh's chance of an easy divorce.

"I understand, son. You can bank on it."

Hampton worked with his maps in arranging the best way for Leigh to travel. In a couple of places, he had selected a slightly longer route because of safety. Pedro was getting excited for they were leaving tomorrow for Fort Sill and Lawton, Oklahoma. He hoped to be lucky enough to find and visit with some of his old Indian friends. Dawn and Little Elk were the two he knew were safe, but there could be more.

Pedro sat in the hotel room all morning with his boss as he worked out the map and directions for her. The young bodyguard had made himself a solemn promise. He felt that he had violated his sweetheart on two different occasions but there would be no more. Leigh Saunders had looked like the twin sister of Running Fox. He decided this was no reason for him to want her but he could not deny that he did. All morning, he was confused and felt down, knowing he had become just another man. He had not been to church lately either, though he did pray often. Somehow, he still felt fear as he prayed to the Good Lord. It had been that way since he had called Toro out and killed him. He was relieved when his boss made a suggestion. "Let's go to lunch. Don't lack too much to be finished with this. We can mail it this afternoon. Anything you want to say, maybe a short note?"

"No, but lunch sounds good."

The following morning, they left for Fort Sill, Oklahoma. Although it was supposed to be a dangerous road, there was no trouble, and the entire journey was made without incident. After taking rooms at a small hotel, they went to the Fort so Hampton could handle his business. Later that day, he saw General Sherman, who was there because of trouble with several Kiowa chiefs. The biggest problem chief was Satanna, the White Cloud. He had been heard to boast after a severe Indian raid, bragging that he had been responsible. Pedro was surprised that it was the Kiowas in trouble and not the Comanches. He knew how they felt about living on a reservation, and then he realized that maybe the Kiowas felt the same way.

At noon on the second day, Drew Hampton had finished his business at the Fort. He took Pedro to the Indian reservation office so that he could inquire about his old friends. He hoped the officers in charge could help him find them. Walking from their buggy, they saw a dark haired young woman go in just ahead of them. As they entered she turned to walk around the railing, facing them. A flicker of remembrance hit them both at the same time, but she was much more sure than was he.

"Pedro? Am I crazy or is it a ghost?"

He stared at her. Dressed like an American woman, she was Indian. She resembled Little Flower. Could it be? "Little Flower?"

"Yes, and you are Pedro, whom I thought was dead."

After a few more minutes of staring at each other, they embraced. Separating, they looked each other over with a smile on their surprised faces. "Wounded Bear had sent me for wood because José was at the other end of the village helping an old woman. I watched the slaughter at a distance. You were not with the women captives when they left, were you?"

She laughed now. "I slipped out of the village when the shooting first started. That night, I almost froze, and the next day when the soldiers went by with the captives, I decided to surrender." Then it dawned on Pedro that his boss was just standing there looking and ignored.

"Gosh, I'm sorry, Mr Hampton. Little Flower, meet my boss, Mr. Drew Hampton. I am his bodyguard."

They spoke and smiled at each other. Then she added, "Boy, I'll bet he's a good one."

Hampton laughed, "Very good. Tell me, was he a good Comanche?"

She looked at Pedro with sparkling eyes. "He went through the training to be a warrior with no trouble. Brown Bear told me one day that he was going to be a great warrior. Every young girl in camp had their eyes on him including Running Fox, the chief's daughter, and you know who else—me!"

Now Pedro knew he was in for a lot of teasing later from his boss. Hampton laughed harder than he had ever seen.

"Come on, Little Flower, you are really fixing me up."

She looked at them both and smiled very sweetly. "Mr. Hampton, don't let him deny it, I swear it is the truth. He even killed a big bull buffalo on his first hunt, was injured, and went after another one until he was ordered to go take care of his leg. I wanted to be with him when he was hurt but I was afraid Running Fox would scratch my eyes out. Fawn said she was killed. I am sorry for that."

At that instant, a handsome army lieutenant came out of one of the offices. "Hi, honey" was his greeting to her. She seemed to blush as she introduced him.

"This is Lieutenant James Corley, my husband. Honey, this is Mr. Hampton and Pedro, who was a Comanche captive when my tribe was wiped out."

Pedro was shocked but very happy for her. He was a tall, intelligent looking, dark haired man. As soon as they all greeted each other, she continued and told the story of how Pedro had been saved, and also what a great warrior he would have been. Pedro could only listen. It was too late to change anything she had said. He would hate to go back to the hotel with his boss for he knew what was coming.

Finally, she asked, "Pedro, do you have any time? We could take my buggy and go visit with Fawn. It is only about fifteen minutes from here?"

At this point, Hampton spoke up, "He needs the rest of the day off to get his head to fit inside that cowboy hat. Take him with you, and I will go back to the hotel. What time do you want me to pick you up?"

Pedro was still speechless, as Little Flower told Hampton she would bring him to the hotel as it was not far. Lt. Corley was very cordial to both men, and invited Hampton in for a visit.

On the way to Fawn's teepee, she told Pedro she had met James when she first came to live at the reservation, and it had been love from the beginning. They have now been married for a year, and she was almost sure a baby is on the way. He had taught her how to read and write English, and she had taught him a lot of the Comanche language. She was sorry for her tribe and people, but as of now, happiness had finally come her way. He told her how happy and proud he was of her, and especially that she was alive. They did not get a chance to talk about Fawn but she did tell him as they arrived at the little Comanche village that Little Elk had died of Cholera over a year ago. Fawn was building a small fire outside as they drove up in the buggy.

"Look who blew in today. Recognize him?"

Fawn looked white as she stared at him. "You, you're Pedro." It was in Comanche as she knew no English. He smiled and hugged her.

While this was going on, Little Flower spoke up quickly, "Your husband is not home, huh?"

Fawn laughed at this. "You right. He is not here, and it will be another day before he returns."

"I won't ask if he is off the reservation," chimed in Little Flower.

"Please don't," laughed Fawn.

It was obvious to Pedro that Little Flower and Fawn were close and that they kept a few things between them. Pedro and

Fawn had a long visit, and Little Flower was also in on the conversation. Pedro knew Fawn had been captured but she really thought, as Little Flower did, that he had been killed. Little Flower saw another Indian woman several teepees down, and left them to go visit. It was obvious she wanted them to be able to speak alone for a while, since her husband was an army officer. Fawn could have guessed what Pedro's first question would be.

"Who are you married to?"

Fawn hesitated as she looked at him. It was almost a look of fear in her eyes. "He was not of our tribe, but was a cousin of my husband. You probably heard of him, most Comanches have. He was not a chief but is strong, great warrior. Ten years ago, he lived in small Comanche village with wife and two children. White men raided camp, raped his wife, little girl and cut off his son's testicles while killing them. So now he believes all white men are evil. It is true savage hatred, and being a great warrior, he has killed many. He promised Great Spirit that he will kill many more. He leaves with small band of warriors, and killing is their way of life. Smart warriors, they not fight unless attack is in their favor. If he thinks it might be even battle, they no fight."

Pedro interrupted her. "Do you love him?"

"Yes, I do. He has promised to never take another wife. You know how I hate that. Also has promised never to borrow one and you know about that. Remember the night I offered myself to you when I was very mad?"

"Is he good to you in other ways?"

Fawn flashed a great big smile. "Yes, in many ways. And Pedro, something else helps in this dull reservation life. He is great lover." After a big smile, she asked, "Do you know his name? I know Wounded Bear told stories about his war cousin."

Pedro looked at her, and answered without a smile, "Yes, I know who he is. Screaming Eagle, also known among the Comanches as The White Hater."

"You are right. I knew you had heard of him. If you ever come to visit, and a black stallion is near the back of the teepee, do not stop. I really do not think there would be trouble, but you never know about him."

Pedro smiled. He had come to respect that gun he carried on his hip. Only another gunman could cause him trouble. The fact that he practiced often, and was faster than ever, gave him a feeling of pride as he protected his boss and good friend, Drew Hampton.

"I understand," was his reply as Little Flower approached.

"I think we better be leaving, Pedro."

Fawn hugged Pedro, and thanked him for looking her up. As they rode off, Little Flower asked, "Did she tell you who her husband is?"

"Yes, I have heard of him."

She looked at Pedro with fear in her eyes. "He is a terrible man. In my eyes, a disgrace to the Comanche people."

"Yes."

With her face still covered with worry and fear, she added, "I hope my husband never crosses his path." Then looking at Pedro, she continued, "The fact that you are half Mexican would not help you."

Pedro was never one to boast but now was the time. "I can handle him and his friends."

"Do not worry about your friend, Pedro."

"I have come a long way in the last two years. In my opinion, he will live longer if he leaves me alone."

Little Flower looked at him with surprised eyes and a little grin. "I have always known for you to tell the truth. I am proud you feel as you do. However, my husband is another matter. He is very smart, but I have doubts about what he could do against Comanches. Thank goodness for the present, as he only does office work. I pray it stays that way."

Then, trying to bring her out of the worried look, Pedro whispered to her, "Did you really care for me?"

Little Flower blushed and smiled at the same time. "You were the first one ever to kiss me. In fact, the only one ever besides my husband. Yes, I was simply crazy about you, but I was afraid of Running Fox."

"I didn't want to put you on the spot, but I needed to see that smile again. I am proud that you cared for me."

"Oh, I cared for you. After you kissed me that night, I didn't sleep for a week, and that is the truth, so help me."

Pedro looked at her but her eyes were straight ahead. "I cannot begin to tell you how happy I am that you married Lieutenant Corley. I am glad you are so happy."

"He is wonderful to me. When he gets to our place, he tries to help with the cooking and everything. Our place is so much better than a teepee. I have all the advantages of a white woman, and there are many."

"Oh, I almost forgot something important. What happened to Amy and little Ross. I saw that they were captured."

"That worked out good. Amy was unhappy at first, but returned to her family, and they adopted little Ross. You might remember, his family had been killed."

"That turned out great."

They continued to talk over old times until she dropped him off at the hotel. It had been a pleasant day, spoiled only by finding out that Fawn had married a mad savage, Screaming Eagle. Even the Comanches knew better than to ever make him a chief.

CHAPTER 30

By the time they left the area, both men were bored, although Hampton had sold a fair amount of jewelry. However, he gave the officers good prices so the profit was small.

Again it was known to be dangerous territory, but they encountered no trouble. After finishing business in Sherman, they headed through the southeast edge of Indian country in Oklahoma, then due north into Fort Smith, Arkansas. It seemed the most dangerous part of the trip had gone off without incident.

Arriving in Fort Smith, Pedro had a letter waiting for him from Jane. The letter really worried him as she wrote of trouble between her mother and father. He was drinking very heavily and when she complained, he had begun to hit her. Jane was very concerned about it, and was afraid of what could happen.

They spent time there and in the surrounding area. Another letter had come from Jane, stating that things were no better. Her mother had received a letter from her brother, who now had seven notches on his gun, and she hopes he never comes home again. She has completely quit writing to him. Jane reminded him of planning their marriage soon, for she was ready to get out and away from her father despite the fact that she loved him. All she needed to be was sixteen years old, for nothing else was holding her.

Arriving in Tipton, Missouri, Pedro was beginning to get homesick for Rainy Roundup and Jane. The following day, a letter came from Jane. When he opened it, it was a shocker, for her father, George Skaag, had died in his sleep. Pedro read it three times before he gave the letter to Hampton. Then Pedro and he had a long talk in reference to the Kid returning to Rainy Roundup, but decided to wait for another letter or so before making a final decision.

Two days later as they were getting ready to leave Tipton, Pedro received the letter he was expecting from Jane. Hampton had a letter from Agnes Skaag. The letter from Jane was very reassuring, and he felt so much better that he was all choked up. Agnes Skaag, being suspicious that Pedro might want to come back, insisted in her letter to Hampton that he keep Pedro on the job until their trip was complete. Everything was under control, and she knew that they would need the money. She told him that she was considering selling the store and café, hoping that she could buy into the horse and cattle ranch that Pedro and Jane were going to try to acquire. She was aware of the fact that by pooling their money, they would have a better chance at purchasing part of what was needed.

When Pedro did not show his boss the love letter from Jane, he only told Pedro the part about him staying on the job. He would write Agnes and make some arrangements with her for the kids future. He loved Pedro as a son, and he would have what he wanted.

They spent considerable time in the Kansas City area. Hampton had arranged to take Pedro through the cattle packing plant there, and it was a highlight of the visit to this busy city. Pedro was beginning to wonder about Drew Hampton and his future mother-in-law. He was receiving almost as many letters as Pedro was getting from Jane. Hampton never volunteered any information about the letters, so Pedro never asked. He could not help but wonder: is Drew Hampton my future father-in-law?

The night before they left the Kansas City area, Hampton took Pedro to an elaborate steak house with music and entertainment. They were seated at a table, and while enjoying a drink, a nice looking brunette came over to Hampton. She leaned over and he nodded yes. She looked over at an attractive young woman near the entrance, and the woman started over to them. Hampton smiled at Pedro as the two women were seated at their table. "My friend is Lucinda Gray, Mr Hampton." This proved to Pedro that this was a preset arrangement.

"Nice to meet you, Lucinda. This is Pedro, and this young lady is Millie Cartwright."

Pedro smiled as he realized they were going to eat together and there was nothing he could do about it. "Nice to meet you both."

Lucinda sat across from Pedro, with Millie across from Hampton. Millie was totally white, but Lucinda was part Negro, with long black hair. She was not dark, and by far the prettiest of the two. It broke up into two separate conversations, and Pedro soon learned that Lucinda Gray was an intelligent young woman with a lot of class. He had been correct, as she soon told him that her mother had been a slave in Georgia, and her father was a white man who was the master of the plantation. Then she admitted they were both hustling, but she would only be one until she could raise enough money to get her a small café. Her mother had taught her to cook, and from the food she had eaten here, they desperately needed some southern cooking in this town. Now Pedro knew he was wrong about the class, but she was intelligent. He was so tired of Kansas City that even he had a couple of drinks while the other three had about four each.

Walking together to the hotel, Pedro informed her in a nice way that he was not interested in anything except going to bed alone. She broke into a hearty laugh, and admitted that his boss had paid for the night. He also told Millie that you probably would not be interested, but he knew you had been very blue lately about your girlfriend. He wanted me to stay with you tonight even it was just for conversation as long as I could keep you awake.

"So, young man, it looks like you are stuck with Lucinda even though she is not attractive to you."

"Lucinda, nobody said you were not attractive. I made myself a promise that my next love session was going to be with my true love."

She thought on that for a moment. "Given half a chance, I bet I could wipe that out of your mind for just tonight. You must love her, and I wish you the best. Let me make a suggestion. Why don't we just go to the room and talk about our lives. Mine has been interesting, and I don't mean about my life here. I also bet you have had an interesting life. My friend says your boss said you were a hell of a bodyguard."

It was not easy to get them up to their rooms, but as usual, Hampton used the never fail method—money. Each couple went into separate rooms. Lucinda Gray was right as she had lived a very interesting life. Pedro learned a lot about southern plantations, and the people who lived on them. She told him things he would never have dreamed about. He did not get into the revenge story but he did tell her about life in the church orphanage and, of course, his life with the Comanches. As with all the others, it was the stories of the Indians that interested her the most. She was very sad as to how his tribe had all been slaughtered. The death of Running Fox was the sorrowful part that almost had her in tears.

Pedro, completely clothed except for his boots, fell asleep around two in the morning. Awakening shortly before daylight, he turned around to see if she had left. What he saw was a shock as she lay asleep by him. The shock part was that she was totally nude. In the semi-darkness, she looked very appealing to him. Lucinda was young, probably not yet nineteen, and her body could attract any man. Three hours later, they could hear Hampton knocking on the door, calling out, "Be downstairs in about a half hour. We have to catch the stage in a couple of hours. I don't know about you two but we need breakfast."

As they started to dress, Lucinda smiled at him. "Not only did you almost miss out, but you would have denied me a great time. Admit it, lover boy, you really got with it."

He smiled but said nothing. Deep down he wanted to kick himself.

Then she needled him again, "Be a sport and admit it."

"You know I enjoyed it very much. It is just that I broke a promise I made to myself."

She smiled as she was slipping into her dress. "I won't tell nobody but Millie. I just want her to know what she missed."

Pedro gave her a pleading look.

"It will be later, if you want. I will make your boss think I am still a virgin for the night."

"I would not ask you to lie. Just play it cool."

Her smile was a sweet one. "Lover boy, you just proved to me that I still like it. I will try to play it cool, but we both know, I could never be cool around you.

Eating breakfast with those three was not exactly the easiest thing he had ever tried to do. Lucinda kept her word and never said anything, but her expressions were enough to put his boss almost in hysterics.

As it turned out, everyone enjoyed the breakfast, even Pedro, after a very questionable beginning. He found out that Lucinda had missed her calling. She was a natural born comedienne and at the end of the meal, both Hampton and Pedro had raised their opinions of her. In one of her serious moments, she had explained very clearly her being a lady of the night was a painful thing in almost all cases. In just a year, she had been beaten, used and not paid, made fun of, and forced to do some acts that were not natural. As she had told Pedro earlier, it was a means to the end. The café was her dream, and by the time they left on the stage, both Hampton and Pedro knew she would have it in the near future.

Their next major stop was to be Abilene, Kansas. A city of cowmen, where the good and the bad mixed frequently. It has been said that there were more thieves, burglars, gunslingers, drunkards, card sharks, whores, and just plain cowhands that ever gathered in one place.

Pedro listened as Hampton told him about Abilene. This, he said, is going to be interesting.

CHAPTER 31

The crowded main street of Abilene, Kansas had probably reached its maximum today. Many trail riders were in town selling their herds to the buyers. However, it appeared at this time, that this year would never match the record year of 1871. The demand was not as good, and the buyers were not offering the top price expected. In fact, there were not as many buyers as before.

On a fairly busy side street, Drew Hampton walked along with his young capable bodyguard. "We need to talk about it, but I just want you to know that I am going to retire in about six or so months."

Then he glanced over to look at the kid's expression. "You don't look too surprised"

The young man smiled at his wonderful boss. "Not really,

I guess I had it figured from some of your remarks lately. What are your plans?"

"Tonight at supper, we will discuss it completely. You know that I am going to take care of you. In fact, you might even be able to help me retire."

Now Pedro did look at him with a lot of surprise written all over his youthful face. For some unknown reason, at that moment, Hampton had turned around to glance back. A face that he feared, was almost breathing down his neck. It was one that he never cared to see again. Hampton had seen this man in action twice and that was enough.

It was Jacoby Jenkins, one of the most feared gunfighters in all the west, having killed close to twenty men. Hoping it was a coincidence that he was following so close, Hampton stepped aside to put out a cigarette. Pedro followed him in stepping aside. Then Jenkins bumped into Pedro and stumbled, and Hampton knew at that minute, it was a fake stumble for he had to go slightly out of the way to bump into Pedro.

"You damn *pelado*, I don't take that crap from any greaser."

Hampton tried to step between them. "Wait, Jenkins," but he was pushed aside by the angry gunfighter.

Pedro moved in, "What just happened when you stumbled was an accident, but keep your hands off him."

Jacoby Jenkins smiled as this kid had just played right into his hands. "You must be old Hampton's guard. You're known as Pedro the Kid, right?"

The kid just stared at him. "Yeah, so?"

A broader smile came across Jenkin's face. "You are nothing but a *pelado*, or do you know what that means? Step out in the street if you've got the guts and lets settle this now

Jacoby Jenkins was a little unnerved when Pedro smiled at him. Didn't this stupid Mexican know who he was?

Again Hampton tried to get into the fracas, "Jacoby, don't do this."

At that moment, Pedro realized who the man was, but at this point, it made no difference. "Whenever you're ready, Jenkins, let's get with it."

What a brash kid, thought the gunfighter.

Then they walked into the street and people around them began to scatter. As Pedro turned to face the famous gunman, he saw Hampton again trying to talk to him. This time he was warned off.

At this moment, Pedro was very glad that he had never neglected working on his fast draw and his accuracy. A quick prayer to God that Jane would get over him and go on with her life. He knew Hampton would send all his money to her. Now he was ready. Maybe this noted gunfighter was too cocky for his own good. Maybe he did not have a chance but Jacoby Jenkins was going to have to prove it to him.

It was at this feared moment that Drew Hampton realized that a friend had told him that Tom Baxter was in town last week. That had to be it. He was trying to get the kid. Pedro had it figured right. Damn, he should have at least warned him or something. Now, it was too late, and he hoped the kid could somehow survive this.

"Anytime," drawled the older man. It was again unnerving to the gunfighter that Pedro had smiled when he was told 'anytime.'

"I'm ready when you are."

This infuriated the famous gunman and they drew together. It sounded like one shot and they both fell with a thud. Hampton ran to Pedro, who had been badly hit, but it appeared to be a little over his heart.

Pedro was conscious for the moment and whispered to Hampton, "Go ask him if…it was…Baxter."

Drew Hampton realized that Pedro was a lot smarter about some things then he was. When he knelt over Jenkins, it was pretty obvious that he was hit very bad. Blood was all over the middle of the chest and coming from his mouth.

"Jacoby, was it Baxter? You just as well tell the truth."

The famous gunman made several attempts to speak. Finally, he got it out, "Yes, and…tell that kid…he's damn good but to…give it up…if he lives…this…" and with that he was gone.

Hampton ran back to Pedro, who was being attended by the doctor. Pedro just looked at his boss.

"You were right, it was Baxter. Jenkins just died."

Pedro, with a scorn on his face, muttered, "If I live, I'm gonna kill that bastard"

Drew Hampton knew he meant it. Pedro never used that type of language before.

Then Pedro lost consciousness. He faded into a deep slumber that brought his mind back to "the day of horror" when he was an eight-year-old. This existing problem had continued all his life since then. A "battle of his conscience" between his powerful love of God that denied him the right to kill and a fiery undeniable feeling for revenge that was uncontrollable at times.

Six days later, Pedro fluttered his eyes as consciousness came back to him. He lay in a daze, and for some time was unable to focus his eyes. For the first few minutes, he could not remember where he was or what had happened. Then it began to come back to him, realizing he had been shot by the famous gunman, Jacoby Jenkins.

"Pedro, Pedro dear." It was a feminine voice, but for the moment, he could not recognize who she was. Again he tried to clear his eyes, and things began to clear a little. Someone with a white dress and black hair was standing over his bed, calling his name out very sweetly.

He stirred slightly, and again she called his name. Then he heard a male voice, and he began to call him by name.

"Pedro, can you hear me?" Pedro nodded his head.

"I am Doctor Clifton. Welcome back."

Pedro tried to smile but was not too successful. Then his eyes cleared more and he could see the doctor, and also the young woman beside him. He could not believe it, but it was Lucinda Gray. This time, the smile came out.

"Howdy Doctor, and Lucinda, is that you?"

Both laughed as they were so glad to see him come out of the unconscious state.

"It's me, Lucinda, in the flesh. I left for Abilene two days after you, and bumped into Mr. Hampton just two days ago. He hired me to come and try to help the fine doc here take care of his young buddy. He should be back soon and will be tickled pink to see you back among the living."

The doctor proceeded to examine him, asking Pedro questions as he did. The youth glanced around the room to see if he could figure out where he was but it was all new to him. The room had a strong type smell, maybe a clean alcoholic one or a similar aroma. He decided it could be a room in the doc's office. Finally, the doctor came with what Pedro wanted to hear.

"I believe that you are going to be fine. The wound looks good, and I see no complications. You are, however, going to have to take it very easy for a while."

"Where am I? In your office or where.?"

"In a small building behind my office. I keep as many as four patients at a time here. I would like to tell you something, may I?"

"Sure, doc, anything."

Doctor Clifton gave him a broad smile. "You did the city of Abilene a real service by putting that killer, Jenkins, away. I have sent quite a few of his victims to the undertaker. Thanks."

Without a smile, Pedro answered, "I never wanted to kill him or anybody else. Someone paid him to take me out, and now I have a goal, and you know what I mean."

"Your goal is obvious. To kill the bastard who hired him. Excuse me, Lucinda, for using such language."

"That's okay, Doctor Clifton, you called him by his proper name."

Even Pedro laughed with them, though it hurt some. Then he began to ask how long he had been there, and about his entire situation. The doctor told him how long, but explained to Pedro, that he could not tell him why, for when it happens, sometimes people never come out of it. Now he understood why they were so excited when he opened his eyes and spoke.

"Young man, relax now for a while, please. Lucinda and I will leave the room. You should not overdue yourself so soon, please."

With this, Pedro was left alone. He tried to sleep and finally dozed off for a short while.

Later, Drew Hampton entered the room. Lucinda had returned just before his arrival, and seeing her smiling face, he took a deep breath. "Hi boss, what's up?"

He looked at Pedro for a moment, then leaned over and kissed his forehead as tears came from his eyes. Pedro never knew a real father before, but now he felt that he had one. Hampton was so choked up that for a moment or so, he was speechless.

"Pedro, I am so glad. I did not see the doctor when I came in. What did he say?"

Lucinda, trying to keep Pedro from talking too much and getting too excited, spoke up, "He examined him, and is happy, so's we is too."

"I better write Jane and Agnes."

"Do they know about it?" quickly asked Pedro.

"No, but they should know. We have to leave out Baxter because they might try to kill him."

With fire in his eyes, Pedro came back with, "I agree, if he hurts either of them, I would want to kill him more than once. I want to kill him myself."

Hampton looked over at Lucinda. "I will write the letter, Pedro, and read it to you. The letter should be addressed to Agnes, for that way she could sort of pad Jane's feelings. We certainly do not want them to come here for fear of the trip through the Indian territory."

Pedro knew how lucky he was to have met Drew Hampton. "Great. Go ask the doctor how long I have to stay here."

Lucinda came with, "You knows the doc just said you have to stay put for a spell."

Hampton, without answering, got up and went to look for the doctor. Hampton was gone for a half hour. When he returned, it was with a smile.

"I am the boss, so now I pull my rank on you. If you heal without any problems, you can ride the stagecoach in about six weeks. Meanwhile, you can start getting up in about a week, providing of course that everything goes well. If Doctor Clifton needs the space, he will transfer you to a place that I have arranged for you. This will be no sooner than two weeks from now as he will want to see you every day until then. Lucinda will be with you, night and day, until we leave. I know what she needs for the café in Kansas City, and she will have it then. Right, young lady?"

"Right, sir, so Pedro, you are going to behave so's I won't have to tie you down." Hampton's deal with Lucinda made Pedro feel even warmer toward him.

Before leaving that evening for the hotel, Hampton looked with a smile at Pedro, and glancing over at Lucinda added, "Remember, she is a nurse, don't try to get well too soon."

All three laughed, then Lucinda chimed in, "I will knows when he's ready for the coach." This brought more laughter.

Leaving, Hampton checked with a man sitting inside where he could see the open area leading to Pedro's bed. He was one of two guards that worked twelve hours each, making sure that none of Jacoby Jenkin's friends came around. While he did not think so, he had been wrong about Tom Baxter, and he was afraid that two mistakes might be one too many.

In his hotel room, he wrote a long letter to Agnes Skaag, not mentioning Tom Baxter, blaming it on Pedro's protection of him. He also did not mention the fact that Pedro had been unconscious for six days. It was a letter that would not upset them to the point of wanting to come to Abilene. He wrote about his retirement party that would be in the Fort Worth area, and that he wanted her to be his escort. It would be held in December, so they had almost four months to get Pedro there in good shape.

Drew Hampton had already made up his mind, though he had never told Pedro. As soon as feasible, he would ask Agnes to marry him. Relaxing in bed that night, he thought about Pedro. That kid is something else, killing Jacoby Jenkins in only his second gunfight. Of course, he had been lucky, as it was really a tie, yet Jacoby was dead and Pedro was very much alive. He decided he was lucky he hired him, not knowing that he would learn to love him as a son.

CHAPTER 32

Two weeks later, a stagecoach was almost out of the Indian reservation area in Oklahoma. There were five passengers, all men, and the driver and guard. It was still September, but almost October, and the weather acted like it was July.

With a stream in sight, just off the supposedly road but in reality a trail in the prairie, the driver and guard strained their eyes hoping it looked deserted enough that they might stop a few moments.

As they cut off the small trail, one of the passengers could be heard, "What the hell are you fellows doing? Isn't this still Indian territory? I haven't seen the Red River yet."

The driver could tell without even looking who was doing the complaining. "Look, Mr. Baxter, we know what we're doing. Just relax, there are no Indians in this section." Tom

Baxter had been happy this entire trip but now he was very nervous, for as long as he knew Indians might be around, he would be afraid.

Everyone got out to stretch their legs and cool off their faces in the stream. The water looked clear and tasted delicious despite the fact it was on the warm side.

Baxter had been on edge for several days now and everyone on the coach disliked him. He knew it but it made no difference. This trip had been a great one. He had been able to purchase a beautiful piece of property near Rainy Roundup for a song and dance price. It had been bought from an elderly woman who took his word for its value. Besides that, it gave him a reason to be in the Kansas area. He knew about when Hampton would be in Abilene, and by personally hiring Jacoby Jenkins with no witnesses within hearing range, he was totally in the clear. That brash kid knew too much about him. With Skaag dead also, he was the only one left of the group who had raided into Mexico. The kid was the only one who knew anything about it. He did not have confirmation yet but was very confident that Jenkins would shoot that smart kid's ass off. A moment later, the sound of howling Indians terrorized his calm thoughts.

From a low spot not seen from the road, a group of Indians rode towards them with breathtaking speed. They had rifles and bows, and soon it was panic near the coach. The driver fell before he got to the coach as the guard shot one Indian off his pony with his pistol. Several of the other passengers quickly tried to surrender as soon as the guard got an arrow through his chest. Baxter tried to crawl off into the bushes, but an Indian had him by the seat of his pants. The Indian laughed as he spoke to the others. There was no pity, as two of the passengers, though unarmed, had been killed and several Indians had the other two backed against a couple of trees. One of the savages walked up to the two men held against the trees, and beat them with a tomahawk. As they fell, they were scalped.

Baxter was shaking like a leaf, but tried to bribe the one holding him. The Indian laughed again, but the one with the tomahawk walked over. There was no smile on his face.

"Spare my life, please, I will make you rich, please!"

The Indian spoke to him in English, "You are a yellow dog, a white scum, like all other whites. I am Screaming Eagle, mightiest of all Comanches, and I am giving my life to killing the white man. All will pay for killing my people. You are next!"

Baxter shuddered with fear as he looked at the fierce, stone faced man with huge shoulders and arms. His dark eyes penetrated and burned into the scared man's face. His skin felt like it was in flames.

"Those fellows, they were white sc…scum, You are right, great warrior. They needed killing. But I…I can be of great help to you and your people. I have big influence with white soldier chief. I will do great favor for you. Tell me what you want, I…can do it. You have my word."

Screaming Eagle smiled, and it appeared Baxter had made a point that interested him. Before he could say anymore, the evil Indian spoke, "So you are big among the whites. Well, well, I will show them what is done to big white men like you."

Then he spoke to the others in Comanche, "Take him to ant hill where we hide. Wait for me."

Baxter was dragged away, while the others finished with the dead ones. They searched them, took what they wanted, scalped the others, untied the horses and chased them away. Then together they pushed over the heavy coach, laughing as if it was all in fun. Bringing the wounded Indian with them, they brought all their horses over to where Baxter was now tied down with his arms and legs spread wide apart. Screaming Eagle told the others that this one was "his."

As Baxter started to beg again, he slapped his mouth shut. "Do not speak, big white scum, you need wind to cry, yellow belly."

With his knife, Screaming Eagle roughly cut the clothing from his body, drawing blood in several places.

Baxter screamed and begged, "You make big mistake. I can help you."

The Indian looked at Baxter with disgust. "I might be

doing something for the whites. You are big disgrace to any color of man, even for whites." Then he began to make fun of Baxter.

In Comanche, he told his men, "Can you see woman wanting him to crawl on her?" This was followed by several moments of loud laughter. Then the mood changed.

With Baxter pleading and crying, Screaming Eagle scalped a small piece of Baxter's head. As ants were beginning to crawl on him, the Indian spoke to the crying man, "I wanted you to live so I can show you what the whites did to my son."

Then he reached down and castrated him. "Until you are found, I do not want you to be hungry," as he stuffed the testicles into Baxter's mouth. Then with a fierce howl, he took his tomahawk and completely mutilated the body of Tom Baxter. Screaming Eagle's own warriors looked at each other as he beat on Baxter with the tomahawk until he was completely exhausted.

Four days later, an army patrol from Fort Sill found the bodies of the seven men. Three days after that, an article appeared in papers around the reservation, telling of the killings and a list of the dead was included. It did not go into detail of the condition of the dead when found. Ironically, on the same page was a small write-up telling of the death of the famous gunman, Jacoby Jenkins. It only listed his killer as being unknown.

Another week later, news of the slaughter was published in an Abilene paper. Lucinda bought a paper, not realizing what the article would mean to Pedro. She returned to their upstairs room above a dress shop, a room picked out by Hampton. It was an out of the way shop, actually in a section of small houses of low income workers.

The only thing Pedro did not like about it was the fact that he could not leave to practice his accuracy. Hampton had laid the law down to him, and when his boss spoke, he listened. He did practice on his fast draw. When Lucinda came in, she put the paper on the bed and it just lay there.

Pedro had gained some weight as Lucinda's cooking agreed with him. He could understand how she would be successful in a café. She served him lunch, and at his insistence that they only eat one full meal a day, it was a light one.

After lunch, they were expecting the doctor. "I never knew that Hampton could be so strict. I can't go practice with my shooting, I can't go to the doctor, I will be glad when this waiting period is over."

Lucinda smiled at him. "You are on edge, young man. I think the doctor will release you today, then maybe the wheel will let up on you."

"I hope so. I wonder if he is afraid that I might slip away to go after Baxter?"

"Oh, he knows you would not go and leave him. Besides that, you fellows leave town in a week."

"You gonna miss me, or is it necessary to ask that?"

Lucinda got up and sat on the bed, picking up the paper. "You have been so well behaved, especially at night, I figured you would not miss me."

Pedro turned a deep pink as she giggled. "You have been wonderful to me. Certainly, I will miss you. I know what my boss does is for the best. I think I will keep you both."

All of a sudden, she howled, "PEDRO, oh Pedro, wait till you read this!"

Quickly he took the paper, with her holding on and pointing to a name toward the bottom of the article. "The Indians killed the bastard," she sang out with rhythm.

Pedro made no comment as he read the entire article, stopping to look again at Baxter's name. "I guess God has his ways of working. He was the only one I have ever wanted to kill. I hated Toro, but I did not really want to kill him."

Reading the article again, he responded with, "I wonder if it was the Comanches? Man oh man, wait till Hampton sees this."

Lucinda interrupted him. "You are a talking machine now. Oh, I hear someone on the steps. It must be the doctor."

CHAPTER 33

Several hours after the doctor left, Drew Hampton came in with one hand full of mail. He had been away for four days and the mail accumulated in his hotel box. "How's my boy?"

"First he was restless, then after the news we read in the paper, he has never stopped talking." She handed him the paper, pointing to the article.

He took it but only glanced at it. "I know all about it. More than is in that article."

Pedro leaned forward with new interest. "Tell me."

Handing Pedro three letters from Jane, one each from Curly Duncan and Leigh Saunders, he began, "All were scalped and killed, but they went to more trouble for Baxter." Then he told them of the position that they had left him in, and what was done to him.

"What do you make of it, Mr. Hampton?"

"There is no way to know what really made them do that to him. Maybe he did something to agitate them. Hell, Pedro, you lived with those Comanches for a long time, what do you think?"

"So they were Comanches. Well, they hate a man who claims to be important. They would rather find out for themselves."

Hampton thought a moment. "Are you saying that maybe Baxter promised big things if they did not kill him?"

"Yes, it's possible. Then again it is hard to figure the Comanche's way of thinking. Many hate the white man and are fierce fighters, so that he may not have had a chance to say anything. They just did it to show superiority, to show how much they really hate the white man. Say, come to think of it, I know a warrior who could pull something like that." Hampton and Lucinda looked at him with puzzled expressions.

"Fawn's husband, Screaming Eagle. There is no Comanche who hates the white man more than he does. He has promised his Great Spirit to kill many white men. Fawn just told me that at the reservation. She said he has a group of bad warriors, and they just go out looking for white men."

Hampton looked at Pedro rather sadly. "You didn't tell me for you did not want me to know how fierce and bad they can be, right?"

"Yes, I did not want to hurt the Comanche image, It's bad enough. I'm sorry, boss." Then Pedro opened his letters from Jane. Hampton had two letters himself, both from Agnes Skaag. It was quiet as Pedro and his boss read their letters. Lucinda started on supper, and since it was going to be gumbo, she knew Hampton would eat with them.

"Jane is all excited about your retirement party, and ahem, about seeing me. She has been catching a lot of fish at my old camp. Agnes has been going with her, and is also fishing."

With a big grin, Hampton answered, "She told me all about that. She also told me that she is willing to be my escort, ahem, at the retirement party."

Pedro looked at him with a surprised expression. "You old

rascal! Is there a chance you might be my daddy in-law?"

Unable to stop grinning, Hampton mumbled, "A damn good chance, I hope. Pedro, please do not say anything to either one yet."

Pedro got up and bowed, in jest. "Yes sir, future papa-in-law. I will abide by the rules."

The letter from Curly Duncan was a happy one. It told of his upcoming marriage to Julie McKeever. I sure hope he is not disappointed, thought Pedro, remembering her statement to him that she would always be available to him whether she was married or not. Once he married Jane, no one could have him, and certainly not one of his friend's wives. His worry was that she would make herself available to someone besides Curly, and his friend deserved better. Maybe it was something she had said on the spur of the moment, and did not really mean it. He sure hoped so.

The fact that he had another letter from Leigh was a surprise. In her last letter, she had told of returning home safely and had wished him well. Opening the letter, he was pleased from the beginning. She had met a nice looking banker, young and wealthy, and guess what? He loved to ride horses. Her family had met him, and they were extremely pleased. She did not believe it was because he was wealthy, for they had realized their pushing efforts had got her into the first failure. Of course, she wrote, the fact that he is wealthy did not hurt their feelings. At the end of the letter, she told him she would not write again. Then an ending note added,

I can guarantee he is not like Stephen. Having a hard time holding him off until we can get married. Hope he takes after a fellow I know by the name of Pedro—and be damn sure you destroy this letter.

With love, Leigh.

Pedro laughed and tore up the letter.

Lucinda grunted, "Next time don't tear it into such small pieces."

Hampton laughed and exclaimed, "That was the one from Leigh. It probably burned his fingers. And believe me, Lucinda,

I'm not kidding." They both had a laugh as Pedro grinned a little as he turned a rosy pink.

Changing the subject, Pedro asked, "When do we leave, boss man?"

"A week today. Because of Indian trouble, we will miss some areas. We have to go back through some of the same places as before. The retirement party is December 15th but we should be there far ahead of time. Jane will be sweet sixteen then so get ready for the noose soon after that."

Pedro had a smile, and a sincere look at the same time. "I am just as ready as she is to tie the knot."

"With all this commotion going on, I forgot to ask. Did the doctor release you today or was it yesterday?"

"Today. He says I am good as new. So can I get out a while tomorrow?"

Hampton studied the kid. "I don't want to punish you, Pedro, but let's don't take any chances."

Pedro smiled at him. "I know you mean well. I will do as you say."

"Thanks."

Later on, they all had their fill of Lucinda's gumbo. Hampton suggested she name the café after that dish. Afterward, he went back to the hotel, and soon after that, Pedro was in his bed for the night. Lucinda came out of the other room, and Pedro happened to glance over at her. Every night she had slept with clothes on, but tonight she was naked. He wondered if she was coming over or waiting for him. Neither made a move so the night passed by. The following morning, nothing was mentioned so things were normal. While eating breakfast, Lucinda told him that the town had dried up. All the cowhands had left, and even the women who hustled them were also gone.

Pedro teased her, "Well, you still have dear old Pedro."

She gave him a look that he would hate to have to describe. "Sleeping in the same house with you is like being in bed with a female virgin. Nothing happens."

Pedro smiled as she began moving the dishes off the table. He got up and dried the dishes as she washed them.

"Ex-lover boy, don't do anything to strain yourself." He continued to grin, but never made any attempt to answer her. It was very obvious she was irritated with him for failing to take advantage of the situation last night. He really liked her and she was cuter than hell when upset. She really did not know how to get mean, especially if she liked someone, and he knew she had some feelings for him.

"I could feel the same way, you know. My bed was only across the room from yours." She gave him a look of sarcasm.

"I was naked, you had on clothes. It meant I was ready for you. If you can not walk across the room, then you don't want me enough. I sure as hell can do without you." Then she slammed the door leading outside, and locked him in as she left.

"Wow, I thought we were kidding. She sure wasn't," Pedro said as he talked aloud to himself.

Several hours later, she returned as Pedro was playing cards at the table. "Would you like a sandwich, or if not, I have a small amount of gumbo left. Which would you prefer?"

"Gumbo, baby doll, and I still have kind feelings for you even if you hate me."

She looked at him without a smile. "Kind feelings is a good word for how you feel about me. That's not what I needed last night."

After this, she did not speak to him as he tried several times to make conversation.

Later that afternoon, Drew Hampton came in and broke the silence. "Another letter from Jane. I got shut out today." He could sense something was wrong between them, but did not ask any questions about it.

Pedro read the letter from Jane, and revealed more than usual. "Now that they have sold the café, Agnes and Jane are really enjoying life. Jane was tickled to tell me that her mother had won the "champion fisherman of all Mexico" title from her by a score of four to three. She said it was in the paper that Tom Baxter was missing. The stagecoach he was riding had not arrived at its destination point."

"Well, they know he is dead by now. Probably won't ever

know the total story unless we tell them later."

Again Lucinda out did herself in preparing the supper. She had fried some fish, southern style, with lots of batter and seasoning, vegetables, and some of the best southern cornbread ever. Neither knew who ate the most, both of them pecked her on the cheek as they left the table. After Hampton left, they were on speaking terms again but when she came to her bed, she wore her night clothes.

Pedro had a tough time going to sleep that night. Now that Baxter was dead, there was probably none of the five killers alive. He felt in his heart it was George Skaag, but he would never ask Jane or her mother. Maybe someday they would volunteer that they were suspicious, but they had just about already done that on the Sunday that he killed Luke and the Sheriff killed Gabby. He wanted to put his gun away. It was a weapon to get revenge, and to make some money. The revenge was certainly obtained, and the money, while not ever enough, was much more than he ever had. The worry was if he would be left alone. Killing Jacoby Jenkins had probably made a name for him, and he felt that someone or more than one would come looking for him. He wasn't afraid, it was just a case of not wanting to kill just to prove he was better. He would pray to be able to marry Jane and have little Janes and little Pedros. Lucinda and Pedro remained good friends, and talked and laughed daily for the rest of the week. Both slept in their own beds with clothes on.

Their last night there together, Lucinda came to her bed without clothes. Pedro took one look, got up, and went over to her. Looking at her nude for a moment, he leaned over and picked her up, carrying her to his bed.

"You were in the wrong bed, doll." Then he undressed as she lay and watched him.

She giggled as she said, "Look how many nights we wasted because I was in the wrong bed."

CHAPTER 34

A month later in a small town in Arkansas, Drew Hampton got into a poker game held in the town's only hotel lobby. A semi saloon with drinks furnished to the poker game and several other tables, it was actually against what Hampton had talked about in regards to trouble. However, he was bored, and with no one around who looked troublesome, he decided to get into the game.

Pedro sat in a large chair that was well located so he could watch at a distance. The game went along smoothly until the only cowboy in the game starting drinking too heavily. He was called Red by the others in the game. Fairly young but very tall and heavy, the red headed cowboy used terrible language as he continued to lose.

Finally, he came up with a good poker hand, and bet

everything he had. Hampton was the only one who stayed with him, and they continued to raise each other. Finally, Red turned over his hand, a full house. Hampton smiled and uncovered four deuces. As he pulled in the chips, the cowboy reached across the table and slapped him across the face.

"That's for the smart ass smile. Here is another one just because I don't like you."

As he landed the second blow, Pedro jerked him from behind. Then he hit the big cowboy with a left, and as the man started his own left, Pedro hit him with an open handed chop on his right shoulder. As Red's arm dropped from numbness, Pedro grabbed it and slung the big fellow across the poker table, with chips, ash trays, and glasses flying everywhere. By the time he hit the floor, Pedro picked him up, walked over to the double swinging doors, and pitched him outside on the boardwalk.

"If you come back in, be damn sure you behave." This brought a lot of laughter, especially from the bouncer, who did not get a chance to get into the action.

It took a while to straighten up the playing area and when things were ready again, Hampton did not want to play but everyone else had been so nice, he stayed in the game.

About fifteen minutes later, the big cowboy came back in with a pistol stuck in his belt. Pedro was standing near the table.

As he approached them, two other cowboys, who had been eating nearby, cut him off. "Red, you are no gun fighter, and we saw that young man practicing outside behind the hotel today. You don't have a chance in hell, even if you were sober."

"You know I am good with a gun."

"Red, you are good for an amateur. He is a pro. Let's go down the street and have a drink at Harry's."

"Yeah," chimed in the other cowboy. "They have a coupla new girls working there now." Red gave them no further argument, and the three turned and walked out.

As they approached their doors in the hotel later that night,

Hampton stopped his friend and bodyguard. "I am sorry I broke our rules tonight. It will not happen again."

"Don't let it bother you. I am just glad those fellows stopped him. I really do not want to kill again unless it is necessary to our safety." "Say, who taught you those moves? You surprised even me."

"Brown Bear and a great young warrior, Blue Tomahawk."

Hampton flashed his friendly smile. "That figures. Everyone was so surprised they stood with their mouths open. Good night, son."

"Good night, sir."

One month later, in Sherman, Texas, Pedro and Hampton stepped off the stage and walked toward their hotel. Pedro carried their two large suitcases and Hampton had the other one. As they neared the door, a young cowboy, looking all the part of being a gunslinger, stepped in front of Pedro.

"Before you go in, if you are known as Pedro the Kid, I believe we have a little business to settle." Pedro set the two suitcases down, and when Hampton tried to step in, told him that he would handle the situation. "My name is Pedro. Don't believe I know you."

The young man smiled, and replied, "You are right, we have never met. However, I believe you killed my buddy, Jacoby Jenkins. Right?"

Now Pedro knew what was coming. "Yes, because he insisted on calling me out. A no good bastard paid him to kill me. Seems he thought I knew too much about his past."

"Well, I feel obligated to even the score for my old buddy. The only way you could have beat him was to draw well before him."

Pedro gave him an icy stare. "Anyone who saw it would tell you we drew together. Really, it was a tie. He just shot a little high." Then he pulled his shirt back to show him the scar.

"Well, in case of ties, we always play them over. I will take his place this time."

"I did not know Jacoby had any friends."

The smile left the man's face. "Stop stalling and let's get this over with." Then Pedro asked, "Mind telling me who you are?"

The smile returned to the man's face. "Danny Dakota, ever hear of me?"

"Truthfully no, but I don't follow gunfighter's names."

"What would you call yourself?"

"A bodyguard. I have called only one man out and had a valid reason. He had raped and killed my mother."

"Are you just plain yellow or what? I called you out five minutes ago."

"Okay, let's do it. At least, you will never be sorry."

Dakota looked at him with a puzzled look and Pedro continued, "You won't have time." No one knew it but that remark shook Danny Dakota. Everything he knew about a gun, Jenkins had taught him, but although he really wanted to try his teacher, he never had the nerve. Now he was about to face the man who had killed his teacher. He had heard that they drew together, but never really had believed it. Now he wondered, as they faced off just twenty feet apart.

Pedro needled him as he had done with Jenkins. "Get with it when you feel lucky." Pedro had always watched the finger of the gunman's hand. There was always a little movement of the trigger finger just a split second before he drew. He had seen it in all the gun fights he had watched, beside the two that he had been in.

After a few more seconds, Danny Dakota drew for the last time. Pedro's lightning fast bullet hit him as he squeezed the trigger, and his bullet was not close to Pedro.

Pedro was not proud of what he had just accomplished. In his heart, it hurt for he had just taken the life of a nice looking young man, probably his age. His prayers would never clear him of the men he had killed. Once he married, he would never wear a pistol again, even if he was called yellow as just now. To people who watched, he was a hero, a "fast gun," but he felt like anything but that. Youngsters gathered around him, and he knew that this alone was bad. A terrible influence on them.

He made his way to his hotel, and never came down to supper.

Later, Hampton brought him a beef sandwich to his room. On December 1, they were only thirty miles from Fort Worth. Pedro sat in the enclosed coffee and lunchroom in the back of the bank as Hampton conducted his business.

There was a cute kid about ten, who asked Pedro all about his gun. He tried to play it down but could not stop the boy from asking questions. The youth had stepped out into the bank to ask his father, who owned the bank, a question.

Suddenly, he came running back in, pointing, "Bank robbers, do something!" Pedro quickly slipped out the back door, opened for air, and motioned for the boy to follow.

They ran around to the side of the building, down the side almost to the front. Pedro stopped and whispered, "You must stay here."

The boy nodded in agreement. The three men were backing out of the door. "Drop your guns," Pedro called out but they did not.

A bullet just shy of his head went by, and then he dropped the close man, and as another turned to shoot at him, Pedro missed in trying not to kill him. This man's bullet burned his side and Pedro fired again. The second man was down as the third tried to mount up, but the shooting had spooked the horses and he fell as the horse ran off. Not as brave as the other two, he came off the ground with his hands up.

The Sheriff and the town Doctor were there in a matter of minutes. Pedro had taken the men's guns, and gave them to the sheriff. The first man shot had only a shoulder wound, but the second man was shot in the stomach. Trying to only wound them did not work too well, Pedro realized.

"How bad are you hit" asked Hampton, as he came running out.

"Not bad, really."

Then the doctor checked him. "Lucky you. The bullet just barely entered and came out on your side. It looks bloody, so we need to clean it up, and bandage it, but you are okay."

"How about that one?" asked Pedro, pointing at the man shot in the stomach.

"It depends on what happened inside. Could be he might not make it, but he probably will be okay."

The banker's son bragged to all his friends that Pedro was his buddy. Again he was a hero for shooting somebody, this time two of them.

Two days later, before leaving town, the banker called in Pedro. He handed him a large amount of cash, "Count it."

Pedro was startled as he finished. "Five hundred dollars! Gee, I can't believe it."

Hampton and the banker laughed. "The sheriff will give me back three hundred of that. It only cost the bank the rest. We saved several thousand."

The bank was happy, Hampton was happy, the sheriff was happy, and Pedro felt that he was the happiest of all. Along with the other two hundred they gave him for capturing the stagecoach robbers, Pedro now had seven hundred dollars in excess of the money he had made working for Hampton. The next stop was Fort Worth and the retirement party. They would be there about ten days early, with Hampton using that time to write to all his customers of his retirement. He had already sent out thirty invitations to his top customers and their wives, all in the immediate area. He did not think it practical to invite customers who lived too far. As for Pedro, it was going to be a time of relaxation, although he had promised to help Hampton write out envelopes and apply stamps.

The closer the time got, the more excited he was about seeing his love, Jane. She was sixteen, and he soon would be twenty. He had met her three years before, and she was nude the first time he laid eyes on her. In the following two years, she had grown into a beauty. Now, it had been a year since he had seen her. He wondered how much she had matured, and if she was still a tomboy. He knew she was beautiful. The day of the wedding, he would wear no gun, then or at no time ever again. Killing his fellow man was a thing of the past for him.

There would no longer be a Pedro the Kid. His revenge had been complete, now he hoped that some way he could say enough prayers and be a good enough person to please God for the rest of his life. Maybe, just maybe, God would someday forgive him.

CHAPTER 35

Pedro and Hampton sat out in front of the hotel, hoping any minute to see the stagecoach pull into town. Both knew it was early but neither wanted that coach to arrive without seeing it.

Last night, Hampton had pulled out his books, and showed Pedro how much money he had accumulated. The youth had never asked, and when told the figure, was happy to the point of being speechless. Hampton also confided in Pedro that he was going to ask Agnes to marry him if she showed the feelings that flowed through her letters. He then asked Pedro an important question. If they did marry, would the young newlyweds be agreeable to go into the horse business with them? Before the Kid could answer, he added that money would never be a problem. Pedro would have preferred to have answered a definite yes before he brought up the part about the money.

Before the night was over, Pedro had broken down and cried for he was overcome with the love and emotion that his wonderful boss had professed. He felt he had come a long way since he was homeless on the night of his mother's death. He had only one regret, feeling the gun was largely responsible for it all. He would have preferred it to be for another reason.

"A buck I spot the coach before you do," jibed Hampton, seeing that Pedro was in a serious deep mood. This usually happened after he was forced to use his very capable gun.

"Bet," smiled Pedro as he came out of the darkness of the moment. With the bet on, both men laughed and teased each other as every wagon that turned toward their hotel was singled out by one or the other. When it did come, an hour or more late, it was Drew Hampton pointing just a split second ahead of the kid. "I thought you were fast," teased Hampton.

"Me too, but you're the best."

When the coach stopped, the two men were standing side by side with a grin that could be seen for a long distance. As the door to the coach opened, it would have been easy to guess who would be the first one out.

A beautiful doll by the name of Jane, who once had tagged herself as "Plain Jane," stepped out of the coach and every man within sight stopped to look. Her very long light brown hair flowed over her shoulders, sparkling blue eyes, the cutest little nose and a figure that would bring envy to most women. She appeared very refined as she approached Pedro. That is until she got about six feet from him. Then she threw her arms straight up into the air, and practically jumped the rest of the way into his waiting arms. For just a moment, he had been afraid that maybe she had become too refined, but thank goodness, she was the same as always—a genuine tomboy. The kiss that followed kept Pedro from even seeing his future mother-in-law get off the coach.

She went straight up to Hampton, first they shook hands and suddenly he was kissing her. Both of them were finely dressed, with Jane's beautiful beige dress a standout while Agnes had a blue pleated skirt topped with a fancy white ruffled blouse that added to her slender, attractive figure. Hampton had arranged for a large room with two beds for the welcomed ladies.

That evening, before going down to dinner, the four of them talked in the room. "How does it feel to be a lady of leisure after all the hard work in your lifetime?" Pedro asked Agnes.

"I'm afraid it is just a little too quiet at times. Jane has taught me to fish, but that has been it."

Jane grinned at her. "Yeah, she grabbed my championship away from me."

After a few laughs, Jane cornered Pedro by the window, as Hampton and Agnes talked on the other side of the room. "Okay, love, tell me about your experiences. You know, the stuff you have been avoiding in your letters."

Pedro turned a little pink and gave her a grin. She looked at him without a grin. "You are still stalling. I gave you permission, that is, unless you overdid it. How many times and what did they look like?"

Pedro hesitated, then, "Sometimes things just happen." Then he hesitated again.

"So she wasn't fat and unattractive. That I can tell by your expressions. Okay, so how many and did you have a good teacher? Something tells me I made a mistake in giving you the idea or the permission."

"No, you were not wrong in giving me the permission. I might have held it from you."

"Love, you are not exactly talking up a storm."

With fear in his eyes, Pedro began, "For better or worse, here goes. Two women. One was a woman of the night. The other was not."

Jane looked at him as sternly as she could, for in reality, she was about to burst out laughing. She did not know anyone could get Pedro this scared. He is absolutely frightened, she thought.

"I want to hear about the one who was not." She had

decided to push this to the limit. Pedro's conscience was killing him for he had to leave Julie McKeever out. They were supposed to attend the wedding in two weeks. Pedro stuttered as he started. "Sh…she was a passenger on the coach with us. That weekend she came to my room with the excuse of having to talk to me. Her husband was only interested in other men, so she was divorcing him. She wanted Hampton to arrange her route back east. While she was in my room, it happened." He could no longer look her in the eyes.

Jane was ready to let up but another question came out. "Was she pretty?"

Pedro just looked at her. "Don't answer that with words. Your face already provided the answer. How about the lady of the night, I'll bet she didn't exactly look like the family dog, right?"

Pedro looked at her, his face so pink it was almost red.

"Right," Jane figured she had put him through enough. After all, she did put the notion in his head. "I will never mention it again, I promise you, Pedro," then with that cute grin added, "as long as you prove you learned something." He smiled as he took her in his arms, and a long kiss followed with Pedro darting his tongue inside her mouth.

"I just got the feeling you learned a lot." Then they both broke into a laugh. Hampton had arranged for a lovely dinner featuring roast wild duck cooked with fresh oranges and brandy.

Before the evening was over, both Jane and Pedro were making eyes at each other as they watched the brewing romance of Hampton and Agnes.

Three nights later, the elaborate retirement party took place. It was a banquet type dinner with beef, venison, geese, chicken and fish all served in three separate main courses with fresh vegetables. Pea soup was first, followed by a delicious salad, and after the main courses came the outstanding strawberry pie and coffee. Jane was amazed at the knowledge Pedro had of the different foods served, and how they were prepared. She later told her mother that she surprisingly was marrying a chef, and maybe they should have kept the café.

The highlight of the night, at the end of his speech to his clientele, Hampton asked Agnes Skaag to rise. When she did, he then announced, "May I very proudly introduce my future wife, the beautiful Agnes Skaag."

After a standing ovation, Hampton added, "Now may I present my future very beautiful daughter, Jane, and her husband-to-be, Pedro Zamora, whom many of you have met since he became my bodyguard. He is without question the finest young man I have ever met and it is with pride that he will soon be my son."

Pedro felt the trickle of a tear roll down his cheek as they stood and were applauded.

CHAPTER 36

At the wedding of Curly Duncan and Julie McKeever, Jane and Pedro danced for the first time. As they struggled through a waltz, Jane thought to herself that while Pedro may have learned about being with women, he certainly had not experienced any dancing. The wedding was held outside of the ranch house at Curly's place, and the turnout was outstanding. Most of Rainy Roundup's population had been invited, and doubtless, almost to the one they had accepted. Pedro was pleased to learn that Jack Harlow had bought the Town Saloon from Baxter's only living relative, an aging aunt. His very capable deputy had taken over as sheriff. Jane had insisted that Pedro dance with the bride, so he reluctantly abided by her desire. As they moved along on the floor, Julie whispered, "I am really in love for the very first time."

"I could not be happier for you."

Then moving in a little closer, she came back with, "I want to clear up a little matter with you. The offer I made to you no longer exists. We were great together but now I am in love. I believe you know what I mean."

"I am thrilled for you, after the hard times you went through. Curly is a great guy and one of my best friends. He had it bad for you."

"You love that little doll so much, you never would have even tried anything, but I wanted you to know how I feel."

Just then Jack Harlow cut in, and Pedro, never feeling better, went back to his love. As they started dancing again, "Now I know, it was the dancing you should have practiced on instead of the other."

Hampton, standing with Agnes, whispered to her, "Have you ever seen anyone as happy as our kids?" as Pedro and Jane laughed over her last remark.

The big day for Jane and Pedro finally arrived. Pedro had gone over to a larger town and arranged for a Catholic priest to come to Rainy Roundup to marry them. It took Drew Hampton, Curly Duncan, Pedro, and ten hired young men several days to fix their wedding location so it could be an acceptable one. Of course, it was the old fishing hole where they had met and fell in love. Once Jane had thought of it, nothing or nobody could have changed her mind, and to make it complete, her "love" felt the very same way.

Jane's mother had ordered her a beautiful white wedding gown, and it arrived just six days before the big day, so that both Jane and Agnes almost had hysterics when it finally came.

Hampton had a piano delivered to the wedding location, so when everything finally fit together, it was more than just a wedding at a fishing hole, but a beautiful affair with the two happiest young people in Rainy Roundup ready for a day that both had looked forward to for so long.

Secretly, Agnes Skaag was relieved that Kelly had not showed up. She had not told him of the wedding, and probably he did not know. Once Kelly realized that his mother would not write again, he had also quit the occasional note that was always little more than a threat. His last letter had been the one threatening Pedro. Thank God that Hampton had convinced him to wear his gun until they had moved to their secret ranch location, which was not decided as of yet. Pedro and Jane would spend time in Mexico, visiting with Pedro's orphanage friends and Sister Theresa. While honeymooning there, Pedro would look for a possible ranch site, while Hampton would use all his influence in learning of a place far northwest of Rainy Roundup. Both Hampton and Pedro preferred Mexico as their first choice.

There are many young women who make beautiful brides, but the beauty of Jane Skaag had become unbelievable. In the very fashionable white dress with the gorgeous veil, Jane was fantastic, and no one appreciated her beauty more than the former orphan, former Comanche captive, former bodyguard now known as Pedro the Kid.

For a young man, Pedro's tenderness toward people he loved made him an easy target for tears to just roll from his eyes. He was determined not to let this happen on this, the happiest day of his life.

When the priest pronounced them man and wife, then added, "Pedro, you may kiss the bride," most people looked with amazement as the kiss almost seemed to last forever.

The wedding was followed by an elegant dinner, but there was no dance. Jane insisted it was not because her love was a poor dancer, but that she wanted everyone to mingle more, adding to the friendship of everyone in Rainy Roundup. When the evening was over, it had been a gala wedding and everyone was happy for the couple.

Hampton had booked passage for them on the stagecoach to Brownsville. From there, at Pedro's request, they would have a nice buggy to be drawn by two horses to go through Matamoros, where the old orphanage and Pedro's original home had been. Then on to Monterey, where Ricardo lived with his wife, and Sister Theresa and some of his young friends still lived at the orphanage there. Part of the trip could have been made by rail, but Jane wanted to experience the stagecoach as her love had for so long. She would never be afraid as long as he was with her.

They would spend the night in the hotel in Rainy Roundup, and the following morning would board the stagecoach. When they closed the door of their room that night, Jane and Pedro were both speechless. They just stood and looked at each other. Having looked forward to their wedding day and night for so long, it was very hard to believe it was really happening. Finally, Pedro broke the ice, "Don't you want me to show you what I learned?"

Trying her best to give him a stern look, she answered, "I agreed not to talk about that. It was a mistake you will probably never let me live down."

Without answering, Pedro took his love into his arms, kissing her until his lips burned. As he held her, she looked into his dark eyes and was swallowed up by them. "I promise never to talk about it."

She giggled, never meaning the attempted stern look in the first place. "You better be good, love, since I agreed to let you. It was a sacrifice on my part. I'm sure you were not bored." Since she followed it with another big grin, he realized she had been teasing him all along.

"I hope you will not be disappointed."

"Well, Mom says it will hurt just at the very beginning. I'm not afraid, old partner." With this she began to open up her suitcase that contained her wedding night gown.

As she took it out, Pedro commented, "What are you going to do with that?"

Jane only giggled again as she headed for the private bathroom they were privileged to have. When she finally came out, the doll was well covered. The gown had a dainty laced collar around the neck, and the next skin below the neck that Pedro could see were her pretty little toes sticking out of the fancy houseshoes.

As she smiled and approached the bed, Pedro was so proud

and happy that he felt his heart would burst with joy and happiness.

As for the groom, he was sitting on the bed with only the bottom of his long underwear on. His muscular arms and burly chest that had very little hair were impressive to her as she stared at him. His curly black hair was slightly mussed making him all the more handsome in her eyes. It was the grin that got to her.

"Are you laughing at my wedding nightgown?" she asked without a smile.

His smile was enhanced. "It is a smile of pride. The day we met was the greatest day of my life."

With a very unlady like jump, she landed beside him in the bed, wrestling him down to plant a lasting kiss on his lips as he offered no resistance.

Following this, she came up with another unlady like move, as she tugged his underwear down his body. Again she had her way, as he offered no resistance in any way. Now, he was totally nude, and she backed out onto the bed, "Goodness gracious!"

Pedro was aroused, and it was a shock to her as she apparently did not expect it. "I don't understand. You said you watched me dress on three different occasions."

Now the tease was going the other way. "Yeah, but it looked different."

As she stood there, Pedro came with, "Well, now that you have put me on exhibition, do you know what the word 'pronto' means?"

She grinned and slowly began to unbutton the top of her nightgown.

Then Pedro continued, "I have not seen you since you were thirteen. Something tells me you will also look different."

"I sure hope so," she added with a bigger grin.

"Pronto, pronto," egged on Pedro, but she still took her time with the buttons. All of a sudden as she reached the bottom button in the middle of her chest, she suddenly jerked the gown over her head, and she was nude.

This time she did not jump toward him, instead she just stood there with that cute grin, letting him fill his eyes with her. Jane had an unbelievable figure, and she knew it. Her mother, the only one to ever see her nude except for the accident when Pedro saw her at thirteen, had raved for a year that she was simply gorgeous.

Although he did not realize it, Pedro's mouth had dropped open, and his expression was one of a person in a daze. The young man had felt that he had seen the utmost in a woman when he had seen Running Fox and her double, Leigh Saunders. Now he realized that while they may have been beautiful, this love of his was something he did not believe possible.

Her perfect breasts, along with that small waist, hips that flowed from the waist and into those curvy gorgeous legs, it all added up to a beauty that took Pedro by surprise. He expected her to be pretty but he wasn't looking for what he had and she was all his. His love for her was so strong that this was just a bonus. She did not have to be this beautiful to hold his love. It had begun as a friendship of a girl and a boy. Her tomboy tactics, the fishing ability, the whistling of beautiful songs, the fact that she could outrun him, that little nose that when she grinned make his heart beat faster, the sparkling personality, the teasing, all added up to true love. He had one regret: those times with Julie, Leigh, and Lucinda. She had suggested it but he enjoyed it more than he really wanted to. He would make it up to her by being the most attentive, loving, faithful husband who ever lived.

When he finally passed the dazed stage, Pedro held up one finger and motioned for her to come to bed. Her grin increased as she slowly slid into the bed. A second later, they were locked in an embrace as their hungry lips tried to eat each other up. His darting tongue was joined by hers, and soon she had crawled on him while never letting up on their kiss. As she kissed his eyes, nose, cheeks, lips, ears, and entire neck, Pedro started to laugh.

She moved back away from him. "Am I doing it all wrong?"

"You may not believe it, but I am laughing at myself. You know, the man of the world. Jane, you know more about loving from just being yourself than I could have ever learned from anyone else."

She grinned and moved close again, rubbing her nose against his. "Honey, what you had with those women was just physical loving. Ours is totally different. Our love is real, it's genuine, it's the way the Good Lord wanted it to be between a husband and wife. Oh, I am sure you will be able to show me some things about how to do it, but the love we have for each other will multiply our feelings."

Again Pedro was partially in a dazed state. This barely sixteen-year-old had just informed him what he had not even thought about. How come she was so much smarter than he was? This time a solid sexy kiss brought him out of his stupor. Pedro decided it was time he become more aggressive, and he forced the kiss as his hands moved over her body. Her breasts were so perfect and firm, and as he fondled them, he could feel her quiver. Then he moved his hands over her entire body and gradually down to her pubic hair and moist places.

She trembled as she whispered, "Oh Pedro, what a wonderful feeling." She did not remain in a relaxed position long as she moved her hands over his body, finding his arousal. Grabbing it at first, she relaxed her hand, and gently fondled it, being surprised at the warmth it generated. Then she moaned "Hmmmmm" as his fingers tenderly penetrated into her private moist places.

Then as he began to suckle her lovely mounds of flesh, his darting tongue circling her rosy red circles around her aroused nipples, she released him, struggling to retain her composure. The pleasure was unbelievable.

Gently, he moved on top of her, whispering, "Honey, let's do it."

Barely able to utter a sound, she was silent for a few moments, then with a small grin, she whispered back, "Give it to me, big boy, but pleeease take it easy at first."

Making love to Jane was a dream come true, and being the

love of his life, Pedro felt he was the luckiest person in the world to have her as his wonderful wife.

A few moments after Jane had absorbed the initial stab of pain, things began to heat up. Pedro started slowly, and soon she responded just as he wanted her to. The loving session was very short as they soon finished together as both felt they had entered the halls of heaven, as nothing in this world could ever equal the true love that had molded them into one.

CHAPTER 37

With Pedro watching like an eagle, the entire trip to Brownsville was uneventful as far as danger was concerned. He had decided when he boarded that first stage in Rainy Roundup the morning after the wedding, if they had trouble, he would not shoot to just wound anybody. Jane, his very precious one, was with him and her life was more important than his.

Going through Matamoros, and the extra five miles to the old church and orphanage did not take long. Pedro was pleased to see the church was open. As they entered it to say some prayers, the strangest feeling went through his body. On his knees, deep into prayer, he realized it was a feeling he had never felt before. Fear, no, that had left a while back. Closeness to God, maybe. He wasn't sure.

Then Jane leaned over and whispered, "I have the strangest feeling. Can't explain it, but I never felt it before."

He looked at her in wonderment. The Good Lord was sending them a feeling that neither could describe. Pedro, at that moment, could feel a chill through his body but it certainly was not fear. "Honey, I have a feeling similar to what you described."

"I want to stay a while, please."

So they stayed and prayed. Then sat back, and Pedro told her all about the church. Leaving there, he took her on a tour of the grounds as the orphanage doors were locked. The fishing stream still looked wonderful and brought back many memories. It was getting late so they spent the night in a small place near the church.

The rest of the visit in this area was a disappointment. Pedro's little home had been torn down, likewise the neighbors houses nearby. There was a large fence that prevented him from taking her to the stream in the back.

The ride to Monterey was a long one. The weather was very cool, so this was a big help to the horses. However, it was the fourth day before they arrived. Pedro immediately studied the map Ricardo had sent him. Before long, they were on the outskirts of the city, nearing the farm.

The two lovers were very impressed as they turned down the private road leading to the farm. The vegetables were all along the side of the road approaching the nice sized home. Rita and her mother were there to greet them, sending one of the children to get Ricardo.

After the death of Rita's father, the family had borrowed money from the bank and built the new house. Besides Rita's two children, Ricardo and Rita had two of their own. Everyone in the family worked hard, yet they still had to hire help.

Ricardo and Pedro hugged each other like long lost brothers. After introductions, Ricardo told Jane that now he understood why his friend was so deeply in love.

"Jane, your husband always had the girls clinging to him."

As she gave him the teasing eye, Pedro came back at

Ricardo. "Come on now, there was only one girl our age at the orphanage."

"Yes, and who was she nuts about?"

Pedro was a little pink as Ricardo, Rita, Jane and Rita's mother all joined in the laughter.

"Yeah, maybe so, but it did not take you long to find a beauty," looking at Rita, as he said it. Ricardo hugged his wife, and they certainly looked happy to Pedro.

It was at the dinner table that Pedro brought up the possibility of their moving to Mexico, to raise horses and cattle. He explained that Jane's mother was marrying the man he had worked for, and that Drew Hampton was the same as a father to him. Ricardo and Rita were just as happy as Pedro and Jane were at the possibility that they might be living in the same area. "The strange thing is that I was offered a piece of property just two days ago that is so perfect that you won't believe it. It is surrounded by good sized hills that would make stealing very difficult. Tomorrow, we will have a look, as it is only about twenty miles from here. The land is reasonable, but still will take a fair amount of money for it is a large area and they will not split it."

Pedro looked at Jane and they nodded to each other. "We do not believe that will be a problem."

Then after a pause, Pedro said, "I want to go to the orphanage also."

"Yes, of course. I'll tell you what might be best. While you and Jane go to the orphanage tomorrow, I will go down to see the owner, who lives a mile from here. Possibly, he would like to go with us the following day."

"We do not want to keep you from your work, Ricardo." Jane commented.

"Honestly, you caught us at a good time. A couple of days off now will not hurt."

"Great," added Pedro.

As Rita showed Jane the guest room, Ricardo pulled Pedro off to the side.

With a smile, he whispered, "You remember how you kidded me about the springs on the bed when I moved in with Rita?"
"Yes," laughed Pedro.
"Well, you don't have to worry. I keep them well oiled."
The wives came out as they laughed. Both refused to tell them what it was about.

Later as they undressed for bed, Pedro told Jane about it. She grinned as she added, "Great, we have not missed a night yet, and for some reason I don't want to miss tonight."

The church and orphanage in Monterey was much larger than the one Pedro had lived in. Ricardo had told Pedro of the death of Father Frankie three years before. He was buried on the grounds and Pedro wanted to visit the grave.

Sister Theresa had no idea that Pedro was coming, so when she opened the door after he had knocked, it was a shock to her to see the lovable boy turned into a man.

"Pedro, what a wonderful surprise."

She put out her hand as if to shake his, but Pedro pushed it aside and took her into his arms. Jane was all smiles as she noticed that both of them had tears rolling down their cheeks. "Wonderful Sister, it is so great to see you."

Then he turned to Jane and brought her forward. "I am proud to introduce you to my very beautiful bride, Jane. This is Sister Theresa, who for six years was a wonderful mother to me."

The two embraced and Jane kissed the Sister, who returned the favor. It had been over six years but the Sister had aged very little. Thank goodness that she was not quite as thin but still could use a little more weight. She put her hands on Pedro's shoulders, looking at him with teary eyes.

"I am so glad you came."

Then Pedro told her of the possibility that they might be moving into the area. That is what it took to bring sparkle to her eyes.

"Jane, if he makes as good a husband as I think he will, you are very fortunate."

"I know, Sister. We were sweethearts for three years before we married." Then Pedro put in his two centavos.

"Sister, when you know this young lady better, you will realize that I was the lucky one."

"Shall I get the children you know?"

"Yes, by all means. Don't tell them it's me, likewise don't tell me who they are. Let's see how this comes out."

While the sister was getting the children, Jane and Pedro waited in her office. "Pedro, if you would like to adopt one if we move here, I am all for it. You owe this orphanage something and I would love to help one of the children."

As the three youths came into the room, Jane was shocked as they were her age or older. Pedro's smile was as broad as it could be. He hesitated to see who would recognize him first, as he knew them all. "Pedro!" yelled out Tomás and Laura at the same time. George also knew and all three hugged him. Then Pedro introduced his wife, and George's comment was, "Pedro really got a beauty," and he gave Jane a warm smile.

Sister Theresa then told of all the children. "María was adopted a year after they moved here. She is married and has a darling boy. Joey was adopted by a family living in Mexico City three years ago, and he still writes me once a month. Millie ran away this year, and we traced her to find out that she had married a young farmer, who she had met at the market while living here. She is fine. I don't know if Ricardo told you but now that he is financially able, George is going to move in with him very soon. Everything is all arranged for the adoption. Although he is eighteen, Ricardo wanted him as a son. They were always very close, you know. We finished more papers last week, and both Laura and Tomás have been adopted by an Anglo family living in Brownsville. They are wealthy, but never could have any children of their own. Father Martínez and I feel real good about that one."

A disappointed Jane looked at Pedro, then spoke to the sister. "Pedro and I really wanted one of them. Are there others?"

The sister smiled at Jane. "I see what you mean, Pedro.

Yes, there are, but take my advice and see what the Good Lord sends you first. You are very young yourself. There will be plenty of time, especially if you move here." Then she hugged Jane again.

Meanwhile, Pedro was the center of attraction with the old buddies of his. George and Tomás were handsome boys, while Laura's blonde curls were still a standout. She was a pretty girl, and from the way Jane looked at her, would have been her selection despite the fact that she was a year older than her. A visit to Father Frankie's grave completed the day for Pedro, especially when the sister gave him a portrait of his beloved priest.

The following day was spent looking over the property with the owner. Pedro and Jane loved it, and the gentleman agreed to hold it until Pedro could get back with Hampton, which would be soon.

CHAPTER 38

Several days after Jane and Pedro returned to Rainy Roundup, Hampton, Agnes Skaag, Jane and Pedro had a long business meeting at the town bank. It was agreed that the two men would leave right away to try and close the deal on the property, providing that Hampton liked it as much as they had. Meanwhile, Agnes and Jane would make preparations for the wedding of Agnes and Drew Hampton. It would be held at Curly Duncan's ranch. It was to be a small affair, and they would not take a honeymoon for the present as it was more important to get everyone to Mexico as soon as possible.

All precautions were taken by the group to assure that no one knew where they were going to settle down. Everyone was led to believe that they were going to a more southwestern part of Texas. The four covered all the bases, and even Curly and

Julie were not told as it was explained to them that it would be safer for them if they did not know exactly. Southwestern Texas was all anyone was told, and that was in confidence although it was not so.

At Hampton's request, Pedro still wore the gun and would do so until they were well away from everyone who knew them. He had not worn the gun once they reached Monterey on their honeymoon, and this would be about when he would discard it for good this time.

While the men were on their trip, Jane and Agnes spent time with Julie and Curly. Several times when Jane and Julie were alone, Jane was questioned by the blonde about her personal life with Pedro. Although she never let on, Jane resented it, and only told her that it was "great." After a couple of attempts, Julie stopped asking, feeling ashamed that she had tried to nose into the couple's personal life. Both men returned from their trip as excited as two little boys. They had closed the deal, and Hampton had surprised Pedro by paying for the property in full. Pedro and Agnes had furnished what they could afford, but it was only a small amount considering what the property cost. Pedro and Hampton had their first argument as the kid insisted he pay some of the cost back gradually, but Hampton would not agree. We are now father and son was his arguing point. It still wasn't settled as yet, but the property was theirs. They had arranged to meet two brothers, well known carpenters, as soon as they returned to Mexico.

The informal quiet wedding was Agnes's idea, as Drew would have given her any type she wanted. Agnes thought it was for the best, and as for the honeymoon, life with him would always be like one compared to what she had gone through with George Skaag.

On the day of the wedding, Agnes wore a beautiful light pink wedding dress, with ruffles and bows. Drew wore a black silk western type suit with black tie and boots. They made an elegant couple, and no one was prouder than Jane and Pedro.

While Jane and Pedro spent the night where the women

had been living, Agnes and Drew Hampton stayed in the hotel. Jane and Pedro had a room at the home of Mrs. Betty Langley, a best friend of Agnes Skaag for many years.

In their private room that night, Jane and Pedro lay in bed, teasing and laughing with each other as usual.
"Wonder what's going on in that hotel room at this exact second?"
Pedro ran his hands over her naked body, then replied, "If you want, I believe I could show you."
Jane laughed as she moved her hands over his body. "Yeah, I can tell you want to show me right now," giggling at the end so much he could hardly understand her. Then she straddled him to prove she had learned the new position he had shown her the other night.

The following morning, Pedro and Jane met the newlyweds in the hotel dining room. On the way over there, Pedro thought about all the teasing he had taken from Hampton so maybe he could get a little revenge.
Seated at the table together, Pedro started on him. "I'll bet you two were so tired you went to sleep as soon as you hit the bed."
Jane giggled as he said it, and it was really something to see the two newlyweds turn pink.
Hampton smiled as he spoke, "I guess I had that coming. I gave Pedro a hard time about his little Indian friend at the reservation."
Jane looked over at Pedro, who immediately defended himself. "I told you about Little Flower in a letter."
With a grin, Jane agreed. "Yeah, but I know you ignored some of my questions."
Hampton laughed as Pedro wondered if he could ever get the best of him.
Then Agnes spoke up, with a smile that showed deep feeling. "I want you two young married people to know that these old folks had a marvelous night. I will never forget it, and something tells me he feels the same way. We have a beautiful

beginning, and now we both plan to keep our marriage on this same high plateau."

"She is one hundred percent right," added Drew as he leaned over to kiss his new bride on the cheek.

Pedro decided to give up on the teasing. He did not want to embarrass Agnes, but he sure would have liked to even the score with his new daddy. He was a prince of a man, and Pedro prayed they would always feel the same about each other. Hampton also knew that he had written to Jane about Little Flower so it was strictly a tease. The next decision was the one to decide what to take and when to leave on their important venture. They had already decided to travel light and buy all new furniture.

CHAPTER 39

TWO YEARS LATER

Two nice ranch houses that were approximately 100 feet apart gave each couple privacy yet they were close enough to get together whenever they so desired. Pedro and Hampton had been very selective in buying stock for their ranch, having made numerous trips into Texas and into deeper Mexico to pick out what they really wanted. They needed a lot more of both horses and cattle but were in no hurry.

Two Mexican families, who were living at the other end of their property, had been allowed to remain there and were hired to work for Hampton and Pedro.

It appeared they had done a great job of covering up Pedro's tracks as no one had come to give them any trouble.

Things were going so well that sometimes it scared Pedro. The big news was that Jane was now seven months pregnant, and doing well. After a miscarriage of their first baby, Jane had been ill and all three were very worried about her. This time, however, she was doing fine, and they watched over her to the point that Jane resented it. She had been a tomboy all her life, playing rough, running or whatever her heart desired and she was not one who desired to be babied, yet she put up with it because of her love and hope for a healthy child.

About that time, in Rainy Roundup, a dusty lone rider came into town. His first stop was the Town Saloon. Carrying his gun low, with the holster tied down, it wasn't hard to recognize that he was a gunman. Not a tall man but certainly a husky one, he stepped up to the bar. "Whiskey, and leave the bottle."

The bartender obliged, as Jack Harlow came out of his office. "Is that you, Kelly?" asked the ex-sheriff.

"Yeah, it's me, Harlow. I don't see a badge, you the new boss here?"

With a stern expression, the ex-sheriff gave him his answer. "Sure am. Don't allow any trouble makers in here."

Kelly faked a small grin. "I agree with that. Personally, I'm just having a coupla drinks."

Harlow continued to give him a hard stare. "What are you doing in this town?"

Kelly gave Harlow a hard look. "I was raised here. Since when did a saloon keeper ask such questions from a customer? Maybe you should put the badge back on, as it fits you better."

"Your family has left this area."

The two men glared at each other. "Yeah, I know. Where did they move to?"

Harlow smiled now. He had talked to Agnes at length, and also to Pedro and Hampton. "They never told me where they were moving to."

"You sure?"

Harlow moved closer. "You wouldn't be calling me a liar, would you?"

Neither man took his eyes off the other.

"No, just asking. But don't you worry, I'll find them."

Finishing his second drink, Kelly Boy paid up, and without another word, he left the saloon. Going across the street into the general store, he asked if they knew where his mother had moved to. Southwest of here was all they knew. Then he thought about Betty Langley. His mother had always confided in her. They were very close, and if she knew, he would know.

He rode his horse out to the edge of town where she lived. Dismounting, he walked through the little picket fence and onto the front porch. He knocked once and got no reply. Then again and harder this time. The door cracked open just a little.

"Yes, who is it?"

"It's Kelly Skaag, Mrs. Langley. I need to talk to you."

Betty Langley was the only one who knew where they were. Agnes wanted someone to know, and she had confided in Betty. However, she had been warned not to tell anyone, especially Kelly.

"What do you need to talk about?" she asked with the door barely cracked.

"Open the door, Mrs. Langley. It's important."

Slowly the door opened, and Kelly walked in. A small frame house with old furniture, Mrs. Langley was a poor widow. "I have an urgent message for my mother. Can you write her for me?"

After a hesitation, she answered, "I don't have an address to write."

"But you know where she moved to, right?"

"No, I don't." She is a poor liar, thought Kelly. "I don't want to hurt you, old lady, but you better tell me, and I mean now."

Mrs. Langley, terrified, backed away.

"Tell me now!"

Then he slapped her and she fell against the wall with one of her pictures falling to the floor. Again he repeated it. "Now!"

"Please don't hurt me, I don't know."

Then he hit her with a harder slap and she tumbled to the floor. "Tell me now!"

She cried as he beat her across the face with his hand. "Okay, okay," she screamed as the blood began to flow from her nose and mouth. He stopped and waited.

"She and the family live about twenty miles out of Monterrey. They have a horse and cattle raising business. She is married again."

"Give me the mailing address. Did she marry some bum who wanted her money?"

"No, he has more money than she does. He is a fine man."

When she handed him the address, he told her, "If you tell anyone I touched you, I will come back and choke you to death. Do you understand? Stay in the house until your wounds heal. I mean it."

She looked at him. "I broke my word. I would be ashamed to tell anyone."

At that, Kelly Boy took off for Mexico.

Several weeks later, when Pedro had gone into town and Hampton was off buying a few horses, Agnes went over to visit her daughter who was now almost eight months. They heard a horse in the front yard.

"Wonder who that is? Pedro could not be back yet, or could he?"

"Maybe."

Just at that moment a knock on the door told them they had a visitor. Opening the door, Agnes almost fainted as she saw Kelly, smiling as he stood at the doorway. He looked older, heavier, and badly in need of a bath. She could see the notches on the handle of his gun. "Hi folks, why does it seem you aren't exactly glad to see dear old Kelly Boy?"

Jane and Agnes stared at him, not knowing exactly what to say. Then their greatest fears were realized.

"Where's your Mexican boy hanging out now that you're gonna have his little greaser?"

Agnes gave him a hard look, while Jane could not even

look at him again. She wanted to claw his mean eyes out for speaking of Pedro like that, but being eight months pregnant she felt almost helpless.

"Kelly, get on your horse and ride out of here before you're sorry."

His mean eyes almost tried to smile. "You covered your tracks pretty good but you left one little mouth, and I made it sing like a bird."

"You beast, did you hurt Betty Langley?"

Now he smiled. "Not really, just a few slaps."

Jane burst in, "That is about your speed. Hurting old women."

"Where's your greasy lover boy? We have something to settle."

"He's not here. Besides that, he gave up gun fighting almost two years ago."

"Good, that makes it easier. I came here to put his notch on my gun. The killer of Jacoby Jenkins and Danny Dakota will be just another notch."

Jane started to cry. "He is wonderful to me. I am your sister, so why must you try to kill him?"

"Did you say try?"

Agnes came with, "He can probably kill you with no practice. Get on your horse and ride out."

As he laughed, Jane took a swing at him, just scraping his jaw. He quickly gave her a hard shove, and luckily she landed on the sofa, though she was shook up. Then Agnes surprised him as she pulled a pistol out of the drawer. Kelly stared at her for a moment.

"Put that gun away. You know you could not shoot your own son, no mother could do that. Hurry, before I show you what I did to your lady friend."

Suddenly Agnes surprised him by smiling. "Did you really come here to kill Pedro?"

With a cocky look, he answered, "I can't think of any better reason."

"You may be right about a mother not being able to kill her own son."

"So put down the gun before I hurt you and your little pet."

With a wild look, Agnes kept the gun on him. He tried to move closer so he could grab it, but she backed away.

"You are a no-good low-down bastard. You are not my real son. Your mother was a cheap whore, who lived with your no-good father before we married. Jane's father was my first husband, a good man killed by Indians. Being desperate when we met, as Jane was a baby less than a year old, we were married quickly. Soon after, I gave in to his insistence to always make you both believe you were really brother and sister."

At this point, Kelly made a move to grab the gun but she fired the pistol, hitting him in the chest, and continued to shoot, emptying the five shell weapon. He lay lifeless on the floor, as Jane screamed and Agnes dropped the gun.

At that exact moment, Pedro came through the door. Seeing Jane lying on the couch, he quickly went to her, as she cried her heart out.

While tears rolled down Agnes's cheeks, she told Pedro of the conversation, including the truth about Kelly Boy. She had no regrets of what she had done. Kelly had never shown his supposed sister any respect, nor his supposed mother any love. Now Pedro and Jane could understand how Agnes had disowned him long ago.

Several hours later, Hampton returned home. After a complete explanation to him, Pedro went after a Mexican official so that Agnes could tell her side of it. The body was buried in a small cemetery miles away, and it bore no name. There were no charges filed against Agnes, and it became a forgotten matter when Jane had her first child, a black-haired little beauty named after her grandmother, Agnes. The day of the killing had put even more of a bond between Agnes and Pedro. She was the mother he had always longed for, and her daughter and granddaughter were the loves of his life. Besides that, he now had a father, a wonderful, caring, loving one. Some people would call him lucky. Pedro knew it was much more than that.